She h   oped out of   air with the second towel.

It streamed long and s____ ___ ___ her back _____ smelled of summer ____ _____ as he blotted thick st___ ____.

"A shower makes ev_____"

Draping the towel o____ ____ ___, __ ____ed, shaking her head enough to make her giggle. Mila Ramirez giggled. Another check in the red-letter-day column on his calendar.

She looked so innocent and needy, and so beautiful and sensual, and he was needy, too, so damn needy. His hands stilled, and his breath locked in his chest, and he lowered his head until his forehead rested against hers. She had stopped breathing, too, and he wondered if she felt the same heat and desire and curiosity and lust that he did. He wondered if she had ever been naked with a man before.

Judging by her edginess and awkwardness when they'd met, he would guess no. He didn't care. He'd never been with a virgin before, but that didn't stop him wanting her, oh, hell, so much.

He wanted to take away the towel that hid her. To look until he'd memorized every part of her. To kiss her. Touch her. Show her. Claim her. He wanted…

* * *

If you're on Twitter, tell us what you think of Harlequin Romantic Suspense! #harlequinromsuspense

Dear Reader,

Thank you for picking up *Killer Secrets*! In my perfect world, everyone would read every book I've written. There's over eighty now, so if you have some time on your hands... But with the incredible number of books available now, the saying "too many books, too little time" has never been more true. Again, thanks for spending a little of your precious time with Mila and Sam.

This is my eighty-(mumble) book and I'm on to the next one, but I still love it dearly. It takes place in a thinly disguised version of my hometown, and the characters are people I know. Okay, I don't actually *know* any serial killers' daughters, but you understand. Murderous parents aside, Mila is like most of us: finding her way, dealing with her past and hopeful about her future. Is it any surprise, given her parents' pastime, that it's murder that brings her and Sam together?

Happy reading!

Marilyn Pappano

KILLER SECRETS

Marilyn Pappano

HARLEQUIN® ROMANTIC SUSPENSE

Recycling programs
for this product may
not exist in your area.

ISBN-13: 978-1-335-45632-8

Killer Secrets

Printed in U.S.A.

Oklahoma, dogs, beaches, books, family and friends: these are a few of **Marilyn Pappano**'s favorite things. She lives in imaginary worlds where she reigns supreme (at least, she does when the characters cooperate) and no matter how wrong things go, she can always set them right. It's her husband's job to keep her grounded in the real world, which makes him her very favorite thing.

Books by Marilyn Pappano

Harlequin Romantic Suspense

Killer Secrets
Detective Defender
Nights with a Thief
Bayou Hero
Undercover in Copper Lake
Copper Lake Encounter
Copper Lake Confidential
Christmas Confidential
"Holiday Protector"
In the Enemy's Arms
Copper Lake Secrets

Silhouette Romantic Suspense

Covert Christmas
"Open Season"
Scandal in Copper Lake
Passion to Die For
Criminal Deception
Protector's Temptation

Visit the Author Profile page at Harlequin.com for more titles.

To my husband, Robert:

What does it say that when I think of crazy people and villains, I think of you?

And when I think of cops and good guys, I also think of you.

And when I think of heroes.

And when I think of love. Forty years...

And we've lived happily-ever-after.

Chapter 1

October 15 was a Thursday, three days after my eleventh birthday. My father came home from work, smelling of cigarette smoke and booze, wearing that big goofy smile that was normally reserved for strangers. He kicked off his shoes, threw his Yankees cap at the hook next to the door and missed, then announced that he was taking me to the mall on Saturday to celebrate.

As with all of his grand pronouncements, he waited for me to show excitement at the prospect, maybe even a little joy, but my face remained in its usual dull set. The idea didn't excite me. It made the hairs on my arms stand on end, churned in my stomach and sent sour little bubbles that burned into my throat. Malls were his favorite hunting grounds: all those shops, all those people, all those escapes. I would gladly give up birthdays and celebrations for the rest of my life if only I never had to set foot in a mall again.

He waited, and I tried to summon a smile, a hint of appreciation, any bit of emotion that would satisfy him, but nothing would come. I just felt sick. I couldn't do it. Not again.

Of course he knew my thoughts. He always did. His jovial mood vanished in a heartbeat, his smile turning to a snarl. His right hand came up automatically, poised to strike my cheek the way he'd done a hundred times before, but with a muscle twitching in his jaw, another at the corner of his eye, he stilled the motion.

He wasn't sparing me. I knew it, and the evil gleam in his eyes showed that he knew I knew. The punishment would come, just not before we went to the mall. He needed me to attract the kind of victim that excited him, and that attraction was always based on sympathy. Poor little waif, separated from her father, big brown eyes, trembling lower lip, fear in her voice—just the thing to kick maternal instincts into high gear. A bruised cheek, a split lip, a black eye—they earned sympathy, too, but not the kind he wanted. Needed.

Though I'd spent my entire life shrinking away from him, tonight I didn't. Not this time. I stood tall and sullen and staring, but inside the shivers had started, and they wouldn't stop for a long, long time. Saturday was only two days away. Some woman whose only fault in life was catching my father's attention was going to suffer horribly and then she was going to die.

And then I would suffer, too, but I wouldn't die. I didn't know if that made me the lucky one. Or the *un*lucky one.

    —Excerpt, *The Unlucky Ones* by Jane Gama

Summer was a hell of a time to be in the lawn care business in Oklahoma.

With the air temperature hovering around ninety-five degrees and the humidity somewhere in the same range, Mila Ramirez was eager to escape the oppressive heat as soon as the battered pickup came to a stop. Opening the door required reaching through the window that wouldn't roll up and grasping the outside handle, sizzling hot in the morning sun. She gave the door a shove with her foot, making it creak, then slid to the ground, her boots making solid clunks on the pavement. If the driveway had been blacktop instead, she was pretty sure they would have sunk into it.

You're the one who wanted an outside job, remember? You should have become a lake ranger instead.

Alejandro and Mario tumbled out on her heels, bearing the smells of sweat, engine oil and unwashed bodies. If she didn't smell just as bad, the odors might have overwhelmed her. As it was, she ignored their stink and her own and headed to the trailer.

Cheap plastic crinkled as Ruben handed out bottles of water from the cooler. He was a sour, taciturn man who worked hard, worked his crew hard and had little interest in chitchat. He had even less interest in Mila. None of the crews at Happy Grass Lawn Service did.

Which suited her fine. Hadn't avoiding attention been one of her goals in life?

She slid the water bottle inside the insulated holder

she wore bandolier-style, then grabbed the favorite of her trimmers and a garden trug filled with tools and headed around the corner of the house. Ruben didn't bother to give them assignments; they'd worked together long enough to know their jobs. This customer was a regular, every Wednesday right after lunch.

The house was somewhere in the high six figures, but she paid it no mind. It was the yard she liked: spacious, more than five acres, with a sparkling blue pool and elaborate flower garden out back. She'd planted the garden herself back in the spring, coaxed the plants to grow from seedlings to strong lush specimens, full of color and fragrance and promise. The irrigation system took care of watering the rest of the week, but on Wednesdays, the plot got her personal attention as she watered and weeded and deadheaded, caring for it as if it were her own.

The silence of the neighborhood was broken by the sound of Ruben's mower starting. He did the front yard, walking diagonally behind a push mower, per the owner's preference. Alejandro used the stand-on mower to take care of both sides of the house, and he and Mario shared the jobs of raking, blowing, Weedwacking and edging.

Mila appreciated the relative silence of the backyard. After typing in the code to the gate, she shifted the trimmer so it didn't damage the flowers on either side of the walkway and wished for a moment that the sun would disappear behind the clouds. Even the ball cap pulled low over her eyes couldn't lessen the glare reflecting off the smooth surface of the pool.

Too bad she couldn't take a dip in it. Even tepid water would feel good right now. At least it would wash away a few layers of grime and perspiration. But that would be a fireable offense. She wasn't so skilled and personable that she could throw away a job, especially one that allowed her to work pretty much on her own. Her crew probably didn't say twenty-five words a day to her, and that was the way she liked it.

Though, at the thought, something twinged inside her. Was that really the way she liked it? Or was it just the only way she knew?

Resolutely, she pushed the question away. A long time ago, she'd adopted her grandmother Jessica's philosophy: *it is what it is*. You took what life gave you, and you made the best of it. That was exactly what they'd been doing for the last fifteen years.

Reaching the back corner of the house, she stopped and let her gaze slide slowly across the vista while contentment chased away the moment of discomfort. The house sat at the top of a hill, with a steep slope starting at the distant edge of the garden. Off to the east rose the slim spires of downtown Tulsa. Just beyond the lower hilltops to the northeast, the town of Cedar Creek sat, compact, a small space crammed with rooftops, power lines and the grid of neatly laid-out city blocks. The valley just past the garden was green with oaks, red cedars and hickories and dotted with gnarled deadfall that indicated too many years since the last cleansing wildfire.

It was a peaceful, quiet place. Until she noticed she wasn't alone. The quiet remained, but the peace disappeared in an instant.

One of the half dozen lounges around the pool was occupied. From this angle, all she could see was tousled dark hair above the chair back. It wasn't unusual to find some clients at home when they arrived, but she'd never seen this client before. His name was Carlyle. She'd taken care of his yard for three years, had planned and planted his garden, but she'd never met him or spoken to him. Like most of their well-heeled customers, he didn't communicate directly with the help if he could avoid it.

Mila hesitated, then cleared her throat. He didn't move. Rolling her eyes at her reluctance to leave her safe, unnoticed spot, she forced herself to put the equipment down, then crossed the stepping-stones to the patio. "Excuse me."

No response.

"Lawn service, Mr. Carlyle."

Still nothing. She rubbed her grubby palms on the legs of her jeans. The dampness of the denim reminded her that she'd started work at six this morning and hadn't been dry since. She wasn't in any condition to approach one of their wealthiest clients.

The deep breath she took was filled with the sweet fragrance of the flowers and a whiff of chlorine from the pool, both expected, plus something else. A tangy, bitter, familiar something that rose like a phantom from long-ago nightmares, that made her muscles go taut and a knot harden in her gut like stone.

The air was utterly still, without even a hint of a breeze to ruffle the dark hair. The oversize chair with its teak frame and plush cushions hid the rest of the person from view, but it couldn't hide the puddle that had collected underneath the chaise. It was fresh and thick and so out of place on the imported rainbow stone, its vivid red hue an obscene contrast with the peaches, tans and purples.

As she stared, something plopped onto the surface of

the blood. Her brain reacted to the ripples, making her aware of the humming of insects. Bees in the garden, she told herself, even as a fat fly lifted off the blood, circled a time or two, then landed again.

Her mind went blank. Her shoulders rounded, her chin drooping. A long time ago, she had believed that if she shrank into herself, if she physically made herself small enough, no one would see her, no one would notice her, but it had rarely actually worked. They had always seen her—her father, at least. Her mother, it seemed, had never noticed her.

The others had seen her. The victims. Even when they were dead, they'd still seen her. Admonished her. Pleaded with her. Blamed her.

She forced a shaky breath. She wasn't a kid anymore, and they *were* all dead. There was nothing they could do to her now, nothing here she couldn't handle. Probably nothing she hadn't seen before.

Alejandro's mower roared louder as he drove toward the fence on her side of the house, then after a rumble that vibrated the ground beneath her feet, he made a tight turn and headed back. He wouldn't hear her if she called. No one ever had. Not even when she screamed.

Nausea rising inside her, Mila forced herself to take a step, another, another, angling off to the left side, the side closest to the gate in case she needed to make a sudden exit. Each step brought the person in the chair into better view, until she could see his feet, his bare legs, the khaki of his shorts. A man, yes. Maybe Mr. Carlyle, maybe not.

Definitely a dead man. The gaping wound that stretched across his throat from one ear to the other left no doubt about that. Neither did the terror in his open eyes. Terror that she'd seen before, on the victims, on her grandmother, on herself.

Oh, God.

Dear God, not again.

Ninety percent of the city of Cedar Creek fell within the rectangular boundaries plotted by its founders over 125 years ago, making it a neat little box that was easy to navigate. Sam Douglas had been born and raised in those twenty-five square miles, gone off for a stint in the army, then come back to work for the Cedar Creek Police Department. He knew every block like the back of his hand, except for the neighborhood he was turning into.

It was a forty-acre section of high-dollar houses on big lots that overlooked the town while security guards and tall iron fences kept out the common folk. The area had fallen under county jurisdiction until five years ago, when the city council got wind that it was being acquired by some luxury developer. The council had moved fast, extending town limits to incorporate the former ranch and getting a nice increase in tax dollars from it. Even though incorporation meant police and fire protection, this was the first call Sam could remember requesting police presence within the hallowed compound.

"Hawk's Aerie." Cullen Simpson, the department's newest hire, snorted. "Who comes up with these names?"

"People who make more money than you and me, bud."

Simpson snorted again. "I'd rather have a nice little house in Texas than a big fancy one looking down on Cedar Creek. They could've at least built in Tulsa, where there's more to do."

"Easier to be a big fish in a little pond."

"Huh?"

"Never mind." Sam showed his credentials to the guard at the gate, then drove slowly down the street. Simpson was from a wide spot in the road in north Texas, so he should have understood the fish comment. Maybe he was just too damn young. The more time Sam spent on this job, the older he felt. He was pretty sure he was going to feel ancient tonight.

There was only one street in the development, splitting five hundred feet in to form a loop with four houses in the middle and six on the outside. The middle houses were just as large as the outer ones, but the lots were smaller, only two or three acres. Even on the lofty premises of Hawk's Aerie, there was *best*, and then there was *best of the best*.

"That must be it there." Simpson pointed ahead, where two police cars, a fire engine and an ambulance were parked. There was also a decrepit pickup truck towing a trailer and bearing a sign saying Happy Grass Lawn Service on its side.

The only happy grass Sam had ever come across was the weed he'd smoked back in his younger days. Who did come up with these names?

He pulled his pickup to the curb, shut off the engine and climbed out as he looked at the lawn service crew idling by their truck: three men gathered together, one woman a dozen feet away. Two of the men were smoking, but none of them were talking. The woman leaned against the faded fender, her feet spread wide, her spine rounded so she stared at the ground. Though there were plenty of people around, she looked alone, with no one to stand with, no one to lean on.

His gut said she was the one who'd found the body, stirring his sympathies. He'd spent two years in combat in Iraq, where he'd seen things no one should ever see, but he still got a jolt at crime scenes. How could someone who probably had zero experience with violence handle getting a view up close and personal?

"Chief." Lois Gideon, the first female officer in Cedar Creek, removed her cap, dragged her fingers through her wet gray hair, then set it back. She wasn't a detective and had no desire to be, but she still pretty much controlled the crime scenes. She was good at it.

"The victim is Evan Carlyle, owner of the house. He's forty-eight, works for a pipeline company in Tulsa, lives here with his wife and two kids. They're out of the country on vacation. Little Bear's out back making a list with locating them at the top." She quirked one eyebrow; Ben Little Bear was a compulsive list maker. People teased him about it, but while things might slip his mind, they never slipped his list.

"The body's out back by the pool," Lois continued. "No sign of a break-in, alarms on the house and the fence, security guard says no one's been in besides those folks—" she gestured toward the lawn service "—and a plumber making a call at a house over there."

"Who found Mr. Carlyle?"

"The woman." Lois checked her notes. "Milagro Ramirez. The 911 call came from the older guy, Ruben Carrasco."

Sam's gaze went to Milagro again. She remained in the same position, as if the clunky boots she wore were the most intriguing thing in her world at the moment…

or, at least, the safest thing. How long would it be before she could close her eyes without picturing Evan Carlyle's lifeless body? How many nightmares would she have, and would there be someone to help her through them?

Not technically his worry, but the Cedar Creek Police Department had a reputation for going above and beyond. *To protect and serve*, their vehicles said, and he believed strongly in doing both.

"Let's see the body."

Lois crossed the fresh-cut grass to the driveway, then took a stone path that led around the side of the house. The gate there stood open, offering a glimpse of a flower garden that would make Sam's father proud. Given that Samuel Douglas had spent the last thirty years running his own nursery, that was saying something. Of course, a man who could afford a ten-thousand-square-foot house for his family of four could also afford to pay someone to create garden magic for him.

Two more of his officers waited in the backyard, along with paramedics, a couple of firemen, the department's senior evidence technician and, at a patio table as far from the scene as he could get, Ben, on his computer. He was the only one doing anything. The victim was beyond help, and the tech knew Sam would want to look over the scene before she started collecting evidence. Though none of them was within ten feet of the body, they all retreated a few steps when he approached.

Sam had seen enough death for twenty people. Sometimes it had been sweet, welcomed, a last breath before peacefully slipping away. That was the way his granddaddy had died, with Sam holding one hand and his cousin Mike holding the other. Sometimes it came as a surprise, just an instant to think *It isn't supposed to hap-*

pen this way before it was over. Some people didn't even get that much—just *poof!* Gone, like a light snuffed out.

Evan Carlyle had had more than enough time to understand that he was going to die. He'd seen it. Felt it. Feared it.

Sam looked a long time, his focus tight, not hearing anything but the buzz of insects, the distant wail of a siren and a muffled dispatch issuing from a radio. Nausea rose inside him, the way it always did, but he forced it down again, the way he always did, and walked away before taking a deep breath. As soon as he cleared that ten-foot mark, the evidence tech moved forward to continue with her tasks.

Sam detoured to the table where his detective worked, sunlight glaring on him. "You need any help, Ben?"

"Not yet. Unless you want to interview the yard service people."

Ben was damn good in the interview situation when it was suspects across the table from him. He was tough, driven, could intimidate the worst of the bad guys and often did without so much as rising from his chair. But when it came to witnesses, the victims, the friends and families, he had trouble finding his stride. "Lois and I will take care of it."

Without looking up from his computer—where the screen showed another list in the making—Ben grunted, and Sam headed back to the gate.

"What now, Chief?"

Simpson fell in step with him at the corner of the house. The newbie had stayed hell and gone from the body. He'd confessed on the way out that he'd never seen a dead person before, had never even been to a funeral, and he wasn't looking forward to the experience. "But I'll get through it," he'd hastened to assure Sam. "I'll get used to it."

"I hope not," Sam had replied. No one but medical examiners and embalmers should ever get used to the sights of violent death, and even they couldn't allow themselves to totally *get used* to it. They had to retain some of their horror, or what purpose was there in living?

"Sit in with Lois while she interviews the men on the yard crew. I'll talk to the woman." As he said it, he looked around. The Hawk's Aerie bulldozers hadn't left a single tree on the property big enough to provide shade to anything more than a cricket. The stoop fronting Carlyle's house was small, and its most notable feature was the sun that shone fully on the three stone steps. "I'm going to the truck. At least we can get some air there. Send her down to me—and make sure she comes."

There weren't so many people on scene that Ms. Ramirez could easily slip off and evade him, but he wouldn't take any chances. If he were a sensitive kind of guy, he could find it downright insulting how many people didn't want to talk to him when a crime was involved— even self-proclaimed honest citizens.

Striding back to the truck, he started the engine, turned the AC on high and watched as Simpson pointed out the pickup to Milagro. With a tiny nod, she pushed away from the pickup and started Sam's way, her head still down, her manner submissive. She was average height, slender, and the hair that hung messily beneath her ball cap was black. Her choice of clothes looked unbearable for working in the heat: jeans, long-sleeved shirt with a T-shirt underneath, work boots that reached above her ankles, a bandanna wrapped around her throat to cover the back of her neck and the ball cap pulled low. The men on the crew were dressed the same. Protection from the sun.

The passenger door opened and, after a hesitation so brief he might have imagined it, she stepped up into the truck. Accompanying her was the overripe scent of hard work. Sam had smelled worse. Hell, *he* smelled worse after every steamy summer run.

As soon as she closed the door, Sam directed most of the air vents to the passenger side. Milagro looked like a rag wrung out then dropped to the ground, with grass clippings clinging to her clothes and what little exposed skin they'd found and coated with layers of dirt. The strongest scent coming from her was that fresh, sharp, not-always pleasant smell of whacked weeds. Smelled like Johnson grass, the invasive weed he'd spent three miserable summers banishing from the farm.

"I'm Chief Douglas." He removed his hat and laid it crown down on the dashboard. "And you are…"

"Milagro Ramirez."

The name alone made him expect to hear an accent and sounds meticulously pronounced. He didn't hear either. She said it exactly the way he would have, her accent indistinguishable, as if she might have been from anywhere but south of the border.

"I understand you found Mr. Carlyle's body."

"Yes." She sat rigid, her spine not touching the seat, and stared at some point in front of the vehicle. The air rushing from the vents blew fine tendrils of her hair and was slowly chasing away the pink that spread across her cheeks.

Was she here illegally? Rumor had it that the guy who owned Happy Grass Lawn Service was too cheap to pay decent wages so he relied on immigrants who had no status and no one to complain to. Or she could have all her papers in order but be in trouble for something totally unrelated. She could be a perfectly law-abiding born-in-the-USA citizen who'd never had contact with the police, or she could distrust cops just for being cops. There was no shortage of that sentiment these days.

And yet he and all the others who did it stuck it out. They were the protectors, the investigators, the defenders, the justice seekers and, sometimes, given the nature of criminals and the extent of the things bad people could do to other people, they were just plain insane.

Though Sam had started the day feeling all law and order, truth, justice and the American way, about now he was thinking he just might be insane.

It didn't take long for Mila's body temperature to drop from borderline heatstroke to shivering like winter in her wet clothing. Her arms had goose bumps and her hands were shaking when she reached out to close the vents until only a thin line of air came out.

For a while she'd been lost in blessed numbness. She'd walked calmly out of the backyard, stopped Ruben and asked him to go with her. He'd taken one look at the body, shooed her away and called 911. Next he'd pushed her down onto the driveway in the miserable bit of shade the pickup provided, thrust a bottle of water into her hand and stopped the other two working. She'd had a few lovely minutes when she saw nothing, thought nothing, remembered nothing, when she was just a drifting soul in a distant universe where no person or thing could follow her.

Then she'd heard the sirens, reminding her of other sirens, other lives, other deaths. The noise and bustle of the first responders had drawn her back into this universe, reminding her to pull herself together. It hadn't been easy gathering all the parts of herself back into a coherent being. Fortunately, these people, this police chief, would find nothing unusual about an *in*coherent being under these circumstances.

She waited for Chief Douglas to begin his interrogation. He was entering information into the computer mounted between them, and she watched peripherally, thinking his big hands were better suited to birthing cattle or catching footballs than typing on laptops. When his fingers went still, she felt his gaze shift to her.

"Are you all right?"

The question surprised her into looking at him. His eyes were blue and serious, and he studied her as if he could read everything he needed to know in her own eyes. Only one person had ever truly read her emotions—she confused her grandmother and her psychologist on a fairly regular basis—and that person was nothing more than dust and bones in a pauper's grave. She would spit on it if she knew where it was.

The chief was still waiting. "Yes. I… I walked into that yard not thinking about anything other than the work and the flowers, and instead I saw—" With a shudder, she raised one hand that she knew would still tremble, would make him sympathetic, because he just had the look of someone who was very sympathetic, then sighed.

"I'm sorry." His voice rang with sincerity.

Guilt twinged deep inside, but she forced it back. She wasn't lying, just playing a role. Any other person in her spot right now would be entitled to sympathy without feeling guilty, and she was pretending to be any other person. "Better me than his wife or kids." Her voice came out small, the way it did when she was trying to shrink out of existence.

That wasn't a play for sympathy. She knew better than most that Carlyle's six- and eight-year-old daughters didn't need to see their dad like that, just as *she* hadn't needed to see her father in all the ways she'd seen him.

Douglas watched her a moment longer before turning his attention to the report template called up on the computer screen. "I need to get some basic information from you."

He asked questions; she answered. Some of her answers were even true. All of them felt true. She had been Milagro Ramirez for so long that it felt genuine. Cassie, Candace, Melanie…all the other names she'd answered to were like a long-distant dream. The name she'd been given at birth wasn't even that. She was no longer any of those girls. She was Milagro, who had never had a mother or a father, who lived happily with her grandmother Jessica, whose life had begun at age eleven.

As she talked and he typed, yet another vehicle parked ahead of them. A man and a woman got out, retrieved a gurney from the back of the van and disappeared around back. Presumably they were from the medical examiner's office. They would put Mr. Carlyle into a body bag, then wheel him back around front, no longer a husband, a father, a boss, just a package, evidence, to be delivered to people who would do even more damage to him than his killer had. They would take specimens and photographs and notes, and then they would send him on to some funeral director who would fix it all so his family wouldn't recoil in shock.

Her stomach heaved.

Mila shifted so she was facing Chief Douglas, so the activity at the house was a blur she couldn't easily follow. He gave the impression of being a big guy, but she doubted he was taller than six feet or heavier than 190 pounds. It was just this air of confidence about him, not boastful or brash but quiet, like *he* knew he could hold his own, and it didn't matter if anyone else knew it.

He wasn't a guy she would look at and think, *Damn, he's gorgeous*, but he was definitely someone she'd look at and think, *He's in charge here.* Authority accompanied that quiet confidence, backed up by the badge, the weapon and the Taser.

But he was good-looking, too. Light brown hair slicked down by the hat he'd worn, earnest blue eyes, a straight nose, a square jaw, a mouth that probably delivered impressive smiles…among other things. If he'd only had dimples, Gramma would melt in a pool at his feet. "I'm sixty-five" she liked to remind Mila. "That's a long way from dead."

And sometimes that was followed by a reminder. *You're a long way from dead, too, sweet girl. You should be grateful for it every single day.*

She was grateful, more some days than others. She knew how fragile life was, how it could be taken on a whim, how the same hand that tickled or soothed or petted could also deliver pain so intense that it stole her tears.

She was very grateful. Mostly.

The chief's cell phone rang, and with an apologetic gesture, he answered it. She narrowed her focus to him. If her attention didn't wander outside this vehicle, it couldn't go where she didn't want it to. Instead, she wondered if he was married. He didn't wear any jewelry, not even a watch, but that didn't mean anything.

What was his first name? She would vote for something wholesome, middle America, untrendy: Joe, Tom, Jack. Gramma had bought her a subscription to the Cedar Creek newspaper, which had surely printed his name a thousand times, along with some personal information, but Mila didn't often read it. She wasn't interested in crime or politics or who got married, had a new baby or won the trout derby out at the lake.

She wasn't interested in the police chief, either.

Really.

He kept the conversation relatively short. "...just the basic info for the reporters—name withheld until next of kin is notified, our investigation continues, so on."

Mila wondered briefly if Chief Douglas and his officers had investigated many murders. As cops, were they good, bad or indifferent? Fifteen years she'd lived in Cedar Creek, and she'd never had any contact with the police, not even a warning. She'd made a point of not being noticed by them, either.

She took a sidelong look at the chief and drily wondered, how was *that* working for her?

In a lot of big police departments, the chief's job was administration, political meeting and greeting, and dealing with the media. Cedar Creek's department was small enough that if Sam wanted to work traffic or act as primary investigator on a routine case, he could. Today, he was grateful to leave this case in Ben and Lois's capable hands. He'd made one too many death notifications, had dealt with one too many grieving family members and friends. He would be satisfied to make his notes on the interview with Milagro Ramirez, turn them over to Ben and get back to the work piled on his desk.

As soon as he dispensed with Ms. Ramirez herself.

"If you'd like me to call your boss and see about getting the rest of the day off…"

Her gaze slid his way quickly, shy or possibly furtive, then shifted forward again. She considered the offer, looking tired and pale and tempted. He didn't know her situation. He did know an unexpected day off resulted in financial hardship for people who counted on every hour's salary to pay their bills. It was a decision she would have to make.

She looked at him again, keeping the eye contact to a minimum. Her hands were clasped in her lap, long fingers, nails cut short, a bandage wrapped around one tip, a bruise discoloring another. Not delicate hands, no polish, almost certainly callused, but capable. Strong. "I—I would appreciate that."

As he picked up his phone, she told him the number. "What's his name?" he asked during the first ring.

"Lawrence."

"First name?"

"Mister."

Ah, one of those people who didn't get overly familiar with his employees. At the moment, that grated on his nerves, but then, his nerves had already been shredded in the few minutes in the backyard.

A woman answered on the third ring, and he asked for her boss. Overhearing her call out "Ed, it's for you," when the man came on the line, Sam adopted what he considered his politics voice.

"Ed, this is Sam Douglas down at the police department. How are you, man? It's been a long time."

Sam didn't know if he'd ever met Ed Lawrence, but he certainly knew his kind. Made his success on the backs of underpaid, overworked employees, somehow convinced himself that they would be nothing without him when it was really the other way around, smarmy and blustery and always looking for anything he might use to increase his sense of self-worth. In a small town, being on a first-name basis with the police chief could be that something.

"Oh, I'm good, Chief, good."

"You heard about the incident out here at Hawk's Aerie, I'm sure. Your employees have been most helpful. I really appreciate it a lot."

"At Happy Grass, we're always glad to help. Glad to help."

Great, a repeater. It was a quirk of cops that too many of them figured if it needed saying one time, it couldn't hurt to say it twice. It was on the short list of things that drove Sam crazy.

"Listen, your worker who found the body…she's pretty shook up by this. You can't imagine what it was like for her."

"Must have been a pretty ugly scene."

Lawrence's voice held a sly, inviting tone that all the put-on sympathy in the world couldn't hide. He would love to share the gruesome details with his buddies while bragging that he got them straight from the police chief himself. That would be worth free rounds at the bar for two or three days, at least.

"Ugly enough that she really needs to take the rest of the day off. You're fine with that, aren't you, Ed? I mean, supporting the community and the police department the way you do, of course you'd want her to go home and deal with this instead of worrying about lawns."

In his peripheral vision, he caught Milagro rolling her eyes. Apparently, she couldn't imagine her boss caring anything about his employees except that they showed up and worked hard. Sam couldn't imagine being that kind of supervisor. Couldn't imagine anyone in his family letting him get away with it before they smacked him back down to size.

"Sure, sure, she can take the day off," Lawrence said. "It'll put us behind schedule, of course, but that's a small price to pay given the circumstances. You just go ahead and tell Maria—"

"Milagro."

"Yes, yes, of course she should deal with this. Tell her I said don't think about work at all today. Tomorrow's plenty soon enough for that."

"I will. And you know, Ed…" Sam adopted Lawrence's insincere good-ole-boy tone. "I would consider it a personal favor if you didn't dock her pay for the time off. She's doing her civic duty, helping the police, and I would just hate to see it cost her more than the emotional trauma she's already been through. You think you could do me that favor, Ed?"

The level of joviality in Lawrence's voice dropped enough to force him to clear his throat to answer, but he came out with the right response. "Of course, Chief. I'm happy to do it. Happy to do it." He pronounced each of the last four words with extra emphasis, like he was trying to convince himself.

"Thanks, Ed. I'll see you around." Sam laid the phone in the console cup holder.

Milagro was watching him again, but this time her gaze didn't dart away and back. Her brows were narrowed, and something that might be the start of a smile curved her lips a bit. He got the impression that she didn't smile much. Lurking beneath the lingering shock and dismay was an intense solemnity that he doubted gave way very often.

What had she been through in her twenty-six years that made her so solemn?

The list of possibilities was too long to consider right now.

She made no comment about the conversation, though she'd clearly heard enough from his end to get the gist of it.

"Do you need to go back to the shop to pick up your car?"

She shook her head.

"How'd you get to work this morning?"

"Ruben picks us up. We're on his way."

"I'll take you home then." When she opened her mouth to argue, he went on, "You're on my way. Buckle up."

She did, and so did he. He pulled out and drove to the driveway, where he rolled the passenger window down. "Simpson, get a ride back with Lois. And Lois, give him the benefit of your years of experience, will you?"

Lois saluted him with a wink and a grin.

After raising the window again, he followed the loop past quiet grand houses and out the gate. He figured

Milagro would be happy if they made the drive in silence, but silence wasn't usually one of his strong suits. "How long have you lived in Cedar Creek?"

Quick glance, hesitation. Yep, she'd rather not chit-chat. "Fifteen years."

"Hmm. I see the same people so often, sometimes I start thinking I know everyone in town. You go to school here?"

"I was homeschooled."

"Church?"

"No." After a moment's pause, he guessed curiosity made her ask, "Do you?"

"Regularly enough that God doesn't forget my face. Every Sam Douglas in town is expected to be there at least twice a month on Sundays."

That caught her attention, as he expected it would. "How many are there?"

"There's me. My father. My grandfather, who's gone now. My cousin Samson. His boy, Sammy. A cousin Samantha. And her son, Samwell. Samantha hyphenates Douglas with her husband's last name for both her and Samwell."

"Maybe your family should look at one of the other twenty-five letters in the alphabet." She folded her arms across her chest, tucking her fingers into the folds of fabric at her elbows.

Wow. A long sentence with a little bit of humor in it. Feeling a sense of accomplishment, he turned the AC lower. "We're a big family. We require a lot of names."

She didn't ask how big. If she had, he would have turned the question back on her. Since she didn't, he turned it back anyway. "Do you have family?"

Her expression turned both pensive and wary, and

though the truck cab left her little room to move, she managed to put some distance between them.

"Look, Milagro, I don't know if you're a citizen, an immigrant or an undocumented worker, and I don't care. You had a shock today. You probably need someone to stay with tonight, just in case. Do you have someone you can call?"

Her face had gone pale once more, but reluctant acceptance replaced the wariness. "Gramma. My grandmother."

"Do you want me to take you to her house?"

"No. She'll come."

He caught a glimpse of that tiny sort-of smile, softened with deep affection.

"She always comes."

Whatever she'd been through, she'd held on to her faith in her grandmother with both hands. That was good. With a family the size of his, it could have been easy for some of the kids to get lost in the crowd, to not have anyone special they could trust no matter what, but with parents and grandparents like his, that hadn't happened to them. He appreciated that it hadn't happened to Milagro, either.

By that time, they'd reached her street. Sam's own house was only six or eight blocks away, across Main Street and in a very similar neighborhood: old houses, some neatly maintained and others looking as if the next strong wind would blow them away. Some of the yards were lush with flowers and vegetable gardens; some looked as if a flock of ravenous chickens had pecked out the last piece of grass and it had never grown back.

Milagro's house was, like his, on the better side of things. It occupied the corner, a decent-size lot with a white-sided house, a deep front porch and a picket fence containing the closest thing he'd ever seen to an English cottage garden. He hadn't expected her to have a pretty yard or a lot of flowers. She did that sort of thing all day. Didn't she want a break from it at night?

The driveway went only as far as the sidewalk, the rest of it having been claimed for plantings. He shifted the truck into Park, then turned to face her. "Are you going to be all right?"

She nodded.

"You'll call your grandmother?"

Another nod.

"Here's my number. If you need anything, even just to talk, call me."

She hesitated before accepting the business card he offered. Then, with a polite nod, she opened the door, got out and walked through the gate and into her garden. She followed the stone path to the porch, never glancing back. There she unlocked the door, opened it to the bare minimum of space she needed to slip through and did just that.

The cop in him wondered about that. Was someone inside she didn't want him to see? Did she have an inside garden that he might have to haul her to jail for? Was she such a bad housekeeper she didn't want anyone to catch a glimpse of the mess? But in those seconds the door was open, he'd heard excited barking and gotten the impression of a yellow-furred mass of energy greeting her. She had a dog, a big one judging from what he'd seen, who'd been locked up all day and probably regarded an open door as an invitation to romp down the streets.

Would she call her grandmother? Would she do it

now or wait until tonight, when it was dark and she was vulnerable and the image of Evan Carlyle's face haunted her even with her eyes squeezed shut?

Her decision to make, he reminded himself. He'd done his duty, both as police chief and as Samuel Douglas's son. The rest was up to her.

Chapter 2

January 1.

Halloween had come and gone, and Thanksgiving, and Christmas. I saw TV sometimes. I knew what those days were like for most people, but I had never had a Halloween costume or anything to feel thankful for. My parents hadn't killed me yet. That should have been something, shouldn't it? The idea of Christmas, of people all over the world celebrating someone's birth… My mother said my being born was the worst thing that ever happened to her. She hated me. He hated me, too.

I didn't hate them. I just wished they were dead.

He took me to the Rose Parade today. I had never seen so many people in one place, tens of thousands of them. We walked down the crowded sidewalks, him grasping my hand so tightly it hurt, his narrow dark eyes sliding from one woman to the next. Did they have any idea, even just a slight disturbance in their souls, that they were in the presence of evil? I knew it. I smelled it, that mix of excitement and lust and sick, sick pleasure. For him, half the fun was the choosing. He never drank before a hunt. The anticipation was his high, his need, his reward.

We walked. He looked. I let my mind wander someplace safer. Sometimes I just stopped being. I was nothing and nowhere. A blink, and I no longer existed. Sometimes I became someone else, a normal girl whose father loved her so much that he'd fought traffic and huge crowds just so she could see the parade. He held my hand so tightly because his heart would be broken if we got separated. Fear, ignited by pure, sweet love.

I didn't pretend very often. It was too nice, and when he poked me to point out his target—our target—the fantasy crashed so hard I was afraid it would squash the hope out of me.

Today I looked at those crowds, those hundreds of thousands of people, and wondered what would happen if I ran right into the middle of them. He was stronger, but I was fast and wiry, and I was more afraid. If I twisted my hand from his, quick and hard, and darted into the street between floats, I could reach the other side. I could run to that group of college kids over there and cry, "This man is not my daddy! Please don't let him take me!"

Better yet, I could disappear. Sometimes when I was allowed to play outside, my mother said I'd never met an obstacle I couldn't go over, around, under or through. I could run and run until my lungs burst, and he wouldn't keep up. Everyone around was taller than me. He would have only a vague idea of where I'd gone, and I would get so far away from him that he would never find me.

Suddenly he jerked me to a stop and bent low to look into my face. His fingers squeezed so viciously around mine that the tips turned red, and after a spike of pain, mine went numb. "You wipe that smile off your face, you stupid little brat. You try to run away, I'll kill you." He yanked hard on my hand, pulling me closer. "You understand?"

I knew what he wanted, and I gave it, a solemn nod.

"You believe me?"

Oh, yes, I believed him.

I'd believed for as long as I could remember that someday my father or my mother was going to kill me.

——Excerpt, *The Unlucky Ones* by Jane Gama

"Hey, Poppy, are you surprised to see me home early?" Mila leaned against the door, held there by the dog's paws on her shoulders, and rubbed the base of her ears. Gramma had rescued the yellow Lab mix from Cedar Creek a few years ago—had seen the puppy perched on a tree stump snagged in the middle of the creek, alternating between whining at the current and barking for help. There had been other people around, but only Gramma had taken action, kicking off her shoes, wading into the waist-deep water and calming the dog for the trip back to shore.

Gramma hadn't wanted a dog, but she'd saved its life, so she'd had to find it a safe home. Where else would that be but with Mila, she'd asked, as if it was the most logical question ever.

She had already given Mila two incredible gifts: unconditional love and escape from the terrors that were her parents. Trusting her with Poppy, with the care and nurturing of another living being, had been the third treasure. Twenty-four years old, and Mila had cried over the big-eyed waterlogged puppy who had climbed into her lap and promptly peed.

The Lab had changed Mila's life. She'd never had a pet before, had been too terrified to even show interest in dogs, cats and hamsters. Showing interest in anything to her father was a one-way trip to pain.

Even over Poppy's happy barking, Mila heard the police chief drive away. She exhaled, tightness easing in her chest and her stomach. He seemed a perfectly decent person, but being away from him made her feel the same way she did after a long swim: like a fish breaching, bursting from the crushing depths of the ocean into fresh, clean, light, sweet air.

He was a cop.

And she was what she was.

Not right. Damaged. A killer.

Numbness spread through her, closing her eyes, but she still saw things. Still heard. Still smelled. Thankfully, Poppy broke the moment by licking Mila's face from the bridge of her nose all the way to her chin. "Ew, Poppy, no dog slobber." Her voice trembled over the words, and she dragged in a breath before catching the dog's face in both hands and pressing a grateful kiss right above her eyes.

"Okay, sweetie, let me get away from the door and maybe I'll find some treats in the kitchen." She caught the dog's front paws and half pulled, half pushed them to the floor. After removing her ball cap and long-sleeved shirt, she bent to unlace her boots and kick them off on the rubber mat next to the door.

Goose bumps rising on her arms—and an odor so unpleasant that even Poppy wrinkled her nose and stepped away—Mila walked across the cool living room, the dining room and into the kitchen. Her land-lord claimed the house had a thousand square feet of living space, but she was convinced that included the front porch, the back stoop and the shaded portion of the backyard. The kitchen's maximum occupancy was one, though that never stopped Poppy from trying, and the bathroom was small enough that a two-by-three-foot rug covered all except the outside edges of the floor. Her bedroom was about ten by twelve feet— enormous compared to the second one, which had room for a twin bed, a night table and a skinny person stand-ing sideways.

She got treats for Poppy before heading to the bath-room. She turned the water to hot, then shed her clothes in the hallway hamper. Once steam drifted on the air, she adjusted the water from scalding to merely breath stealing and stepped into the glass-enclosed shower.

The water streamed down her, washing away sweat and grime and the tensions she wore like a second skin. She luxuriated in it for one minute, three, five, then washed her hair and scrubbed her body. When she'd started working at Happy Grass, she had welcomed long days in the sun, wearing only short shorts and a tank top. That first day, Ruben had looked at her and shaken his head chasteningly. That day she'd burned despite her olive-toned skin and a zillion-SPF sunblock. She'd quickly adopted Ruben's ways.

Her brown skin and black hair helped her live up to the name she and Gramma had chosen so long ago. People heard the name, looked at her and thought, *Yes, she looks like a Milagro Ramirez*. Even Chief Douglas had seemed surprised when he'd heard her unaccented voice.

She had no accent because she came from everywhere and nowhere.

Someday, she hoped to hear Oklahoma in her voice.

After shutting off the water, she pushed the shower door, but it moved only a few inches before stopping. Poppy lounged on the bath mat, her yellow hair drifting in the air. Mila coaxed her back enough so she could step out, throw on some clothes and then let her into the fenced backyard and watched her through the window over the sink. The garden there was as elaborate as the one out front, and if blooms escaped the dog's huge feet only to fall victim to the sweep of her brushy tail, it was a small price to pay for having her.

One word in that thought stuck in Mila's brain, refusing to fall away into oblivion as the others had. *Victim.* Evan Carlyle's image appeared, as sharp and clear as it had been in the relentless glare of the midday sun, his body slack, his neck gaping, his eyes… It was always the eyes that stayed with her. A dead body wasn't obscenely different from a living one, just a shell for a soul that had been ripped away. But something about the eyes… The spirit left them last, watching her, accusing her.

"It wasn't my fault!"

The words exploded from her with such emotion that Poppy, curiously sniffing a frog, directed her gaze to the window, her head tilted to one side, concern on her goofy, doggy face. Mila wanted to tell her it was all right, to go back to her exploring. She wanted to pet her and thank her for caring. She wanted to drop to the ground beside her and wrap her arms tightly around her neck and let her wild hair tickle her nose.

But fear held her at the sink, on the inside looking out. That had been her life for eleven years: no friends, no family, no school, no everyday dealings with the world. Her father had left her home when he worked or drank. Her mother had left her home when she grocery shopped or paid bills or drank. Most of their neighbors in the towns where they'd lived had never known Mila existed. She didn't go to the doctor when she was sick or play in the yard or get too close to a window where someone might see. The only people who'd ever seen her were the victims.

For eleven years. An eternity.

When the cell rang, it startled Mila. Her head whipped toward the hall, where the phone was still tucked in the pocket of her jeans. Her breathing was heavy, and her hands shook, but her feet were rooted to the floor.

You try to run away, I'll kill you.

The ringing stopped, but it would start again in seconds. The only person who ever called her was Gramma, and Gramma wouldn't be deterred by voice mail.

Fifteen years ago, Gramma hadn't been deterred by time or distance or the obvious message that her daughter wanted nothing to do with her. She hadn't even been deterred by the evil in the flesh that was her son-in-law. She'd come to Mila's rescue, same as she'd done with Poppy, and given her a chance at living. Real life. Not cowering in isolated fear.

The ring sounded again, and so did the faint, faraway whisper. This time it didn't frighten Mila. After all, she *had* run away, and he had died in the process.

That was one death she would proudly take credit for.

Dashing into the hallway, she grabbed the phone and held it to her ear. "Hi, Gramma. I'm glad you called."

When Sam walked into the squad room at the station the next morning, Ben Little Bear was typing at his computer. He looked comfortable, like he'd been there awhile and intended to stay a good long while longer.

Sam sat down in the chair next to the desk, its ancient wood creaking beneath his weight, and put his hat on the next desk. It was the most beat-up one they had and had gone unused for as long as he could remember. According to his predecessor, some chief long ago had gotten it in the hopes of one day being fully staffed. Operating on a budget, that had never happened.

"What do you have on the Carlyle case?"

Ben saved his work, then swiveled to face him. "The State Department located the wife and kids in Rome. The embassy notified her, and they're helping expedite their return home. I talked to his boss. He said Carlyle was a solid manager, got along with everyone. He seemed happy in his marriage and adored his daughters. No problems at work, no disgruntled employees, no ex-wife, no money problems, no problems of any kind that he knew of."

"Basically, no reason for anyone to want to kill him."

Ben nodded. "Funny how many times we hear that about people who have, indeed, been killed."

A person who didn't think in terms of resolving issues with murder was always puzzled by someone who did. Sam had learned to understand the thought processes, the motivations, but it still amazed him that people chose murder.

"There was no sign of forced entry," Ben went on, and Sam swore he could almost see him ticking items off a mental list. "You need a code to get into the house and another for the backyard. I'll have to get a list from the wife of everyone who knows the codes, but obviously the yard service and probably the pool service have the gate code. Pool service isn't due until Friday, and I've confirmed the yard people's whereabouts for the morning. They were out at that private school on Highway 117 for three hours, then ate lunch at Scott's, where they're regulars. Cameras show them arriving at 11:05 and leaving at eleven thirty. Guard has them logged in at Hawk's Aerie at 11:42. The 911 call came in six minutes later."

There was nothing like a routine that allowed a person to document practically every minute of their day, Sam thought, then wondered…how was Milagro?

She'd been on his mind ever since he'd driven away from her house yesterday. Had she called her grandmother? Had she managed a peaceful night? Was she back at work this morning? It wouldn't be a bad thing if she was. In his experience, the best way to deal with trauma was by keeping busy.

And maybe she was one of the lucky ones whose spirits were strong enough to cope, to adjust, to say a prayer, take a deep breath and go on doing what they had to do. Though she'd seemed fragile enough to shatter in a breeze yesterday, he suspected she was much stronger than that.

But he would check in on her later today just to be sure. It wasn't an unusual action for him to take. In fact, witnesses to violent crimes pretty much always got a well-being check a day or two later. Usually it was the detective handling their case or Lois, but Sam made some of them. He would make this one.

"We got a lot of fingerprints," Ben said, drawing Sam's attention back to the case. "Most of them belong to the same four people, presumably the family. There was no sign of a struggle, no skin under his fingernails, no obvious attempt to get his cell phone out of his pocket. My guess is he let someone in, and after he sat down, the person came up behind him. Surprised him. A sharp blade, no hesitation marks. By the time he realized what was happening, it was too late."

As Sam stood and retrieved his hat, he asked, "Why was he home yesterday?"

"He told his assistant Tuesday night that he was working from home Wednesday. He's done it before, but it's an occasional thing."

Maybe he'd planned on having a late night Tuesday. Maybe he was having company who was staying over for breakfast. Maybe he was taking advantage of his wife and kids being out of the country.

Or maybe he'd just wanted to sit by the beautiful

pool and enjoy the beautiful view he worked long hours to pay for.

"You're thorough, Detective."

"You might be as thorough if you made a list from time to time," Ben replied, giving a rare smile. As if an afterthought, he added, "Sir."

"I may stumble a bit without your endless lists, but I always wind up in the same place."

"Yeah, well, stumbling isn't my thing."

From her desk outside his office, his secretary called, "Telephone, Chief."

"Got it." Sam returned Ben's smirk. "Keep me updated. If you need anything—"

In unison, they said, "Lois will be the first to know."

With a nod, Sam headed to his office and picked up the phone. "Chief Douglas. What can I do for you?"

"Morning, Chief, good morning. This is Ed. I just wanted to check in and make sure my employees cooperated fully with you yesterday. I give 'em a job and I treat 'em like family, but that gives me certain expectations of them, you know."

No, Sam didn't know. He wasn't even sure whom he was talking to. His work involved a lot of phone conversations, double that yesterday, and he couldn't place the unctuous, smarmy...

Oh, hell. Ed Lawrence of Happy Grass was the kind of guy Sam wanted to forget as soon as their business was done, but no, he'd buddied up to Lawrence to be sure Milagro got some time off without losing pay. Now Lawrence was going to return the favor by buddying up to Sam. Damn.

"Hang on, Ed. I just this minute walked in the door. Let me get settled." He set the phone down, closed the door and set his hat in its designated spot atop an old oak filing cabinet. Finally he sat down behind the desk and took up the phone. "Sorry about that, Ed. I'm here."

"Don't apologize. People always call at inconvenient times. Some of the worst times. I could tell you…but I won't." He cleared his throat and slid into what Sam pegged as his faux-concerned voice. "I just wanted to be sure my crew was cooperative with you yesterday. They're good workers, but they've got their quirks. You know, pretending they don't speak English sometimes when you know damn well they do, or sticking together like it's them against me, or freaking out when they have any interactions with the police. My workers are all here legally, Chief, don't doubt that a second, no, sir, not one second. I've got copies of their papers. Now if it happens to turn out that some of those papers aren't real, well, you can't blame me for that. I did what I was supposed to."

Sam barely resisted a snort. If Ed Lawrence was the man he thought, any false papers had probably been obtained at his behest, thereby covering his ass while leaving everyone else out to hang.

When Lawrence took a noisy breath, Sam grabbed hold of the pretext for his call. "Everyone was fully cooperative, Ed. They lived up to your expectations."

"Good, good. So…the dead guy—I mean, the victim. Ruben says it was Evan Carlyle. Well, actually, what he said was that they found him at the Carlyle house. Was it Evan?"

Bracing the phone between his shoulder and ear, Sam picked up a thick pile of messages and ruffled the edges. Milagro had intimated that Lawrence didn't encourage familiarity with his employees. He doubted Evan Carlyle had, either.

"You know I can't confirm that. An official announcement will be made once the next of kin have been notified."

"But you can confirm that his throat was cut, can't you?"

Sam sighed. In the reality of crime scenes, there was no such thing as private information versus public. Too many people saw the body: in this instance, the lawn service crew, the police, the crime scene investigators, the ambulance and fire crews, the team from the medical examiner's office. And everyone talked. Lois, Ben and Simpson had surely told other officers what they'd seen. Ruben and the rest of his crew had likely told their families or friends, and hopefully Milagro had told her grandmother.

"Officially, I can't confirm anything. When Detective Little Bear has information to share, he'll contact the media."

Lawrence's chuckle held a hint of disappointment. "Aw, Chief, you know everyone shares a few tidbits with their buddies."

"I know, but as chief, I don't have that luxury." Before the wheedling could continue, Sam asked, "How was Ms. Ramirez this morning?"

"Who—oh, Maria. She was fine." His tone clearly said he'd paid no attention to her. How long had she worked there that her boss still didn't know her name? Happy Grass wasn't a large company. Even if Lawrence did nothing more than sign her paycheck every two weeks, he should know her name.

Thankfully, someone in the background shouted for

Lawrence's attention. With a remark about how he never could catch a break, he hung up, and Sam heaved a sigh of relief. He made a mental note to check with Milagro in another few weeks. With Lawrence now acting like they were buddies, she'd damn sure better get paid for her few hours off.

Mila liked to think she didn't spook easily, but mid-morning on Thursday, when she had to walk into the first fenced-in backyard, she'd hesitated so long that Ruben had come over and led the way. The second time Alejandro had accompanied her and then Mario.

None of them had mentioned yesterday's discovery. None of them had teased or scorned her hesitancy. They hadn't said much of anything at all, but she'd appreciated their actions. She hadn't had a lot of experience with simple courtesies, and today they'd made her throat swell and her eyes sting.

She stood up from the bed she was weeding, arched her back and grunted as a soothing crack sounded in her spine. *You're making old woman sounds*, Gramma warned her. *I'm the one who should be creaking and popping.*

Gramma had come straight to her house after yesterday's phone call, making the five-minute drive in two and a half minutes. She'd burst through the front door, greeted Poppy, then wrapped her arms around Mila and rocked her back and forth, stroking her hair, calling her *baby* and *sweet girl* and whispering that everything was all right now.

And everything *had* been all right, because Gramma was there. She was the rock in Mila's life. Once, when Mila had told her she was her hero, Gramma had laughed and said, *Except the tights are support hose these days, and the cape looks more like a hairdresser's than a superhero's.*

Having Gramma in her life made Mila the luckiest person in the world.

"Milagro."

Her startle reflex was sharper than usual, though an instant after the surprise, she recognized Mario's voice. He stood just inside the gate, his brows raised in question. She nodded and began gathering her tools, along with the pop-up mesh tub that held the weeds. She would be the first drop-off today, a fact she appreciated since they'd already worked an hour longer than usual. Poppy would be even more excited than usual, both with her greeting and her need to get outside.

Most of the equipment was already loaded in the trailer. Ruben secured his weed trimmer while she stuffed her tools into their spot, then they both climbed inside the truck and headed out of the neighborhood. The silence was comfortable, she realized with surprise. She'd always lived mostly in silence, and she'd always been acutely aware that it wasn't exactly normal. But the crew wasn't quiet because they were angry or suspicious or plotting. They were tired, thinking about a shower and dinner and a good night's sleep, just as she was. It was familiar. Normal.

When Ruben turned the old pickup onto her block, he glanced her way. "Huh."

She looked at him, then ahead. A white pickup truck with police department markings was parked across the street from her house. Chief Douglas. *Huh*, indeed.

Her mouth went dry, her stomach clenching hard. Did he have more questions? Pretty much everyone involved with a murder was looked at closely. Had they looked at her? Had they found out that Milagro Ramirez had formed out of thin air fifteen years ago, that before then she hadn't existed? Did they wonder what she was hiding and if it had anything to do with the dead man she'd discovered?

Ruben pulled up to the curb opposite the police chief. She got out of the pickup, holding the door so Alejandro could move from the back seat to the front. Before letting go, she managed an action that was more grimace than smile and said, "Thanks, Ruben. Goodbye." She didn't look to see if all three men were staring at her. She'd never said thank you, goodbye, hello or anything else voluntary to them.

No wonder they were never chatty with her.

She wanted to go straight inside her house and lock the door, but it would be futile. If Douglas could be put off that easily, he wouldn't be police chief. With a deep breath to control the queasiness in her stomach, she turned to face his truck. The engine was shut off, the windows rolled down to let in the stifling heat, stirred only by the occasional rustle of wind. The sun was at just the right angle to shine in the driver's side window, making the cab significantly warmer than the outside air, enough to make sweat glisten on his forehead.

It wasn't a bad look on him.

He got out, closing the door with a thud, and crossed the street to join her.

"You should have waited on the porch. At least you would have had shade and a breeze," she said, not realizing until after she'd spoken that a greeting of some sort would have been polite.

Being polite had never been one of her goals, regret-

fully. Not being noticed had always been far more important to her—and to her survival.

"I would have, but my going on the porch and knocking on the door made your dog crazy. I figured if I didn't
go away, he was going to come right through the door."

"She," Mila corrected automatically as she opened
the gate, then led the way to the porch. "Poppy is excitable."

"To say the least. What breed is she?"

"Mostly yellow Lab. Maybe something wiry. She
lives in a perpetual bad-hair day." At the top of the
steps, she stopped. Poppy's barks demanded attention,
but Mila didn't yet know why the police chief was here,
and she didn't want to invite him into her house. No one
but Gramma had been inside in the three years she'd
lived there, and there were things in there she preferred
no one else saw.

Awkwardly, she faced him again. He'd stopped one
step below her, putting them on eye level and much
closer than she'd expected. He still had that undeniable
air of authority about him…and he was still handsome.
His eyes were as blue as she'd remembered, his mouth
as full of promise, and without crease marks from his
hat, his hair looked soft and smooth, though shorter
than she usually liked.

Hmm. She hadn't realized she had a preference in
men's hairstyles.

He smelled faintly of sweat and sunshine and cologne, reminding her that *she* smelled like a rotting garbage heap under the fires of hell and didn't look much
better. Her clothes were soaked and stinky, and her face
was dirty and baked dry. It felt as if too much expres-

sion might actually crack her skin. This wasn't a bad time to wish, for the ten thousandth time, for invisibility.

Poppy's barks and bangs at the door were frantic, though not an indication of doggy emergency. She acted much the same when Mila came back from the bathroom or returned from getting the mail on the porch. She and Gramma were the only creatures in the whole world who were always happy to see Mila.

But Chief Douglas wasn't here because he was happy to see her. He'd come about the body, or about information they'd found on her—or hadn't found on her. It wasn't a social call. Just police business, and she'd spent her life not getting involved in police business.

Scuffing her feet uncomfortably, she fixed her gaze on the flowers visible over the chief's shoulder and politely—blankly might be a better description—asked, "Was there something you needed?"

Peripherally she caught a glimpse of his expression: friendly, sincere. No suspicion or doubt or accusations. "I wanted to see how you're doing. Any problems last night or today?"

She blinked. Seriously? The chief of police was taking time from his day to see how she was coping with finding a body? Of course Gramma would check, and the crew going into the backyards with her had been their way of checking, but what kind of police officer did that? What kind of *chief*?

"I—I'm okay." She confirmed the words with a shrug that felt jerky rather than assuring. With some sort of obligation pressing her, she went on. "I still see…you can't *un*see… But it's—it's all right."

Did that sound as bad to him as it did to her? Embarrassment flushed her face, heat creeping down her throat. A man was dead, and no matter that she hadn't known him, it wasn't all right. She'd never known any of those women when she was a kid, and their deaths would never be all right.

But she felt responsible for their deaths. With Evan Carlyle, she'd just been in the wrong place at the wrong time.

Chief Douglas seemed to understand what she meant. When she sneaked a look, there was no censure in his eyes. "No problems sleeping? No nightmares?"

"A few." She avoided his face and took another step back. She wasn't lying, though it felt like a lie. She'd had two nightmares, waking soaked with sweat, Gramma at her side and Poppy resting her head on her thigh. But the nightmares hadn't been about Carlyle. Seeing him had triggered them, but the faces in her dreams were women whose names she'd never known and the parents she wished she'd never known. If she'd been a regular person, finding Carlyle's body would have been nothing more than a blip on her radar.

Poppy banged the door hard, and Mila gestured that way. "The baby really needs to go out. Do you mind…?"

She meant *Can you say what you want and go?* He interpreted it as *Can you give me a moment, then we'll talk?* With an expansive gesture, he pointed toward the door. "Go ahead. I'll wait here."

Her breath grew tight again. She unlocked the door, then, out of habit, opened it just enough to slide through. Poppy had never met a stranger at the house before, and though Mila was pretty sure the sweet puppy didn't have it in her to bite someone, she wasn't so sure about knocking them to the ground and loving them to death.

"Hey, Poppy, baby," she greeted, rubbing her hands

over the dog's ears and face and shoulders. "I know I'm late. Do you need to go out? Please need to go out because if you don't, that means I'm gonna be finding puddles somewhere. Come on, sweetie. I'll race you to the door."

Chapter 3

Everything was my fault. They told me that every day, that I was a bad girl, that I made them do bad things, that everything wrong in their lives was because of me, but they never told me what I was doing wrong. If they had, I would have fixed it. I would have changed. I didn't want to be bad. I didn't want to make them be bad.

I didn't want anyone else to die because of me.

My father liked to play a game with me. He stood me against a wall, the heels of my shoes pressed against the baseboard, my shoulders against the Sheetrock. "Don't you say a word," he said. "If you do, I'll have to punish you. Do you understand?"

I knew what was going to happen next. I racked my brain to find a way around it, to avoid the slap that would jar my teeth so they felt like they'd come loose in my jaw. I obeyed him. I didn't say a word. I just nodded, slowly, because I knew it was the wrong thing to do but it was also the only thing I could think of.

He bent, his face inches from mine, his breath smelling of beer and whatever food he'd last eaten. "Do you understand?"

Tears of fear and dread and helplessness started forming. I nodded again, and he bent so close his nose practically touched mine.

"I don't know why you make me do this. Your mother says you're stupid, but I don't think you're stupid. I think you do it on purpose. I think you like to make me mad. You know I don't like yelling at you, and I damn sure don't like punishing you, but you do it anyway. You make me do it anyway." By then, his eyes were glittering with hate and insanity. He was a mean man and a crazy man, and I didn't know which one was worse.

"One more time," he breathed, his voice more dangerous the softer it got. "If you say a word, I will punish you. Do…you…understand?"

I couldn't hold it back no matter how I tried. I knew, no matter what my choice, the result would be the same, whether I said a word, whether I didn't. "Yes!" I cried.

The next thing I knew, I was on the floor, certain that this time he'd broken my jaw, my cheekbone, a tooth or two. He stood over me, staring down at me with such disgust. "One simple thing," he said, and he called me by whatever name they'd given me that month. "I just wanted you to do one

simple thing, and you couldn't. It's your fault. It's
always your damned fault. But you'd better learn,
brat. You'd better learn good, because next time I
won't go so easy on you."

Then he walked away, leaving me on the floor,
crying as quietly as I could. He was right. It had
happened so many times. I should have been able
to figure out the right thing to do by now.

But I was stupid. I was bad. And everything
was all my fault.

—Excerpt, *The Unlucky Ones* by Jane Gama

Listening through the door, Sam smiled. So Milagro might not be polished at human interaction—or
maybe it was man/woman or cop/woman-who-didn't-
like-cops—but she obviously adored her dog. He hadn't
had a pet in a long time, but he believed that, in general,
people who loved pets couldn't be all bad.

Sure, and now he would meet up with a serial killer
who volunteered at the animal shelter and adopted and
lovingly cared for all the animals his budget could afford, while carving up people as if they meant nothing.

After Poppy thundered away from the door, Sam
took a seat in one of the rockers. He didn't mind the
heat of the day so much. It was summer in Oklahoma—
expected. It was when they reached this part of summer, when the temperature after 10:00 p.m. was still in
the eighties and the humidity was just as high, that he
got tired of it and started wishing for fall. Trouble was,
neither spring nor fall lasted nearly as long in Oklahoma as they should. Some years, sleep in late and you
missed them.

He hadn't intended to wait for Milagro when he

stopped by half an hour ago. Knock on the door, exchange a few quick words, then home to shower, dinner and maybe an entire evening in front of the TV in his boxers. But some part of him had decided to wait while sweat began breaking out all over. The back of his shirt was soaked, and if he took his shoes off, he would leave wet prints wherever he went.

And still he'd waited.

This was a much nicer place to wait. The chair was comfortable, old and creaky, probably a family antique passed through the generations. The flowers filled the air with a dozen fragrances. Two brilliantly colored hummingbirds darted from bloom to bloom, the larger one trying to commandeer the smaller one's choices. When the little guy whirled and scolded him before chasing him away, Sam laughed. He always rooted for the little guy.

"Well, aren't you a handsome addition to the garden."

Sam shifted his attention to the woman standing on the walk to the side of the house. She wore a sleeveless shirt, yoga pants in eye-popping colors and running shoes in enough hues to match something in everybody's closet. Her gray hair was pulled back from her face with a band, and a turquoise activity monitor circled her left wrist. She was pretty, fit, older than his parents and twice as spry.

"I appreciate the compliment."

Instead of walking to the corner and around to the gate, the woman carefully swung one leg over the fence, found good footing, then swung the other over. "Mila hates when I do that. She thinks I'm going to hurt something. I don't know whether she worries it'll be me or her plants."

"Mila?"

"Milagro. Spanish for *miracle*. Did you know that?"

"I didn't." He'd seen a lot of things in his career involving kids. It was sweet to think that a pair of parents had loved their baby girl enough to name her Miracle. Though he liked the nickname, too.

She wove through the beds before climbing the steps and plopping into the other rocker. "I'm Jessica Ramirez. Mila's gramma."

Ah. Sam took the hand she offered and found her grip strong and her squeeze firm.

"This, young man, is where you say—"

Grinning, Sam interrupted. "I'm Sam Douglas. It's nice to meet you, Ms. Ramirez."

"See, I knew you'd get it with a nudge. Is she home? No, she must be, or Poppy would be dismantling the front door." She rocked a few times, her head tilted to one side. "Why are you here this evening, Chief?"

"I just stopped by to…" To see if Mila was all right, and she'd said she was. He'd asked about nightmares, and she'd admitted to a couple. That really was the end of their conversation, unless he could come up with something else before she walked out the door. He could throw together a couple of quick questions of a cop-ly nature, nothing really important but enough to satisfy her and her grandmother.

Jessica was still looking at him, one thin brow arched high. "You stopped by to…?"

"Sorry. I got distracted."

Her broad smile hinted that she'd already guessed at reasons for him to be there and was happy with the one she'd chosen. She didn't comment on how pretty her granddaughter was or mention that she was single, though. Instead, she replied from a totally different angle. "If you kept lists like that nice young Detective Little Bear does, you wouldn't get distracted so easily."

Sam's eyes widened. "You know Detective Little Bear?"

Quietly in the background came a rattle, then the door opened and Mila stepped out. When she saw her grandmother, Sam wasn't sure whether it was dismay or resignation on her features. Was Jessica the type to embarrass her with old stories or on the constant search for a potential bridegroom whether Mila wanted one or not? Sam's aunt Leah was in year three of a campaign with no end to get her five daughters married off, and her behavior had gotten downright desperate.

"I work at one of the antiques stores downtown," Jessica said. "Called A Long Time Ago. We had a couple of incidents that Detective Little Bear took care of for us."

Sam remembered: two cases of malicious mischief. Two teenage girls had left nearly a thousand dollars' of damage in their wake, then posted pictures of themselves in the midst of the mess on Facebook.

"You never mentioned that, Gramma." Mila went to lean against the porch post. When Sam started to rise to offer his chair, she shook her head.

Jessica lifted her chin and smiled smugly. "I do not tell you of all my interactions with lawmen. Or with men in general, for that fact. A grandmother's got to have some secrets, don't you agree, Chief?"

"If people didn't keep secrets, I'd be out of a job."

Jessica's smile broadened at his words. Mila's eyes darkened, and she stared down at the floor.

Sam had assumed Mila just wasn't a social person until he'd met Jessica. Then he'd thought maybe, with a grandmother so friendly and larger-than-life, Mila had never had the chance to develop conversational skills. When Jessica was around, he doubted there were many moments for anyone else to jump in on a subject.

"None of my secrets are policeworthy, I'm afraid, are they, sweet girl?" Jessica went on. "More along the lines of that old bat living next door to me will never know that these baby blue eyes aren't my natural color, and I will deny having a face-lift until the day I die. And if you forget to bury me in my Spanx and my five-inch red high heels, Mila, you'll have to wear them for the rest of your unnatural life."

Jessica's accent was more Southern than the women in his family, but Sam could practically hear his aunts Loretta and Leah and Goldie in her. It was thanks to them that he even knew what Spanx was. The only good thing about acquiring the knowledge was they hadn't tried to show him. Goldie would have—"They cover as much as my shorts do!" she'd protested when his mother made her stop.

Thank you, Jesus.

"If you're not here, you're going to have trouble making me wear those red torture devices." Mila slid to the top step, her back against the post. "Besides, you're not dying for a long while, Gramma." There was a hitch in her voice, a little quaver, and a responding hitch to Jessica's smile.

Instead of making a big deal about it, though, Jessica laughed. "I tell you, Mila, heaven's not ready for me and hell can't handle me, so I'm going to be around a good long time. Now…all three of us are sitting here in slightly less than pristine states, and I don't know about y'all, but my stomach's reminding me it's about dinnertime, so here's my suggestion. Let's each of us go to our own homes, clean up and meet back here, and I will provide dinner. Does that work for you, Chief?"

"Sam."

"Thank you. You can call me Jessica."

Sam hesitated. There wasn't a single reason why he should have dinner with the Ramirez women…and more important, no reason why he shouldn't. Yes, Mila was very loosely involved on the very periphery of a case, but it wasn't even his case. He got invited to dinner by people in town more often than he really wanted just because he was chief, and if he could eat with the mayor and his wife—who was the most abysmal cook in the entire county—he could share a meal with Jessica and Mila. He could assure himself that Mila wasn't just giving the right responses to his questions, that she really was doing okay or if she needed help to cope.

"I'm older than your mama, son. I don't think the gossips will find anything to talk about," Jessica said. "Just agree and give me a ride home so I can get back with the food."

He looked at Mila, whose expression was somewhere between normal, resigned and panicked. Yeah, he would bet on his cop instincts that Jessica was looking for someone to share Mila's life, even if Mila did seem perfectly happy with Poppy and no one else. But if she didn't absolutely hate the idea…

She looked up, caught his gaze on her and gave the tiniest of shrugs. It wasn't a glowing agreement—*oh, sure, great, stay and have dinner with us*—but it wasn't a frantic *please go away* signal, either.

"Come on then, Jessica," he said. "I'll give you that ride."

* * *

"What do you think they'll talk about?" Mila watched the pickup drive away, Gramma leaning forward to wave, then closed the front door. Poppy watched her, posture alert, ready to spring this way or that, even drooling a bit in anticipation of a treat.

Gramma had tried over the years to push her into some friendships. A person needed to be around people their own age, she'd insisted as she gently, lovingly shoved Mila forward. *It's the normal way of life.*

Mila and *normal* didn't belong, no matter what the age.

"Don't you want a best friend?" Gramma had asked in frustration. "Don't you want a boyfriend someday?"

Mila had lied, told her no. It wasn't that she didn't *want.* It was that she didn't know how to be a best friend or a girlfriend. Relationships required trust, and the only person Mila had ever trusted in her entire life was Gramma.

And now Gramma wanted her to be friendly with Chief Douglas.

Her stomach flip-flopped. She did her best to never let Gramma down, but encouraging any sort of relationship between her and the chief seemed a one-way trip to disaster.

Vaguely queasy, Mila showered, dressed in a summer dress, dried her hair, then with Poppy on her heels, she made a round of the living room. She swept an entire bookshelf clean of files, correspondence, printed pages and notebooks. In the tiny second bedroom, she crabbed sideways between the bed and the wall to dump her load into the mostly empty closet. There was a box, filled with copies of a single book; a file box with documents and statements; and a battered old photo album.

Her secrets.

Her life.

She closed the door, feeling marginally safer. This weekend she would put a dead bolt on that door. Then she wouldn't have to worry about anyone who came here learning a single thing about her. She'd been tortured by the details of her life forever. No one else deserved to suffer.

Stepping outside onto the back porch, she debated whether it was cool enough to eat there. There really was no option inside for three people, especially one who seemed to take up as much space as...Sam, she tried experimentally. It was a nice name—strong, nononsense. And like most first names, it felt very personal to her. Maybe she would stick with Chief.

With the ceiling fan turned on, the porch was bearable. She did a quick sweep of the old floorboards, then dragged over a stepladder to stretch out the mosquito netting that hung at the four corners, puddling the creamy net on the floor.

With lights hanging around the perimeter of the porch, the fan and the sweet, luscious fragrances of the flowers, the space was welcoming. A little cramped, but with Gramma there, it would be bearable.

She had just put the stepladder away when Chief Douglas knocked at the front door. She knew it was him because Poppy was howling excitedly and because Gramma never knocked; she jiggled the doorknob even though she'd been the one to teach Mila to always, always lock her doors.

Her breath caught in her chest. She'd talked more

in the last two days than in the past month. Her sparse supply of words was used up. Why couldn't Gramma have asked him to pick her up on the way back? She could talk to anyone.

Another knock pushed Mila through the kitchen and to the front door. She grabbed Poppy by the collar, twisted the lock, then backed away, dragging the dog with her. "Come in."

The chief opened the door and stepped inside slowly, careful to close it before Poppy had a chance to escape. His gaze went from her to the eighty-pound dog straining hard to check him out, her barks turning sharp, her nails digging into the floor as she tried to twist free. "Hey, Poppy." He crouched, a sensible distance between them. "You've got a big voice, don't you, sweetie? What are you so excited about? Are you not used to having strangers come to your house?"

Poppy stopped barking so she could listen to him, her head tilted to one side. She still pulled, but with determination, not frantic dancing. She was sniffing so fast and hard that it was a wonder she wasn't light-headed— though, really, based on her usual behavior, how would Mila know?—and drool puddled on the floor in front of her.

"Go ahead and let go of her," Chief Douglas—Sam— said.

"She'll knock you over."

"Nah, I don't fall so easily."

Both cautious and curious, Mila released her hold on Poppy's collar, and the dog made that sensible distance look like millimeters. Since the chief had wisely gotten on her level, she didn't leap at him, but neither did she stop in time. Her body slammed into his, but he was prepared, absorbing the shock. Poppy couldn't decide whether to hyperventilate while sniffing every inch of him or to enjoy the good scratching he was giving, so she contorted herself this way and that to take advantage of both.

"She's a beautiful girl," he remarked, his focus on the dog's ecstatic behavior. "Your grandmother said she rescued her."

"Some boys threw her in Cedar Creek," Mila answered, her gaze focused on *his* behavior. She'd never known she was a dog person until the day she got Poppy. Obviously the chief was, too. "Gramma pulled her out. The boys ran off, no one claimed her and she became mine."

A scowl lined his forehead. "I wish she'd called me."

"What would you have done?"

He looked up and grinned. "I may not know every single resident in town, but I know all the troublemakers." Disappointing Poppy to no end, he finally stood. The dog pressed herself to his side so he could continue scratching with one hand. "One lesson everyone needs to learn—misbehavior has consequences."

Chills skipped down Mila's bare arms. She'd learned consequences long before she could pronounce the word. In her family, breathing too loudly had had consequences. So had getting hungry between meals or having to go to the bathroom when they were traveling.

Still rubbing Poppy's ears, the chief—Sam—glanced around the tiny room. Books filled the shelves, the newspaper sat on the coffee table with a few magazines and pictures hung on the walls. She thought most people would just see the love seat, comfy chair and television and never notice that there was nothing truly personal in the room. They wouldn't think that Mila could live here or anyone else…or no one, for that matter. It could be staged to suit anyone.

She gathered from the intent look in the chief's eyes that he did notice.

"I like your grandmother's apartment," he said when his gaze came back to her.

She grabbed the lifeline he'd unwittingly thrown. "Then you've seen why I choose to make my space a little more bland."

He chuckled. "It's kind of like walking into an explosion in a paint store, isn't it? It's, um…"

"Eye-searingly bright?" she supplied drily, and he nodded. "Gramma's not a subdued person." She lived in a top-floor apartment of a downtown office building, and every inch of space was filled with stuff. New, old, in prime condition or about to fall apart, cheap, pricey, someone else's antique, someone else's trash… if it spoke to her, it went home to live with her.

"If it makes her happy, that's what matters. It does make this—" he gestured around the room "—more soothing to the spirit."

Mila liked the idea of her space soothing the spirit. It made her smile even as a beep sounded outside. "That's Gramma's signal that she wants help carrying something. I'll be right back—"

She'd taken only a few steps when he moved. "Keep the dog from making a break for it. I'll do the lifting."

Poppy whimpered a time or two when he stepped out the door, then nuzzled against Mila. "Ah, you ignore me from the moment he knocks, but now that he's gone for a minute, you want my attention again, huh? You're easy, Poppy."

And a good thing she was, because the last word anyone would ever use describe Mila was *easy*.

Jessica Ramirez drove a bright orange vintage convertible Bug. Of course. What other car could possibly suit her as well? She was standing in the street, bent over the back seat when Sam reached the sidewalk. Looking up, she grinned. "You don't look any the worse for wear after meeting Poppy."

"I grew up on a farm with a lot of big animals." He pulled a laundry basket from the front seat with various dishes tucked inside between thick towels, then picked up an insulated tote bag that clinked when he shifted it.

"Siblings?"

"Cousins. There are more Douglases around here than you can…"

"Shake a stick at?" Carefully Jessica balanced her own laundry basket. "I never understood that saying, but it's older than I am, and that's says a lot. Have you lived here all your life?"

"Since I was a twinkle in my daddy's eyes."

Stepping onto the sidewalk, she bumped her shoulder against his. "Now that one I understand. Let's avoid the sweet beast and go straight around to the back porch. I'm sure that's where Mila plans to put us."

Sam followed her across the garden, through a tall gate on the south side of the house and into the backyard. Like the front, it was all flowers and colors and sweet smells. The sun stretched long shadows over the beds and the path, a lone mimosa tree in the middle making a dappled pattern. A string of lights illuminated the porch, a gauzy island of white, thanks to the thin…

"Mosquito netting?" he asked.

"Ugh, the little buggers go crazy for me." Jessica climbed the steps, then shouldered aside an opening in the net so he could enter. "The only way I can be outside after dark without becoming a meal for them is if I'm going a hundred miles an hour in my little car." Then she grimaced. "Oh. Cop. Forget I said that."

Laughing, he set the basket on a worn wood cabinet against the wall. Jessica deposited hers there, as well, then gestured toward the dining table and the chair pushed into the outside corner. "Have a seat there, if you will. When Mila and I have a dinner party, we like to wait on our guest instead of climbing over him every time we need something."

It was a tight fit back in that corner, but it would give him the prettiest view: the two women. No Douglas ever turned down the chance to look at pretty women, his uncle Hank preached, and Sam agreed.

As he settled in, the back door opened and Poppy shot out. Sam wondered if she would upend the table to get to him, or rip the yards of mosquito netting right down from their hooks, but she skidded to a stop at the top of the steps, waiting politely until Mila parted the overlapping fabric. Trotting into the yard, Poppy lowered her nose to the ground and disappeared down the path.

Every day was an adventure for Poppy. Hell, every hour was.

"Sit, Mila," Jessica commanded. "My food—I get to serve."

Mila took the chair to Sam's right, crossing her legs, smelling of jasmine and vanilla. While he'd helped Jessica, she'd put her hair up off her neck in a style that was messy and careless and touchable and tempting.

She wasn't wearing makeup—apparently didn't need it, because her skin tone was smooth and even, her lashes were dark and curly, and her lips were tinged a natural pinkish shade.

She was prettier than he'd noticed yesterday. Of course, yesterday she'd looked one scare away from collapsing into a heap. She was back in control of herself today. Not her circumstances, necessarily—he knew well that if left to her own choices, she wouldn't have invited him to dinner this evening—but her eyes weren't haunted now, and she didn't seem so weary and worn.

"Your garden is beautiful," he said as he spread his napkin over his lap. "If you ever get tired of working for Lawrence—" a tiny wrinkle appeared between her eyes "—you could go into business as a landscaper. I really like your bluebonnets and the coneflowers. The golden esperanzas are gorgeous, too."

Her gaze shifted to his. "You know flowers?"

"Depends on who's asking. If my mom says, 'Go get me ten flats of apricot zinnias,' I forget what color apricot is and what zinnias look like. If you ask, 'Do you like the apricots better than the thumbelinas right next to them?' my answer would be yes, though thumbelinas are awfully pretty, too."

The faint hint of a smile stirred across her face. Okay, so if all else failed, he could talk flowers with her until his store of knowledge ran out. Should've paid more attention all those times he'd helped out his parents.

Jessica handed a dinner plate across the table to him, heaped with smoky ribs and thick slabs of bologna bearing grill marks and a glaze of barbecue sauce. Around the sides she'd tucked in fresh cherry tomatoes sprinkled with herbs and a light dressing, potato salad and a mound of vegetable salad. After handing a smaller serving to Mila and setting a third one at her own place, she passed around tall glasses of iced tea and added a loaf of Rainbo white sandwich bread and a roll of paper towels for napkins. Flashbacks to meals on the farm.

"You don't happen to run a restaurant," Sam said tentatively. He gestured to the food and considered the relatively quick manner she'd pulled it all together.

"No, but I always thought I'd be good at it. I do like to be prepared for any circumstance."

Between them, he noticed, Mila was trying not to smile. He fixed his gaze on her. "What's her secret?"

It was the wrong question to ask. Her lips went flat, the light faded from her eyes, and the muscles in her jaw clenched so tight that he expected to hear her teeth grinding. After a moment and a helpless look at Jessica, her wariness—almost fear—changed to panic. "I'm sorry. I didn't— I wasn't—"

Jessica reached across and gripped her granddaughter's hand tightly in hers. "Aw, there's no secret," she said, sounding almost as natural as before. "I do like to be prepared for everything, and that includes knowing where to buy the best home-style ribs and potato salad—at Reasor's and that new little deli across from the courthouse—plus always having a crop of fresh cherry tomatoes in my roof garden and keeping the ingredients for sauerkraut salad on hand. That's the way we host in this family, isn't it, Mila?"

Mila's response was unconvincing, but Sam pretended, like her grandmother, that he didn't notice anything unusual. "Sauerkraut salad," he repeated, forking it apart. "Is it like coleslaw?"

"Were you a detective before you became police chief?"

"Yes, ma'am."

"Then detect. Take a bite."

He obeyed, tasting sauerkraut, sugar and vinegar, bell pepper, onion, and pimiento. "Wow. Way better than coleslaw." He complimented everything else as he tasted it, keeping up with his end of the conversation while some part of his mind stayed locked on the episode with Mila. Whose secrets had she been conditioned to keep, and how bad had the punishment for letting them slip been?

He couldn't imagine Jessica Ramirez ever mistreating her granddaughter. Instinct never led him wrong, and it said Jessica loved Mila dearly and would protect her with her life. What was it Mila had said about her yesterday? *She'll come. She always comes.* And with such intense affection.

So the next likely person for forcing secret keeping would be Mila's mother or father. There'd been no mention of them, and honestly Sam hadn't thought anything of it. His family was extraordinarily close, all ten or twelve dozen of them, but of course, others weren't so blessed—or cursed. Things had gone sour between Lois and her side of the family after she'd become a cop. Ben Little Bear hadn't heard from his younger brother in ten years. There was nothing unusual about Mila being close to her grandmother while her parents were out of the picture.

The only thing that would make it unusual was *why* her parents were out of the picture. Had they abandoned her? Had she abandoned them? Had they died when she was too young to live on her own? Were they in jail, in a hospital, out of the country, out of touch?

An inquisitive nature was a requirement for his job. He couldn't be satisfied with the normal flow of information between people. He had to be curious, spot questions that might never come up, find inconsistencies in stories, recognize lies, know when reactions didn't match stimuli and be just damn nosy about everything and everyone. He was snoopy, his mom said. Terminally curious, his grandfather called it.

Mila's reaction had been odd, and of course he'd like to know what had caused it, but in the overall scheme of things, it was okay to let it go. It was perfectly okay to forget it, to focus on the good food, the good company and the small things that drew her out—talking about flowers, her grandmother and, of course, Poppy.

He was off duty tonight. No cop-ly intuition, no inherent need to arrange everything in neat facts. He was having dinner with a woman he liked a lot and her granddaughter, whom he thought he might also like a lot in whole other ways, and he was going to enjoy it.

There was always time to wonder later.

Mila had learned the hopefulness in writing during a ninth-grade assignment in her online school. "Write your best vacation experience," the teacher had said, in a thousand words. Mila had never actually been on a vacation, so she'd created one out of thin air. It wasn't much, just the kind of getaway that she and Gramma might have taken if they'd had the money and Gramma hadn't worked two jobs most of the time to support them. She'd researched cabins for rent in the state parks, picked one and created a fantasy weekend of boating, fishing and hiking in the woods. The paper had earned an A and a comment of "lovely" from the instructor.

With that, she'd learned that words could take you to other places, other lives, other outcomes. They could give voice to the emotions eating her raw inside and make her feel better at the same time. For a kid as strange as she was, they could give her friends— not the kind she went shopping or to movies with, the kind who knew everything about her, but online friends who lived elsewhere, who didn't know her real name or where she lived or how old she was or if she was even a girl, but they chose to take her on faith.

They'd given her a way to start coping with her nightmares—catharsis, her psychologist called it—and now she wondered if they might give her a way to cope with the new issues in her life.

Sam Douglas in particular.

Don't you want a boyfriend someday? Mila had always said no. She had always lied. More than anything in the world, she wanted to be normal, and that meant friends and best friends and boyfriends and dating and falling in love and getting married and having kids.

The thought of all that made her skin tingle and her lungs tighten. She couldn't handle that many people, that much complexity, that many opportunities to hurt or be hurt. But everything in life started with one step. Choose a plant. Dig a hole. Put it in. Water. Water. Water. Watch it grow. Feed it. Clip the blossoms to enjoy inside. Deadhead it. Water it more.

Friend–best friend–boyfriend–dating–love–marriage– kids surely must be the same way. There was only one step she had to take first, before any of the rest of it could become even a remote possibility.

She had to open herself up. Gramma told her so. Her psychologist told her so. Common sense told her so. Granted, Gramma, her psychologist and common sense didn't know how incredibly difficult a first step that was, and she did, because she'd been trying and failing for fifteen years. It was so much less scary alone in her little house with Poppy. If she let no one in, then no one could hurt her. If no one saw how vulnerable she was, no one would take advantage of her. If she didn't ask anyone to trust her, no one could expect her to trust them.

No one could be disappointed in her. No one could ever see how damaged she was. How afraid she was. How lonely she was.

She sat on her front porch, the sun barely lighting the Monday-morning sky, with a cup of iced coffee in one hand, her feet propped on the porch railing and a notebook leaning against her knees. It was a cheap spiral notebook, bought at Walmart in a back-to-school sale. She'd filled a few pages this morning with her jumbled thoughts, trying to find some order.

She hadn't found it by the time Ruben pulled up, but her mind was calmer. Sliding to her feet, she set the book and ink pen just inside the door on the end table, called goodbye to Poppy, and locked up before hurrying to the truck.

In her mind, she practiced words that came naturally to everyone in her world except her. She climbed into the front seat, yanked the door shut and balanced her coffee, breathed deeply, stared straight ahead and said, "Good morning."

A moment's silence, then Alejandro muttered something, and Ruben grunted.

Again she breathed deeply. That wasn't as hard as she'd thought it might be. If she'd learned it when she was little, like most kids, it would have been as easy as breathing.

They'd gone a mile or so when Ruben flicked his gaze her way. "Good weekend?"

If she hadn't seen him look at her, she wouldn't have considered he might be talking to her. "Yes," she said. "Uh, yeah."

How about that? She'd made small talk.

Their second client on Mondays was the worst one. Mr. Greeley had invested wisely and retired at fifty. With Mrs. Greeley long since moved on to husband number two and having taken the kids with her, he didn't seem to have anything to keep him busy besides harassing the help. He told his housekeeper how to mop the kitchen floor, argued the pH of the water with the pool service, insisted Mila deadhead at a precise forty-degree angle and pestered every other soul who set foot on his property.

She'd once overheard Mario tell Alejandro that what the man needed was a woman. What he needed was a purpose in life. He should go back to work, volunteer at some charity, give himself a reason to get out of bed in the morning so he didn't have to berate others to feel useful. Who retired at fifty—in this case, quit living at fifty—just because he could?

Because the Greeley yard was large and had thirty-eight trees to trim around—Mario had counted them—Mila started out on the stand-on mower. It beat walking behind a push mower, like Ruben, but by the time she finished her portion of the lawn, her shoulders and upper back were aching and sweat drenched her T-shirt and overshirt. She was happy to escape to the back of the house with her gardening tools, this time including— God save her—a ruler. Mr. Greeley wanted the mulch exactly three and a half inches deep in every bed and on every path, so every week, she measured, raked and leveled them.

In businesses like theirs, Gramma said, quirky people paid the bills. *Don't grouse about them. Celebrate them.*

Of course, a lot of people thought Gramma was quirky. Mila, on the other hand, they considered just plain odd.

The housekeeper came out of the kitchen while Mila was finishing one of the beds. She smiled, nodded and proceeded to the pots on the patios that were lush with herbs. With a pair of small shears, she snipped stalks and stems into the small basket she carried, then turned toward the vegetable garden at the back edge. "I just get some tomatoes," she said with another smile and a heavy South Asian accent.

Mila nodded and continued to her own destination, the shrubs that marched across the back edge of the yard. She passed the garden, its tall fence intended to protect it from wildlife. She had watched quietly last week as a deer gracefully leaped in, snacked to her heart's content, then leaped out again and disappeared into the trees. Mr. Greeley might be able to control the rest of the world with his demands, but the deer wasn't impressed by how much money he had.

She approached the line of blue junipers, far too uniform for her tastes. She liked freedom, flow and movement, not the unnatural precision of too much pruning. And that was why she had her own garden: most customers didn't care what she liked. They paid her boss so she would do what *they* liked.

She was inspecting the junipers when she heard the first sound: a sharp intake of breath from the garden area. Turning, she looked for the housekeeper, who might reach five foot two on tiptoe, but saw no sign of her behind the plentiful tomato, corn and okra plants.

Then came a bloodcurdling scream, a rustle of plants swaying, small feet pounding on the path. Mila, her own feet frozen to the ground, followed the woman's progress by the plants she bumped or mowed over on her way to the gate. Wild-eyed, she burst through the gate, looked frantically around, then ran to Mila, grabbing her arms, speaking rapidly in a language Mila didn't understand.

Mario came running from around front, followed by Ruben. An instant later, the powerful roar of Alejandro's mower shut off, and he joined the men. Ruben's gaze met Mila's as he handed the hysterical housekeeper to Mario, then beckoned Mila to go with him.

I don't want to. Please don't make me. I don't want to see, I'll do anything you say, I'll be good, just please don't make me look. The little-girl whimper was sharp and raw, echoing in her brain even as she forced herself to take the first step, then the next.

Ruben went first, around the fence, through the gate, along the main path where rows branched off to the left. Corn, okra, cucumbers, lettuce, bell peppers and, last, tomatoes, planted where the taller plants helped protect them from the midday sun. She counted six, seven varieties—heirloom, hybrid, giant beefsteaks to tiny grapes, red, yellow, green and striped.

Finally she had no choice but to look at the cause of

the housekeeper's scream. Mr. Greeley lay on his back across the path, tomatoes spilled from a trug that lay on its side and red stains, too many of them, marking his shirt. Still sticking out of the center of his chest was the source of those stains: a wicked sharp pair of pruning shears, the pivot and a portion of the shank buried in his flesh.

Mila couldn't breathe. She couldn't think. She couldn't run far, far away and hide. She could only stare, could only feel the vicious ache in her own chest, could only remember…too much, too much, just too damn much.

God help me, why is this happening again?

Chapter 4

It was raining the night my parents died. Dark clouds threatened all day, but the storm had held off until the skies were black. I stood at a side window, unable to see anything, but my skin prickled, and every breath I took was an effort. As lightning flashed a brilliant warning in the night, thunder erupted, vibrating through the ground and the floor and right up into my body.

The storm had arrived.

My mother's eyes glittered with excitement as she pulled on her slicker. She took hold of my arm and dragged me across the kitchen toward the back door. My terror found its voice as I dug in my heels. "Let go. I don't want to—"

"Your father warned you, but you wouldn't listen. Now you're going to see just what you're making him do." She opened the back door and shoved me to my knees at the bottom of the steps. By the time I stood up, she was beside me again, her nails biting into my skin.

It was twenty yards to the barn, lit only by the flashes from the sky. I lost my balance, sliding in the mud, but her forward momentum kept me upright. As water soaked my clothes and turned my dingy sneakers brown, I thought, *She'll punish me for this tomorrow. "How did you get your shoes so dirty? You are so stupid. You do it just to cause me trouble."*

Maybe I was stupid. Just ahead, behind big wooden doors, my father waited with his next victim, and I worried about shoes? He intended to force me to watch his sick game to the end, and all I could think about was my own problems?

God wasn't a name heard often in our house, and when it was used, it was a curse rather than a prayer. I didn't know how to pray, beyond what my grandmother had taught me when I was five. Those were the only words I could put in coherent order. *Now I lay me down to sleep.*

The door was just ahead. I wanted to stop. To break and run. To hide under my bed and hope that this time when they moved on—they always moved on after every victim—they would forget to take me with them. If I made myself small enough and quiet enough, if I pretended I was invisible, if I prayed…

I pray the Lord my soul to keep.

If they made me watch this tonight, I wasn't

sure I would still have a soul come morning. Some things were just too fragile to survive.

If I should die before I wake...

My mother had to let go of me to shove open the wide heavy doors, spilling out yellow light into the storm. He was in there, but I didn't see him right away. I tried not to see anything, but I didn't have a choice. She was there, hands tied above her head, in the middle of the large space. Her mouth was taped; her eyes were huge and fearful and her breathing was a pained gasp that hurt me to hear. She knew I'd gotten her into this, and she looked at me as if I could save her.

I pray the Lord my soul to take.

I couldn't save her. I couldn't save myself. All I could do was pray the Lord my soul to take. And hers. Right now. A lightning strike, a funnel cloud swooping out of the sky to carry us away.

Because the real storm was yet to come.

—Excerpt, *The Unlucky Ones* by Jane Gama

"Chief, Lois is looking for us."

Sam looked up as Ben Little Bear strode out of Judge Watson's second-floor courtroom. The hearing he'd appeared for had already started; Ben should have been on the stand the past five minutes. Instead, he was heading for the stairs and obviously had no doubt that Sam would follow.

"What's up?" Only an emergency could get an officer off Judge Watson's stand, and the old coot had a different definition of the word than everyone else did.

Their boots clunked on the marble stairs, the noise bouncing off the high ceiling and echoing off the walls.

The Cedar County Courthouse was more than a hundred years old, built at a time when marble and stone and intricate woodwork had been within a small city's reach. It was one of the beauties of Cedar Creek architecture.

Ben reached the first floor before glancing back. "We have another murder. That makes three in four years. Two in five days."

Sam's gut tightened. Cedar Creek's violent crime mostly ran along the lines of burglaries, robberies, drug deals gone bad, assaults and domestic disputes. It was enough to keep the department busy, but not enough to overly worry the town council or the residents.

"That's not all." Ben pushed one of the heavy doors open, then held it for Sam. "Guess who was there when the body was found."

Sam hated statements like that. If the answers weren't obvious, no one would say them in the first place. Adjusting his hat against the glaring sun, he matched his stride to Ben's as they headed for the police department, a minute's walk away across the town square.

"Mila," he murmured more to himself than Ben. *Why?* Of the twenty-five thousand people in town, why her?

"Milagro Ramirez." Ben's confirmation was flat. "Quite a coincidence, huh."

Lois was waiting at the foot of the broad steps that led into police headquarters. She looked as grim on the outside as Sam felt inside. "Victim is Curt Greeley. Lives out at the old Burnett place set back off Highway 66. Remember, he fought the extension of the city limits out there. Said if he'd wanted to be in the city, he would have bought in the city."

And had been pretty pissed off about losing the fight. "I remember. He said he'd have the council's jobs and mine, too."

Ben snorted derisively. "If we had a dollar for every time someone's told us that…"

"Hell, no one wants our job," Lois said, covering the ground to the parking lot with long strides. "Not for what they pay us. Tucker and Simpson were first on the scene, Sam, and Fire Rescue's out there, too, though there's no one to resuscitate except maybe the woman. She was awfully shaken."

"Yeah," Ben said. "Maybe."

Sam cast him a look before angling off to his truck, parked in his reserved space. He didn't wait to get his seat belt fastened before flipping on the lights and siren and shifting into gear.

It was Ben's job to be suspicious, he reminded himself as he headed west down a side street with less traffic than First Street. It was *his* job, too, but Mila wasn't the cold-blooded killer type. She'd had no motive to kill Evan Carlyle, and even though Curt Greeley was one of the meanest SOBs in town, people managed to deal with him every day without resorting to murder. He was sure Mila gritted her teeth, made an effort not to offend him and escaped his company as quickly as possible. Just like everyone else did.

Sam's phone rang, and he glanced at caller ID before answering. "Yeah, Ben." The car radios were handy, as were the microphones clipped onto their uniforms, but cells were great for convenience and privacy.

"What do you know about Greeley?"

"He was buddies with my uncle Hank and my cousin Zee back in the day. He was arrogant and obnoxious, and the more money he made, the worse he got. Even Zee wouldn't have anything to do with him after a while."

Ben's grunt was simple but enough. Zee was a well-known waste of space who would hang out with a rabid skunk if the skunk could put up with him. Zee had no standards. When he dropped a person, that person had no hope. He'd become the lowest of the low.

"Family?" Ben asked.

"Used to be. Wife left him about eight years ago and took the kids. Very ugly, very public. Rumor said it was a huge blow to his ego because he'd never lost anything before, and it left him a little unhinged."

"Enemies?"

"Everyone who ever met the man."

"Great. No one with an obvious grudge against the first victim, everyone with a grudge against the second."

"Better start making those lists, Ben," Sam teased before disconnecting. The Greeley house was little more than a mile past the edge of town, barely a quarter mile inside the new city limits. He shut off the siren but kept the lights on as he turned into the long drive.

The house was a bona fide Southern mansion, rescued from a hundred years' neglect on the banks of the Mississippi River in southern Louisiana and moved to its current location. Even back in the '50s, the move had cost a fortune, but the doctor behind it had spared no expense. His beloved wife had had a thing for the Deep South, and he'd been happy to bring a small portion of it to Oklahoma for her.

Sam's mom had called the doctor and his wife a true love story. After their deaths, Curt and Charlaine

Greeley had bought the place. He seriously doubted the story they'd lived out had had much love in it. Curt had been all about power and control and humiliating the people around him.

Sam pulled off the driveway and parked in the grass next to the Fire Rescue truck, giving them room to leave if they got a call. The familiar Happy Grass pickup was parked closest to the garage, a fire engine behind them, an ambulance to the side. Its rear doors were open, and the paramedics were fussing over a dark-haired woman wrapped in a cotton blanket. Mila?

No. The instant the thought occurred to him, she stepped into view, with her coworkers beside the pickup truck. Her expression was troubled, her shoulders rounded, but truthfully, she looked no worse than the three men with her. No more invested.

As Sam approached the ambulance, Cullen Simpson met him. *He* looked sweaty, pale and green around the gills. The kid had gone off and seen his first dead body. It had to happen sometime, but Sam wouldn't have minded if he'd gotten more experience first.

"Where's Tucker?"

Simpson's Adam's apple bobbed. "Out back with the body."

"You okay?"

This time he bobbed his entire head, but he didn't look at all convincing. "Mr. Greeley's body was found by the housekeeper, Luna—Lushan—Lu—"

With a thin unsteady smile, the woman leaning against the bumper of the ambulance offered her hand. "Lunasha Ajmera."

Sam shook hands with her, automatically assessing her. She was short, round, probably in her early to mid-sixties. She radiated caring and security. She looked motherly. Grandmotherly.

He introduced Ben and Lois to the woman, then circled the ambulance and headed for the lawn crew. The men instinctively drifted away, moving to the shade provided by the garage overhang, leaving Mila standing in the harsh sun.

"We've got to quit meeting like this," she said.

Sam was surprised. He hadn't been sure she had a sense of humor, especially one that bordered on inappropriate given the circumstances. She seemed to regret the comment quickly enough, pressing her lips into a thin line and directing her gaze off in the distance.

"Sounds good to me. But then we'll have to find other places to meet."

This time the surprise was hers. She looked at him from the corners of her eyes, her brows arched upward. Thinking his comment was even more inappropriate?

He gestured toward a grove of crape myrtles on the east side of the lawn, and they began walking that way. Lines showed how far the crew had gotten in cutting the grass before the discovery, and the fresh scents drifted up with every step they took.

"What happened?" He pulled an ink pen from his shirt pocket and a notebook from his hip pocket, flipping it open to a clean page. While they walked, his notes would be a crappy shorthand that no one but him could read, but it was enough to get the point across.

Mila removed her ball cap and swiped her sleeve across her face. Her hair was in a braid today that hung between her shoulder blades, the black glossy and glinting in the sun. "I was in the backyard getting ready to trim the junipers. Mr. Greeley likes them to be uniform. The housekeeper—"

"Lunasha."

"She was clipping herbs when I went out back. She said she was going to get some tomatoes from the garden. I heard a gasp, and then she screamed. She came tearing out of the garden, out the gate, and grabbed me. I couldn't understand what she was saying."

His first impression had been wrong. Mila was shaken. Her flat narrative was proof of that. The way she stood utterly motionless. The emotional disconnect that wrapped itself around her.

"Did you know Mr. Greeley was home?"

"I didn't think about it. I had my ruler. I was prepared." She stepped into the grove, weaving around the trees and took a seat on the concrete bench in their shade.

"Your ruler?"

She gazed up at him before moving over a few inches on the bench, making room for him. "Did you know him?"

"I did."

"He was…difficult."

"He was." Sam sat down beside her, far enough away that they couldn't accidentally touch.

"He wanted us to 'fix' all these crapes as soon as they finished blooming this year. There wasn't enough structure to them. He wanted them pruned to the same size, the same shape. He wanted the blossoms in each group to be identical in color. He wanted strict regimentation in both his yard and his gardens."

Bracing his notebook on his knee, Sam glanced around at the trees. The bark peeling from the trunks was his favorite part of the crape myrtle, but their free-form shape and lush flowers made them gorgeous. They belonged here, growing rampant with the Southern mansion, but it didn't surprise him at all that Greeley had wanted them under tight control or gone. He'd given pretty much the same order to everyone in his life, and everyone had chosen gone.

But now he was gone. The crapes had been saved.

"Did you talk with him often?"

"No. When our crew took on this property, he gave us tutorials on how to do our jobs—how short to cut the grass, how deep the mulch should be, exactly where to make cuts when trimming branches, how far apart to plant this tomato plant from that one. He checked on us about once a month to make sure we haven't forgotten."

Jeez. Sam had just developed a new level of respect for all the service people in the world. He dealt with plenty of demanding, overbearing and just plain mean people himself, but at least he had some measure of protection from the badge he wore and the title he carried. He'd worked for a chief who stood up for his officers, and Sam made sure his officers knew he had their backs.

He was pretty damn sure Mila's boss didn't stick up for his crews. He was also pretty damn sure they didn't get paid extra for dealing with a jerk like Greeley, even though the boss did.

Ben called him on the radio, and Sam answered, then stood. "I need to go out back. Can you wait here? I have some more questions."

She nodded, and again he became aware of that sense of distance about her. As if she was holding herself together in some way he didn't understand. Like she wasn't here in the blazing sun being asked about the second murder in five days, but somewhere…else.

He would like to be somewhere else with her.

Maybe someday. But right now he had a body to examine.

Last night, Gramma had called Mila during the news when the latest lottery winner was announced. She bought a ticket religiously, just one, and always called Mila during the drawing so she could share the thrill of winning with her. Every one of those lottery tickets had been losers, though, and Mila always ended the conversation with "Better luck next time."

"You bet," Gramma always replied. "We'll win someday, pretty girl. We'll be so rich we'll buy our own state. Our own country. I'm thinking England."

Being rich, at least for Mr. Carlyle and Mr. Greeley, hadn't ended the way fantasies were supposed to. When Gramma won the lottery and they bought England, they were supposed to live happily ever after. Everything was supposed to go their way. Otherwise, what was the point?

Though she felt selfish for even thinking it, Mila wondered how far behind schedule this would put them. Presumably, like last week, they wouldn't be allowed to finish the job since it was now a crime scene. The officers would question each of them in their own time, and if they hadn't already, sooner or later they would wonder at the coincidence of two murders committed while the same group of people was around. Evan Carlyle hadn't been dead long before she'd found him, and neither had Mr. Greeley. She and Ruben had both seen the last trickles of blood seeping from his wounds.

Goose bumps rising on her arms, she took a long look around. Traffic buzzed by on the highway, barely visible. The front and sides of Greeley's property were fenced in, but the gate from the highway was always open. The nearest houses were out of sight, but she'd heard sounds before—dogs barking, a chain saw, music—suggesting that the neighbors were a short walk through the woods. There could be a back road that left the property in that direction, or someone with a four-wheeler could have made his own trail.

A murderer showing up at her place of work twice. What were the odds of that?

She was so lost in the ugliness of that thought that Sam's reappearance startled her. He must have noticed that her mind was wandering, because he'd stopped at the edge of the copse, giving her a moment to notice him. If he'd just suddenly appeared on the path in front of her, she might have managed a scream at least as impressive as Lunasha's had been.

Once he had her attention, he sat down again, as far toward the end of the bench as he could get, then shifted to face her. His expression was grave, his eyes shadowed. "Greeley was still alive when you—when you saw him."

Mila nodded.

"You didn't see anyone around who didn't belong? No vehicles anywhere? No sense of someone watching?"

She shook her head. So the killer could have been in the yard, could have been interrupted in his escape by Lunasha or Mila. That made an already disturbing experience even more so.

"Did you leave the body alone after finding it?"

"Ruben waited with him." He hadn't said anything beyond instructing Alejandro and Mario to take the women around front. She'd suspected he'd found it disrespectful to leave the man sprawled there alone on the path. Ruben was never subservient but always respectful, even though many of their customers couldn't tell the difference.

Sam—*Oh, now you call him Sam, when this situation certainly calls for Chief*—the chief wiped away sweat that had beaded on his upper lip. "So this makes two of your clients."

So it was sooner rather than later. Mila's insides clenched, but she forced a steady nod.

"Do you have any idea if they knew each other?"

"No."

"How long had they been Happy Grass customers?"

"This was our first year with Mr. Greeley. Probably would have been our last. He was never happy with anyone, and he changed services every season. We already had the Carlyle account when I started three years ago."

"What do you know about the rest of your crew?"

Her gaze went to the driveway, where officers were questioning her coworkers. "I'm comfortable with them."

The honesty of the statement surprised her and, judging by the arch of his brows, the chief, too. Did he understand from the time they'd spent together how important that was to her? She wanted him to, more than she could explain, so she went on talking to keep herself from watching for his responses. Though his pen scribbling across the notebook didn't thrill her, surely that was something most people would find disconcerting, and not just those with secrets to keep.

"They're hard workers. They never shirk their duties. They've never missed a day of work in the time I've been with them except Alejandro, who took a few days off when his son was born early and was in the neonatal unit at Hillcrest. They treat me the same way they treat each other. We're efficient."

Being treated no differently…that was important, too. But she thought that, perhaps, only a person who *was* different could fully appreciate it.

"Tell me about your boss."

She said the first thing that came to mind. "Once you've ruled us out, he's the next obvious connection between Mr. Carlyle and Mr. Greeley."

One corner of his mouth turned up. "Do you know anything about Ed Lawrence's working relationship with his clients? Any problems?"

"No." She took a deep breath, preparing to say more right now than she'd said at one time in longer than she could remember. Silence and *no* came so easily to her, but she wanted him to think of her as cooperative.

She didn't want to be investigated as a possible suspect.

She didn't want everyone, or anyone, to ever know the truth about her.

"As police chief, it's important for you to get along with people—the ones you work for, the ones who work for you, the ones you arrest, the ones you protect. You have social relationships with your employees, your bosses, your constituents. You know their spouses' names, their kids' names, what sports teams they support and what churches they attend.

"Happy Grass isn't like that. Mr. Lawrence walks through the yard in the morning before we all head out on our routes, and he can't call one of us by name. My crew alone is from Panama, Bolivia and Italy, and for me, Ramirez is just a name I got from Gramma. No Latina blood to go with it. But Mr. Lawrence thinks we're all Mexican. There are four women on the crews at Happy Grass. One is Cherokee, one is Asian American, one is a blue-eyed, corn-fed blonde from Nebraska. To the boss, we're all 'that little Mexican gal, Maria.' The only interest he has in us is getting the best work possible for the lowest pay acceptable."

Sam needed a moment to finish his notes, and she watched as black ink filled line after line in the narrow notebook. She couldn't make out his handwriting beyond the date and time he'd printed at the top of the page. But that was all right. If he made comments to pursue later or questioned her veracity or honesty, she didn't want to know.

His pen had stopped moving for a moment before she realized it. She lifted her gaze to his. His next question, though, wasn't what she'd expected. "So why do you work for him?"

Her mouth opened, then closed again. She had a pat answer to that question: she loved being outside and taking care of plants. The few people who asked were perplexed by the idea of wanting to be out in triple-digit temperatures and high humidity or the thought of doing someone else's menial work, or they were just grateful someone was willing to do the dirty work so they didn't have to.

Gramma had never asked. She knew after eleven years of mostly indoor prisons, Mila needed the freedom of standing in the sun and the shade and the rain, of not having to hide if anyone came along, of not being forced to pretend she didn't exist. It was far more than just a job to her. It was part of her sanity.

Which made her response sound incredibly lame. "I—I really like what I do."

"But you could do it for someone a hell of a lot better than Ed Lawrence."

And there was the untold reason she liked her job: she already had it. She'd made it through the application and the interview and the background check, shabby as they were. How did she know, if she went elsewhere, they wouldn't have a more extensive application and interview and a more intensive background check? Who could guarantee they wouldn't find out that her Social Security number was a sham, that her name was fake, that her life was made up out of whole cloth?

She fit as well at Happy Grass as she was ever going to, and Mr. Lawrence didn't care about her past, future or present. He was less emotionally invested in her than he was in the other tools of his trade: the mowers, the trimmers, the trucks.

She hoped her shrug appeared casual, because it felt to her like spasmodic twitches. "As long as someone's there to put my proper name on my paycheck, I'm fine. I work with my crew, Chief. They're the important ones."

A hawk soared across the sky, wings outstretched, needing virtually no effort to ride the currents, majestic and free. She had dreamed of freedom for so long that having it still sometimes felt like a dream. She still woke some nights, caught halfway between sleep and awareness, and went into a panic at the sight of the night-light or the open curtains where someone might see in. Those nights, when her heart stopped pounding, when her breathing slowed from laboring freight train to shallow and easy, she got out of bed, turned on other lights and stood at the window. Sometimes she even went outside and walked through the backyard, the mulch and pebbles dirtying the bottoms of her feet, and on very rare occasions, the little girl inside her wept with joy that she could do it without fear.

The chief watched the hawk, too, until the bird disappeared over the woods. Then he settled his gaze on her. "You can call me Sam."

She'd discovered today that she could. She just didn't think she should. Despite her freedom, there were still so many things she couldn't do. "I don't think so."

"Why not? I've been to your house three times now. I met your grandmother—who, by the way, gave me permission to call her Gramma. I had dinner at your house." He paused, then grinned. "Poppy likes me. You can't ask for a better endorsement than that."

Poppy and Gramma did like him, and their opinions meant more to her than anyone else's. "But you're the chief of police, and I'm…"

"A subject in a case?"

Sooner rather than later, she reminded herself, her heart kicking into high gear. Trembling started inside her, working its way out, tiny little tremors in fingers and muscles and—

"I said *subject*. Not *suspect*. A subject is just someone involved in a case in some manner—a witness, a friend, a coworker, a paramedic, a firefighter. Just because I've questioned you a couple times as a subject doesn't mean we have to stay on formal terms. If it does, I'll let Detective Little Bear or Officer Gideon ask any further questions."

She considered it a long moment before saying, "All

right." It took another breath, another quick tightening of her nerves, for her to actually say it. "Sam."

He grinned again, satisfied and authoritative and handsome, and she couldn't help but think that she'd just taken a very big step.

She hoped it didn't end in her falling on her face.

Sam finished writing his report and grabbed a bottle of water from the lounge refrigerator before heading into the conference room. He was a few minutes late, but operating on a strict schedule was pretty much impossible in the cop business. Ben was the only one waiting, his laptop in front of him. Lois, Tucker, Simpson and Daniel Harper would join them as soon as they could.

"You look annoyed," Sam remarked as he sat down across from Ben. Truthfully, he looked the same way as always—stoic and long-suffering—but a few tics gave him away to anyone who'd grown up with him. His eyes were a shade narrower than usual, and his jaw was clenched tight enough to show the slender line of muscle on each side. He also held his head cocked slightly to the side and was less willing than usual to make eye contact.

"You know Ed Lawrence?" Ben pushed his laptop a few inches way, straightened his head and kneaded his neck with one hand.

"Only over the phone."

"Huh. To hear him tell it, you're best buds. After I left the Greeley place, I went out to Happy Grass to talk to him. He offered to fire those four employees effective immediately if you thought he should. In fact, he offered to fire all his 'brown' employees." With his dark skin and Creek Indian ancestry, Ben didn't have to make clear what he thought of Lawrence's offer. "Of course, he'd be out of business in a day if he did."

"Did you learn anything from him?"

"He's a snake. Even his office girl—his words, not mine—doesn't care much for him, and she's married to him." Ben leaned back as Lois came in, carrying a tray of homemade cookies. "He says he gets along great with all his clients and that Greeley couldn't have been happier with the job his people were doing."

Lois snorted disbelievingly. "Curt Greeley was never happy, and Ed Lawrence doesn't tell the truth unless there's something in it for him." She sat next to Ben, then slid the cookies to a spot exactly in front of Sam. As soon as he reached for one, though, she pulled the tray back. "Tell us about Mee-lah-gro."

He tried to scowl at her, but it was a lot like trying to scowl at his mother. He'd be lucky if she didn't grab him by the ear and tweak it until he danced in pain. "She goes by Mila, and she's not a killer."

"Is that your cop-ly side talking or the manly side?"

"I trust my intuition."

"Yes, but has your intuition ever told you something about a woman that you didn't want to hear?"

"No."

"Liar. Remember that lawyer you went out with? We all tried to warn you." She exchanged grins with Ben. "That woman was too kinky for handcuffs. I don't know where she got her ideas, but she was a dirty, dirty girl—and you knew it before things got weird."

Sam hated it when he couldn't argue with Lois. On the surface, Beth DePuy had seemed amazingly right for him. She was an assistant district attorney—he arrested criminals, and she prosecuted them. They'd had everything in common. His mother had loved her. His father had been half *in* love with her. Everyone thought they were perfect.

Though all along Sam had had a niggling little suspicion that something wasn't right.

Too kinky for handcuffs. That about summed it up.

Thankfully, the other officers filed in then. Lois had no qualms about picking on him in private or with Ben, but she never mocked her boss in front of other employees.

Each officer shared whatever information they'd learned in turn, then Sam looked around the table, shifting his gaze between the two detectives. "Are the cases connected?"

"The victims had only two things in common," Daniel said. "They both had money, and they used the same lawn service. But from what I heard, Greeley's used every big lawn service in town and a few in Tulsa."

"So you think it's a coincidence they were both killed shortly before the same lawn crew found them." That came from Ben.

Harper shrugged. "Coincidences happen. That's why someone made up the word. Two different guys. Two different circumstances. Two different weapons. Two different killers."

"Both men were killed in their backyards," Ben said. "Not vastly different circumstances. And killers don't always use the same weapon. Maybe he wasn't intending to kill Greeley today—just checking out the place. Maybe Greeley surprised him, and the killer used the only weapon available."

"Yeah, like anyone takes scissors to the garden with them," Daniel said.

"You're not a gardener, son, are you?" Lois shook her head with mock despair. Daniel had grown up in Los Angeles, and she was still giving him a hard time about it. "Yes, people use scissors or shears. You can damage the stalks by breaking off stems. And Greeley was compulsive. One of the yard guys said he made them measure the grass before and after they cut it and use a level when they raked the mulch to make sure it was even."

"And they had to use the blowers to clear the dust off the driveway," Simpson added, "all the way out to the highway. The old guy would drive out onto the shoulder of the road, and the others would blow the blacktop clean and then they could leave."

Ah, to be as young as Simpson again. Sam knew from last week's reports that Ruben Carrasco was only fifty-two. Outdoor work and tough living had weathered his skin and stooped his posture, but fifty-two was no longer nearly as old to Sam as it used to be.

"Theories?" he asked, directing the question to the room in general but intending it for Ben. He was the most experienced, had the best intuition. Daniel had the makings of a good detective, but he had some learning to do. His thoughts went first to the obvious before he opened his mind enough to let the evidence lead him.

Ben let Daniel go first. The younger detective shrugged. "Ordinarily, I'd say in a small town like this, rich people would know each other, socialize together and such, but it sounds like Greeley kept to himself other than making people who had to deal with him miserable. There doesn't appear to be any reason for Carlyle to deal with him."

"Maybe it was coincidence," Lois conceded.

"Greeley isn't the only one here who's tough to deal with," Sam pointed out.

Ben nodded. "Ed Lawrence is a piece of work, and right now his company is our only connection between the victims."

"You think someone's killing his customers to get back at him for something?" Simpson's voice was full of skepticism, and Tucker and Daniel clearly shared it. Hell, Sam did, too, to some extent. It wasn't logical or rational or reasonable, but it usually took a twisted mind to make murder any of those things. Logical people solved their disputes in rational ways. Reasonable people were repulsed by the idea of killing for any reason but the most extreme. Self-defense. Protecting someone else. Getting backed into a corner with no other way out.

"I think right now Happy Grass is the only connection we've uncovered between the victims," Ben said in his patient, dogged way. "We can't say that it matters, but we can't ignore it, either. Maybe it's coincidence that both men were found by the same Happy Grass crew. Stranger things have happened. My great-aunt Weezer won half a million dollars on the only lottery ticket she ever bought. What are the odds?"

"Your aunt Weezer won half a million dollars?" Tucker asked. "But she still drives that crappy old Ford and goes grocery shopping in her robe."

"When I was growing up, we called it a housecoat," Lois said, rolling her eyes. "And the difference is, she doesn't buy it at the dollar store anymore. She gets it at Walmart."

Sam rolled his eyes, too. Sometimes he felt like the only grown-up in the room—and when everyone was wearing a gun, that wasn't a feeling he welcomed. He let them talk for a few minutes before bringing the conversation back to the subject. "Okay, right now we keep our minds open. Ed Lawrence or his business could somehow be involved in these killings, or maybe we should all go buy lottery tickets. Anything's possible, right?"

After all, even though she'd seemed like she'd rather bite off her tongue, Mila had called him by his name, and for her, he was pretty sure, that was a huge step forward. Who knew? Sometime she might even smile at him, and somewhere down the line, she might do a whole lot more.

Anything was damn well possible.

Chapter 5

I tried to warn the last woman.

My father picked her from the girls' clothing department in the biggest store at the mall: a pretty blonde, wearing jeans and an emerald green sweater, her hair pulled back. She wasn't curvy like my mother, but not thin like me, either. Solid. That was my first thought. She looked like someone who could take care of herself, but I knew she couldn't. Not this time.

He told me where he'd be, then pushed me toward her. The sick swirling in my stomach made my steps halting, like the commands couldn't get from my brain to my legs without coming apart on the way. I stumbled over the carpet that formed passages around the store, tripped over the tile where the clothing racks stood. I wanted to run out of the store and right into the street. If I was lucky, a car would hit me, and he and my mother would run off without me. I would lie to the doctors and the police about my name, and if they ever came back looking for me, they would never find me.

Or the car hitting me would kill me. Either way, I would be free.

From the corner where he lurked, he made an impatient gesture. I saw it from the corner of my eye. I knew better than to look his way, to draw anyone's attention his way.

The woman lifted a dress from the rack, holding it at arm's length, tilting her head to study it. It was the purest, cleanest white I'd ever seen, about my size, with a rounded neck, sleeves that went to the elbow, a dropped waist with a wide ribbon so pale that I couldn't tell if it was pink or blue. I'd never had a dress like that. For just a moment, I coveted it. Coveted her. Surely a woman who bought a girl a dress like that would love her and take care of her and never make her cry.

I moved around a rack of T-shirts, turning so that my father was behind me. I was taking too long. He would be mad at me when we left, but I didn't care. He was always mad at me. I watched as she put the white dress back and picked up one the color of spring grass. Green wasn't my favorite color, but I wanted that dress, too, just because she'd picked it.

I could feel him staring at me, could feel the anger and impatience and hatred building. I couldn't move any slower without stopping. I reached the dress rack, nausea rising inside me. I never had to pretend to be afraid or to cry. That came naturally because I knew what was going to happen, because of him, because of me, and I wanted to die.

I just wanted to die easy, but I knew that wouldn't happen. He would never make it easy.

Before I could find my voice, she glanced at me. Smiled. Turned the dress so I could see it. "Do you like this?"

I nodded mutely.

"It's for my niece. Her birthday is next week. She'll be ten."

Bile worked its way up my throat and into my mouth. I swallowed it back, grimacing at the taste.

"Are you okay?" Her brows furrowed, and she swept her gaze around the area. "Where's your mom? Who are you with?"

"I—I—my father." I took a breath, a shallow one, and my lip began to tremble, along with my voice, as words spilled out. "He's over there. He sent me to get you, to trick you into going outside with him. Please walk away. Please just go, go out to your car and leave. If you don't, he'll take you and he'll hurt you. Please…"

Please please please.

—Excerpt, *The Unlucky Ones* by Jane Gama

Mila got home late again Monday evening, and Poppy was howling her displeasure to anyone in a two-hundred-foot radius. She rushed the dog into the backyard, turned the shower on, then let the dog in for cookies and fresh water. Mila bathed quickly, too antsy to spend a lot of time under the water. After the day she'd had, the best thing for her and Poppy both would be a walk, and she knew exactly where to go.

Dressed in shorts and a tank top and flip-flops that felt like nothingness after an entire hot day in boots, she looped Poppy's leash over her wrist and walked a block east to Main Street, then turned north. The real main street, First, was downtown and home to A Long Time Ago and Gramma's apartment. It wasn't likely Mila would catch her in the store—the only times the downtown businesses kept late hours was on Thursdays—but Poppy was behaving so well that checking the easiest choice was worth the extra block's walk if she was wrong.

There was little traffic downtown. That was logical, given that everything was closed and the nearest bar on First Street was six or eight blocks east. Gramma had plenty of neighbors living above the businesses down here, but they must have been enjoying the air-conditioning instead of the warm evening.

Mila didn't need to look in the doors of A Long Time Ago to see the shop was empty. Few lights were left on inside, and the heavier, pricier pieces that stayed outside on display were all pushed together and locked with a heavy chain. That didn't stop Poppy from eagerly sniffing each piece, leading Mila in a circle around the bunch twice.

"Do you know a dog's sense of smell is a thousand to ten thousand times better than ours?"

The hairs on the back of Mila's neck stood on end. She couldn't tell whether the raspy voice was male or female, and when she turned to face the stocky figure, she still wasn't sure. A rush of shock went through her, followed by guilt and shame.

It was hard to say anything about the woman—she thought—besides *God bless her*. Her hair was like straw and grew in every direction, and the skin on her face was shiny, tight, the colors mottled in shades of purple and red. The symmetry of her face was askew, as if doctors had rebuilt it with no idea of how she'd looked before. The scars continued down her throat and beneath the collar of her shirt and picked up again on her left arm. She wore a plain white glove on that hand.

What terrible burns she'd suffered, and what incredible strength she must have had to fight her way back from them.

Abruptly Mila remembered the woman's question about dogs, and she held Poppy a little tighter so she wouldn't suddenly decide she needed to climb and sniff all over the stranger. "I'm not surprised. She can smell the bread drawer opening from a mile away."

The woman smiled, just a stretching of taut skin, then glanced around. "This is a lovely downtown. I can't believe no one besides us is out here enjoying it. I hear almost all of these buildings have apartments upstairs."

Mila considered for a moment that she'd exhausted her supply of chitchat. Even the friendliest clerks at the grocery store were satisfied with a line or two. But the woman showed no inclination to move on, and learning to be more…well, just *more* included learning to be friendlier. "Do you live here?"

"I'm passing through. I'm driving the Mother Road and doing some sightseeing along the way. Started in Chicago and I plan to stay with it all the way to the Pacific Ocean."

"That's nice." Though not to Mila. Route 66 passed through Arizona, New Mexico and California, states where she'd lived with her parents. They'd lived along the Mother Road, too, in big cities and small towns that had sprung up when the highway was built, faded away when the interstate replaced it, and they now survived on nostalgia. She would be happy if she never set foot in those states again. "Are you traveling alone?"

That curious stretch of a smile once more crossed the woman's face. "I am. It's the only way to make sure I don't get pissed off at my traveling companion. Though if I had a girl as beautiful as she is, I'd have brought her along." She nodded to Poppy but made no effort to approach her. Mila appreciated it.

Now she had exhausted her chitchat. "Well, good luck with your trip. We, uh, we should get going." She tugged the leash, and Poppy happily began moving again. Instead of walking to the corner, then crossing the street, Mila trotted across in the middle of the block. This being-friendly stuff wasn't as easy as people thought. Something about the woman made her feel vaguely anxious.

It wasn't the scars or the odd, eerie sound of her voice. Mila wasn't that superficial. It was just that her whole life she'd avoided unnecessary contact with strangers, and it was going to take a long time, she feared, before it felt as nonthreatening to her as it apparently was to everyone else.

She and Poppy set a good pace, crossing the intersection and walking the few hundred feet to Gramma's building. When she stopped to open the door, she glanced back down the street and saw the woman, her stride stiff, returning back the way she'd come. She struck Mila as alone and sad.

One different person projecting her feelings onto another different person.

Though there was an elevator, Poppy spent every ride barking fiercely at the lights, so they took the stairs, Mila huffing somewhere around three and a half floors, Poppy still going strong at five. Before Mila could summon the energy to knock, Poppy did it for her, banging her tail against the wood before offering a big, deep *woof!*

"Jessica! Your great-grandbaby's here to drool all over everything!" came a shout from the apartment behind them. Wynona Novak, also known as the old bat next door, had a voice that could cut through steel. Poor Poppy cringed and rubbed at first one ear, then the other, and Mila wanted to do the same.

Gramma opened the door, smiled and cupped both hands over the dog's ears. "Better her drooling than you dribbling everywhere!" she bellowed. Then her smile grew even bigger. "I'm so happy to see you." She snuggled with Poppy before giving Mila a hug, too.

"I see things are the same with Mrs. Novak."

Gramma wagged one finger. "If she didn't have her nose in my business…"

If Mrs. Novak hadn't had her nose in Gramma's business, Mila thought, Gramma would still have *her* nose in Mrs. Novak's.

"What are you two doing out and about?"

Mila waited until they were inside, the door closed, the leash unclipped from Poppy's collar before grimly answering with her own question. "Did you hear the news?"

"I didn't get home until they were already doing the weather, which was just a lot of still hot, still dry, still a burn ban. Good Lord, it's July in Oklahoma. Do they really need a weather forecast every single day?" Gramma went to the kitchen, got a treat for Poppy, then opened the refrigerator before slowly stepping away, letting it fall shut again without noticing. "Though I did hear something at the store… What was it? Oh! That rich old coot who lives in the Scarlett O'Hara house died today. Shirley said he had more money than God and more enemies than—"

Gramma broke off and stared at her. "Oh, my sweet child, don't tell me… You weren't…" She pressed both palms to her cheeks. "You didn't find his body, did you?"

"No. His housekeeper did." Before her grandmother could relax, she went on. "But I was standing about fifteen feet away. Gramma, do you think—"

"No!" The word burst out with such force that it startled all three of them. Poppy whined and moved to press against Mila's legs, and Gramma's shocked expression sent chills through her. That thought hadn't occurred to her yet, and Mila was sorry she'd put it in her mind.

"Sweetie, I'm sorry. I didn't mean—" Gramma gripped her hands so tightly that just seeing it made Mila's own fingers ache. "It's just… I know we don't talk about this. Maybe we should, I don't know. Dr. Fleischer always said to leave it up to you, that if you wanted to discuss it, you would, but you never did, and it was just easier not bringing it up myself. But, Mila, this can't have anything to do with them. They're dead, and I thank God for it every day of my life. I would regret even giving birth to her, but if I hadn't, I never would have had you, and I can't even imagine how much less my life would be without you in it."

Emotion rose in Mila's chest, clogging her throat. She knew what her life would have been like if her grandmother hadn't rescued her. More brutality, more abuse, more victims, until it was her turn. Even then, she'd known her father wanted to kill her, known her mother wanted to see it. She'd known they were saving her for last.

Gramma came around the counter and wrapped her arms tightly around her. "They're dead," she whispered, "and no one on this earth knows what they did but you and me and Dr. Fleischer, and he will never, ever tell. There's no way this can have anything to do with them, none at all. It's just a horrible, horrible thing that you've gotten caught up in."

Mila relaxed in her embrace, her grandmother's shudders making it difficult to feel her own. She was right. There was no way these two deaths could be connected to her parents. The murders they'd committed, if not perfect, had at least gone undetected. They'd changed locations and identities so often that they had spent the last fifteen years buried under names not even remotely connected to their own. They were beyond wreaking any more havoc on her life.

This was a horrible thing she'd just been caught up in, and she had survived far more horrible things before.

She would survive this.

Growing up on the farm, Sam had never had to worry about staying in shape. He'd had a lot of chores, and in their every free minute, he and his cousins had run wild. He'd played baseball and football, and when he'd decided to join the army, he'd taken up running.

Choosing an occupation where people were likely to shoot at him made it seem a wise idea.

These days staying in shape didn't come as easily as it had back then. Sitting behind a desk or in a vehicle didn't tend to burn calories as efficiently as chasing cows or hauling hay, though wrestling with a suspect usually got his blood pumping. So he'd gone back to running, which would be okay if he could just find that damn runner's high he'd heard so much about…

He stopped hearing his footsteps pounding the downtown sidewalk when a door on the next block opened and a big yellow dog raced outside, dragging her owner with her. Where did Mila find the energy to wrangle the animal for a walk after the day she'd had?

He kicked up his speed a few notches and indulged for a moment in pure vanity, wishing he wasn't sweaty and smelly and out of breath and sure as hell not looking his best, but screw ego. He took his chances where he found them.

She and Poppy had reached the intersection of First and Main and turned south by the time he caught up. He could tell when she heard him by the way her muscles tightened and how she moved to the outside edge of the sidewalk. Her fingers curled tightly around Poppy's leash, leaving him plenty of room to pass…and herself plenty of room to move away if need be.

Was that because of the two murders, or had she needed to get away before? He hated either possibility but hoped for the first one.

Poppy was the first to look at him, her mouth curving into a goofy smile of recognition as she leaped toward him without care for the fact that she and her owner were attached. Mila stumbled at the sudden jerk, then caught her balance by grabbing the no-parking sign ahead of her.

Damn. He would have been glad to steady her.

"Hey, Poppy, pretty girl." Sam crouched to scratch the dog's ears, amused by the way she twisted to get his fingers in just the right spots. She was downright orgiastic, body trembling, tail swirling, legs giving way beneath her body. She was delighted and didn't care who knew it.

Looking up at Mila, he grinned. "Enjoying this nice cool evening?"

She looked at the time and temperature display on the bank across the street. "It's eighty-nine degrees."

"Thirteen degrees cooler than it was at noon."

"But still eighty-nine degrees. Most people are sprawled in near unconsciousness in their air-conditioned houses trying to avoid heatstroke."

"Well, we're obviously not most people, are we?" He straightened and swiped his sleeve across his face. Since the shirt was dripping wet itself, mostly he succeeded in rearranging the sweat drops. "Mind if I walk with you?"

"Don't you need to keep your heart rate up?" She let go of the street sign and began walking again, still hugging the curb.

"My heart rate's not settling down for a while. Trust me."

She made a noise that might have been an aborted laugh or a derisive snort. He chose to think she'd come *that* close to laughing.

He liked that she seemed to find it easier to talk to him this evening. Her gaze had actually met his right from the start, and some of that tension had drained from her body. She looked… His gaze went sideways to her. Softer. Prettier.

Every time he saw her, he thought she was prettier than before. At this rate, it wouldn't be long before he was using words like *beautiful* and *gorgeous* and *sexy*.

And *innocent*. In shorts and flip-flops that made her legs look a mile long and a thin white shirt that molded to her breasts, with her hair collected into a ponytail high on top of her head, she looked young and sweet and small-town wholesome good.

Not too young, though—only nine years younger than him—and sweet and small-town wholesome good were two of his favorite things.

"Did you guys have a better afternoon than your morning turned out to be?"

"We did. Was your afternoon worse?"

"How could it get worse?"

"Someone had to tell Mr. Greeley's family, and rumor is someone had to talk to Mr. Lawrence."

"Ben Little Bear in both cases. Greeley didn't have any close family. His ex-wife said the appropriate things and seemed to genuinely regret having to tell their children. They're teenagers. Sad they had to lose their father this way."

Mila looked right and left before stepping off the curb to cross Elm, then shifted her gaze to the sidewalk as if it was a threat. The downtown sidewalks were over a century old, but they were decently maintained. She wasn't likely to trip on a crack and take a header if she didn't watch like a hawk.

Maybe Greeley's kids were harder to think about than his death or his ex-wife. Maybe she had a tender spot for kids, especially since her own parents weren't around. There'd been that moment at dinner last week, when he'd asked about Jessica's secret for dinner and Mila had...

Well, if it had been anyone else, he would have just said she got upset. But she was so controlled, it carried more weight than just upset. More like meltdown.

At odd moments, he still found himself wondering why.

Deliberately Sam changed the subject. "Did I tell you my dad owns a plant nursery?"

That made her look at him, her brows both tilted up. "Douglas Plant Farm? Is that him?"

He nodded. "Mom helps out part-time, but she makes him pay her. She says being a Douglas and working for free would make people think she's *the* Douglas, and she doesn't want that responsibility on her shoulders. This way it's clear she's one of the sheep, not the shepherd."

She almost smiled again. "Most of the plants in my garden came from there. I had to order some online, and my crape myrtles are all volunteers from our old house before Gramma and I both moved, but I bought the rest there."

"If you want to keep shopping quick and easy, don't tell Mom you know me. She's inordinately interested in every female I meet between the ages of twenty and forty. On the other hand, if you want first dibs on some of the cool stuff Dad gets, drop my name. He'll set it aside for you."

Her mouth twitched, and he asked, "What? What's that twitch?"

"I've never name-dropped once in my life. I never knew any names *to* drop."

Though she said the words in her usual tone, Sam got the impression that she meant them very seriously. She'd never had many friends, many people to trust. The first time he'd seen her, he'd thought she was totally alone in the midst of the crowd. Every meeting since had helped solidify the feeling. A woman her age should be dating, partying, hanging out with friends, clubbing until the early hours. She should be keeping company with someone other than her dog and her grandmother, no matter how lovely they both were. She shouldn't be so isolated.

Unless she liked isolation, but Sam didn't really think that was the case.

As they passed an open lot, Poppy spotted a rabbit and veered hard in that direction. Sam grabbed hold of the leash when Mila stumbled, taking the pressure off her wrist. "Would she know what to do with a rabbit if she caught it?"

"With Poppy, who knows?"

He tugged on the leash, and she relinquished it to him in case of future bunny attacks. "You know, you can train her not to pull or run or jump with a few treats and a little discipline."

"Discipline is highly overrated." Her voice and expression were equally flat, her gaze narrow, but after a moment, she swallowed hard, exhaled and forced a lighter tone. "Isn't pulling and running and jumping what puppies are supposed to do?"

Again questions about her parents came to the forefront of his mind. Too much discipline? Was that the reason her grandmother had done at least part of her raising?

Just the thought set every protective instinct inside him on high alert, but he kept them under control and

instead lightly said, "I think pulling, running and jumping is what we're all supposed to do until we get too old
or too tired or too creaky or too fat."

She gave him a long look that roused awareness,
from the tiny sweat-coated pores on the surface of his
skin all the way deep down inside him. He had no idea
what she wanted to find, but if it was good, he hoped it
was there with lights flashing. If it was something that
might make her keep her distance from him, he hoped
it had never been.

"Well," she said softly. "You don't qualify on any of
those."

Pathetic as it was, he thought it was a damn nice
compliment. If she ever truly complimented him, he'd
be as delighted as Poppy and act just as silly.

He looked forward to it.

Mila drew to a stop at the next intersection. The
post office, a marvel of drab government construction,
was catty-corner from them, and her house was a short
block behind it. She didn't mind walking farther, but
her stomach was threatening to rumble, and Poppy was
past her usual dinnertime, too.

It would be really easy to say, "You want to get something to eat?" At least, it should be. But there was little
food in her house besides canned soup, ramen noodles and frozen dinners, so her invitation would have
to mean ordering delivery or going out. She had never
asked anyone besides Gramma to do either with her.

She looked down the street ahead—a fried-chicken
place, an ice-cream shop with burgers and a Chinese
buffet were the only offerings in sight—then glanced
toward her house. It was quiet. She loved it for its quiet.

It was her retreat from a world that was too much for her…but she'd retreated for far too long. Years ago, Dr. Fleischer had told her healing would come, and with it, she would find her way into the life she was meant to live. Even at eleven, she'd known the life she was meant to live: hidden away, left alone by anyone and everyone but Gramma. She'd wanted to be safe, and she had been.

But she was twenty-six years old, and she'd never had the chance to pull, run and jump. She hadn't been too old, too tired, too creaky or too fat.

Just too afraid.

Always afraid.

Sam didn't question her stillness. He watched with patience and interest and a little hope on his face. He didn't want to end the evening here, saying goodbye like casual acquaintances. She could see that as clearly as if they were acting in a scene and she held his script. Problem was, no one had provided *her* with a script. Could she really risk inviting him to have dinner with her? What if she was misreading him and he said no?

What if she wasn't misreading him and he said yes? She could hold up her end of a conversation only in rare moments, and dinner would be committing to at least an hour more together. Could she count on Poppy to entertain him if she couldn't?

She would never know if she never tried.

"Would you like—" Hearing an echo, she broke off. He'd spoken at the same time she had, said the same words. He stopped, too, a grin brightening his eyes, and gestured for her to go on. She shifted her feet uneasily, looked once more toward her house, her haven, her isolated retreat, then forced the best smile she could manage. "Would you like to get some dinner?"

His grin got bigger. "I don't think they'll want me looking and smelling like this, but we could pick up something to take to your house, or to my house if you want. I live a few blocks that way." He pointed to the east. "Of course, if you don't want to eat with me looking and smelling like this—"

She interrupted him with a shake of her head. If she gave him time to shower and clean up, she might lose her nerve. "Those places set their standards too high. They don't want Poppy in there, either. Taking something back to the house—my house—is good." She was already nervous over the idea of sharing a meal with him without Gramma as a buffer. Having that meal at his house, where he lived, slept, read, watched TV…that was one step farther than she could manage.

"Good." He gestured ahead of them. "You choose."

Her immediate impulse was to demur. What if she chose chicken and he wanted Chinese? What if he hated Chinese but ate it anyway because it was the first word to make it out of her mouth? What if indecision was one of the little things that drove him nuts?

"Hamburgers." Her voice was less substantial than she would have liked. Quickly she cleared her throat and added, "Poppy loves ice cream on hot days."

"A girl after my own heart," he teased.

It was two and a half blocks to Braum's, and Sam filled most of it with normal chatter, lamenting the ugly post office, remarking that it used to be in the beautiful old building downtown that now housed the police department, commenting on a lovely house and the busyness of the liquor store and the building that had once been the church home to dozens of Douglases before they'd moved into a newer—also uglier—facility on the edge of town. There wasn't much for Mila to say besides *hmm* and *nice*, and it was easily the highlight of her week.

Maybe her whole life.

The parking lot at the ice-cream shop was filled with vintage cars, their hoods raised, people talking engines and restoration and good ole days. Several of them greeted Sam, a couple including Mila in their nods, and he returned their hellos. At the curb, he stopped and pulled a debit card from his pocket. "You want to stay out here with Poppy or go in and get the food?"

Staying in the parking lot with friendly people around? That was a no-brainer. "What do you want?"

"Double cheeseburger with jalapeños and fries. Don't forget Poppy's ice cream."

She withdrew her own debit card, but he took her hand, laid his card in it and folded her fingers over it. "It was your grandmother's treat last time. This time it's mine."

The instant his fingers made contact with hers, she lost the ability to move. Instinct told her to pull away—she wasn't a touchy-feely person at all—but all her muscles had gone rigid while every nerve in her body was firing off neurons and sparks and tiny, strange, delicious little electric shocks. It was…

The first time any man besides a doctor or dentist had ever touched her.

Ever.

It was incredible.

An older man standing next to an even older pickup called Sam's name, and he squeezed her hand before letting go. "Get Poppy a carton of ice cream. Maybe she'll share with us for dessert."

Unable to speak over the swelling in her throat, she nodded, stiffly turned and walked into the restaurant. The chill inside was a shock to a system already in shock. She shivered, goose bumps raising everywhere, went to place their order, then got a tub of ice cream from the freezer. While she waited for the food, she watched out the plate glass windows as Sam chatted with a group of the car enthusiasts. His hair stood on end, his shirt clung to his body and his smile was worthy of preserving forever.

Just the sight roused an ache in her chest for all the things she'd never had. All the things her parents had taken from her.

They're dead, Gramma reminded her.

Dead. They couldn't hurt her anymore.

Unless she let them. Unless she stayed hidden away the rest of her life. Unless she chose solitude over people.

Because it was a choice. The easiest one she'd ever made, but also the hardest. She was safe, all right. No one knew anything about her past because no one knew *her*. No one could hurt or shame or hate her, but that also meant no one could like her, love her, hug her, laugh with her, cry with her. Life with her parents had been a prison, but the life she chose now was also a prison. Not as ugly, not terrifying, not one with a death sentence hanging over her head, but a prison all the same.

Maybe it was time to plan the greatest escape in the history of escapes.

A teenage employee came around the counter to where Mila waited against the wall. "Ma'am, here's your food," she said in a bored voice that suggested it wasn't the first time she'd said it. She handed over two bags, hot food in one and ice cream in the other, then hurried back to her spot.

The intense smells of greasy meat, jalapeños, onions and French fries made Mila's stomach growl. She and Poppy were going to be such happy girls this evening.

It took only a second to locate Sam, bent over a flame-red car, peering at the engine as if he fully understood what he was looking at. Cars and engines weren't on her list of interests, so she waited until he noticed her. He smiled, said good-night to his friends and they left.

"I take it Poppy loves hamburgers." He was walking on the far inside of the sidewalk, the leash wrapped repeatedly around his wrist to restrict her bounds and contortions.

"She loves them. And French fries. And peach ice cream is her absolute favorite."

"Aw, man, homemade peach ice cream at the Porter Peach Festival. It's in July every year. Have we missed it?"

"I have no idea." With her uneasiness in crowds, she never went to any of the local festivals. Bad things could happen in crowds. But as Mr. Carlyle and Mr. Greeley had found out, bad things could happen alone in your own backyard.

Poppy didn't dally this time, making Mila glad she carried the food. Being on the receiving end of the pooch's jerks and twirls and excited leaps could make for sore muscles sometimes. And while her muscles were in good shape, thanks to her job, Sam's were a whole lot better.

At her house, she fished her keys from her pocket and unlocked the door. Poppy shoved her way in as soon as her nose could clear the space and trotted to the kitchen for water. Mila checked the thermometer hanging near a set of wind chimes. "Wow, it's cooled all the way down to eighty-six. You want to eat out here, on the back porch, or gee, I actually do have a dining table inside."

Sam made an exaggerated face. "Will I sound like a sissy voting for the dining table? Especially if there's an air-conditioning vent nearby. I'm so ready to cool down that I might just ask you to turn the hose on me."

"There's a vent and a fan." She went inside, crossed the living room in a few strides and stepped into the dining room. Like so much else about the house, it was tiny, really more of an alcove that provided passage between living room and kitchen. The table was hand-made, oak with a worn golden glow, three boards nailed across the top, four sturdy rectangular legs. The seams between the boards were uneven and marred with chips and scratches, and the two oak chairs showed the same wear and tear.

She set the food down, stashed the ice cream in the freezer and filled Poppy's food dish. After gathering napkins and drinks, she returned to the dining room and took the seat closest to the wall, the one that left little maneuvering space to get in and out.

"Nice table. Family heirloom?" Sam ran his fingers across the top after he settled into the other chair.

"Someone's family. Not ours." She thought she'd said it carelessly enough to go unnoticed, but turned out, she could have chosen any number of better answers, because the next response from him was the one that seemed most logical in hindsight. It was one she'd rather never answer with anyone, especially a police officer.

A police chief. A gorgeous, handsome police chief who made her insides flutter.

"Tell me about your family."

Sam kept his tone even, conversational, as if it was the most natural question to ask a woman over dinner. And, really, even though Mila's jaw had gone tight and an emotion he couldn't identify had come into her eyes, it *was* natural. Asking and answering questions about themselves—that was how people got to know each other. That was how they determined if they liked each other. He knew he was attracted to Mila physically—he'd swear that brief touch of her hand had scorched the shape of her fingers into his brain—and he was interested in her as a person, but he couldn't know if it went beyond that if he didn't find out things about her.

The pointless things. The silly things. The things that made her smile and laugh and want to tear out her hair. The pet peeves, the favorite books, the movies she loved and the music she hated.

Knowing she was pretty, isolated, emotionally distant but dearly loved her grandmother and her dog… those were important, but not enough. He wasn't sure anything less than everything would be enough.

"I'm not asking for life histories. I don't need to know that you potty trained early—though my mother would proudly tell you that I did—or if you walked late. I don't want to know if there are more Ramirezes around somewhere than there are Douglases here, or what they do or how they think or what their politics are. Just a general overview will be enough." For right now.

With the tremor in her hands only slightly visible, she plucked off a piece of hamburger and lowered her hand beneath the table. He didn't need to have Poppy sitting on his right foot, tail thumping in anticipation, to know she was slipping the food to the dog.

Her hand didn't reappear—he suspected she was holding on to Poppy for comfort—but her gaze slowly lifted to his face. She didn't meet his eyes, but at least she came close. "My parents died when I was eleven, and Gramma took me in. They were both only children, so there are no aunts or uncles or cousins, and my grandfather had already died, so Gramma just sort of focused on getting me grown up. It took…" She drew a deep breath, and her gaze made a fleeting connection with his. "It took longer than she expected."

Huh, she'd made a joke. He didn't point it out, didn't want to make her self-conscious, but he did smile. "You strike me as someone who was probably all grown-up at birth. I suspect, in truth, you were helping raise Jessica."

"She has a certain enthusiasm for life," she admitted.

"That must be where you get it from."

She lifted her hand back to the table and picked up her hamburger, slowly chewing a bite. "What makes you think I even got it?"

"Look at this place." He tilted his head to indicate the house. "Well, outside more than inside, but you've made it gorgeous. My dad would be jealous of your yard, and he's used to being the king of beautiful yards. You're a big part of your gramma's life, and you adopted Poppy because she needed somebody in her life. You love life, too. You just love it more quietly than Jessica and the baby do."

His words pleased her. That was easy to see in the depths of her eyes. They also made her uncomfortable, easy to see in the sudden awkwardness of her movements. She wasn't used to compliments. Or having dinner alone with a man in her house. Or letting anyone get close. Or sharing her space with anyone besides the dog—certainly not with someone who really wanted to invade her space.

Wanted to be invited to invade it.

He shifted the conversation to an inane discussion of the weather and the town and bits of information about people she'd come into contact with in the past week. Still, he wondered about her parents—how they died, how traumatic it had been for her, what the eleven years of her life with them had been like. Had she loved them even more dearly than Jessica? Had they spoiled her rotten and doted on her the way little kids should be doted on? Had their deaths devastated her?

But then there was that meltdown last week, and the flat, stiff way she'd said, "Discipline is overrated."

Though the happy-loving-precious family was a pretty picture, something about it just felt wrong.

And there was a deeply ingrained, vital part of him that needed very much to put things right for everyone. That was why he'd joined the army. That was why he'd become a cop.

It wasn't why he was so drawn to Mila. Oh, it was part of it. She was vulnerable, and he was protective. But she was more than that, and he felt more than that. He was looking forward to finding out what.

They finished their dinner, sharing bits and pieces with Poppy. When Mila gathered the wrappers and showed her there really was nothing left, the dog slunk into the kitchen and ate the dry food she'd apparently reserved as a last resort. Sam drank iced tea, brewed in a canning jar, and Mila drank iced coffee, brewed in a second glass jar, turned caramel by the cream she stirred in, smelling strong and sweet.

For a while, they just sat, listening to the quiet broken by Poppy's snores and the occasional car passing outside. Night had fallen, and the only light on in the house was in the kitchen, white rays tinged with yellow that gleamed off the old oak table and gave the dining room a sense of intimacy.

After a time, Mila yawned. She flushed, and one of her quick, barely there smiles flashed. "Sorry. I'm usually up by five."

"That's way too early in the morning."

"What time do you get up?"

He shrugged with a smile. "Five, if I'm going to run. Five forty-five if I'm not. I try to be in the office by seven thirty, but it seems to take me longer with each passing year."

"You don't run morning and evening." She raised one brow to provide the question mark that escaped her voice.

"Oh, no. I only go at night if I've missed a couple of mornings. You know, if you slack off one day, it's harder to get back out the next."

Scooting her chair back a few inches, she crossed her legs. "I don't run."

"No, you just do hard work twelve hours a day in hundred-degree heat."

"When your work is seasonal, you do it when it comes."

"So spring's busy because you're planting and fertilizing and seeding. Summer's busy because all your spring work is coming to fruition. In fall, you plant more, seed more, fertilize more, rake and get ready for winter. Then do you get to take winter off?"

"Part of it. Happy Grass lets most of its people go for the coldest months, but we're still getting ready in November, and we start working on gardens in January or February—planning, layouts, ordering. I do whatever work is needed with the crew, but the gardens and shrubs are my primary job."

Sam's arms were resting on the solid tabletop, the left one bent so he could support his head on his palm. He watched the faint shadows shift over her face with her every movement. Watched her mouth form the words that described her job. Watched the slight actions of her hands that indicated she was inclined to talk with them but not this time.

"What?" she prompted, and he realized she'd quit talking a moment ago but he hadn't quit watching her, and the smile he wore, he was pretty sure, was as goofy as Poppy's.

"I like listening to you."

Even in the dim light, he saw the flush return to her cheeks. "I—I don't usually talk a lot."

"I know. And that's fine. Usually at work, I have so many people talking at me all at the same time that I have to hide in my office with the door locked to get just one moment of silence. But you're different. I actually want to hear what you have to say."

She didn't know how to react to that. She uncrossed her legs. Crossed them back the other way. Rested her hands on the table, loosely clasped. Let them go to brush at her bangs. "I…"

Poppy trotted to her side, and Mila gratefully turned her attention to her, rubbing the spot between her shoulders, and gave up looking for a response. There was something sweet about the image they made, big yellow dog and slender dark-haired woman, but something sad, too: a grown woman needing comfort from a dog.

Somberly he scooted his chair back and stood up. "I should go."

The look she gave him was tinged with relief, which also made him sad. But there was something more, wistfulness or maybe even regret, and he shared that.

They walked to the front door, the three of them. Realizing the door was going to open at any moment, Poppy lunged forward, the swish of her tail wiping the table there clean. Mila scolded her in a voice that was so sweet of course it negated the words coming out of her mouth while Sam bent to scoop up the fallen items: an ink pen, a spiral notebook, a stack of magazines and a book. The dust jacket was familiar, since the same book sat on his coffee table at home. *The Unlucky Ones* by Jane Gama.

"I wouldn't have figured you for crime stories." Granted, she'd probably bought it before Carlyle's death, and it had probably sat there waiting its turn to be read. It had that sort of pristine stiffness unread books had.

Was that a shudder ricocheting through her, or merely the strain of holding back her excited dog? "I read everything."

"I have it at home but haven't started it yet. Lois said she had to quit halfway through. It gave her nightmares." He paused. "Have you had any more?"

She shook her head, her lower lip caught between her teeth.

He glanced at the book again, its stark cover declaring it the true story of a girl's life with serial killer parents. The name was a pseudonym, the author's real identity well hidden, which had created a buzz regarding its real truth that was, according to Lois, better publicity than the publisher could have paid for. She hadn't decided for herself before having to give it up.

Shrugging it off, he set the book and everything else back on the table and fixed his gaze on Mila. "Well."

She was still biting her lip, stirring the need for him to brush his fingertip across it, to ease her teeth apart and then, oh, hell, maybe she could bite *his* lip.

He was in a damn pitiful state.

"Thank you for dinner."

"You're welcome." He opened the door, and she pulled so hard against Poppy's force that she would lose her balance and fall on her butt if the dog suddenly relaxed.

"I—I'll see you…?"

He grinned to ease her uncertainty and to express his own relief. "Absolutely." Then, because he couldn't kiss her good-night or squeeze her hand or anything like that, not yet, he did the next best thing. "Sweet dreams, Mila."

Chapter 6

The storm was violent. The power flickered and went off, but there was no peace in the darkness. He had anticipated this, had lit lanterns all around the barn. The rafters shook under the force of the winds, bits of straw and dust sprinkling onto us from the loft above. My mother, trusting I wouldn't flee, slowly walked toward the victim, a look of such ecstasy on her face. Her gaze moved over her like a caress. It was the first time I'd ever seen a remotely happy expression on her, and the fact that it was caused by the sight of a bound woman about to die sickened me.

The air crackled around me, and I jerked my head up, looking out the door. The hairs on my arms stood on end, and I swore the hair on my head tried to rise, too. A brilliant light flared outside, followed immediately by a deafening crash that unsteadied me. Sulfur and smoke filled the air, first pungent and fresh, then the wet, bitter smell of flames quickly extinguished. The giant oak tree in the backyard had been struck by lightning. The earth still trembled, little shock waves that kept time with the pounding of my heart.

I didn't want to be here, didn't want to be here, didn't want to be—

A scream exploded into the air, pain and anguish and terror. I jerked back around to see that he'd started. He held a knife in his hand, and blood dripped from his fingers. I wouldn't look at her, couldn't, or at least I tried not to, but my gaze was drawn to her no matter how I struggled.

Now I lay me…

It was my fault, because I tried to warn her. He knew even from so far away that I had changed the script, that I wasn't doing my poor-lost-lamb routine, that I was trying to get her to run. What made me think I could change anything? He always knew. He could look at me, he said, and see exactly what I was thinking, feeling, planning, and I believed him.

Please let his hand slip. Instead of just cutting her, let him slice an artery. Let her death be quick and easy. Take his joy from it. Take my pain from it.

It was a prayer, but I didn't know to whom. God didn't listen to me the other times. Why should he? If I'm not worth my own father's attention except when he was mad, why in the world would any god give me his attention?

Another scream ripped through the air, stronger, more desperate, its echo as sharp edged and tormented as the scream itself. It made the air vibrate, made me vibrate, just like when the tree had fallen, life ending in violence, only this time it went on and on inside my head, my chest, my soul, my very being. My throat went hoarse, my mouth dry, and that was when I realized.

The scream was coming from me.

—Excerpt, *The Unlucky Ones* by Jane Gama

It was lovely to have a plain, ordinary day at work on Tuesday. True, Mila's workmates were more somber than usual, and she thought everyone felt the same edginess she did each time they arrived at a new job. But the heat was especially overpowering—114 degrees, according to the bank sign when they passed it midafternoon— and the heat index was north of a hundred, too. By the time she got home, she was too wrung out to do anything more than take care of Poppy, eat dinner and write a few pages in her notebook.

Pages all about Sam and confusion and new feelings and old feelings.

Lord, she wished she really had begun life the same day Mila Ramirez sprang into being. Without all the family baggage dragging her down, she could have made friends, had a first crush, a first date, a first kiss, all well before the age of twenty-six. But she hadn't. And all those wonderful, lovely firsts were still out there, waiting to happen.

Wednesday morning a storm blew through, springing up out of nowhere as Oklahoma storms often did, a few cracks of thunder, a few flashes of lightning and a deluge of rain before moving on as quickly as it had formed. The pavement steamed, and the air hung heavier than it had before.

It seemed appropriate, since they were turning in to the Carlyle driveway.

After shutting off the engine, Ruben sat there a moment. They all looked at the house, no different than it had been the dozens of other times they'd seen it but seeming somehow so. There was actually one difference, Mila noted: a for-sale sign planted near the front curb.

She swallowed hard before reaching outside the window to grab the door handle. It creaked open, helped along with a kick on the lower panel. No one said anything as they got out, gathered their equipment and scattered to their tasks.

Mila was on her way to the backyard—unwillingly, though she didn't voice it to Ruben or the others or even herself—when a car door sounded behind her. They rarely ran into anyone in this neighborhood. Either both spouses worked to pay for the big houses or one worked while the other did whatever people with money did to fill their time.

It wasn't a resident. The shield and decals on the white pickup made that clear. She didn't overtly react as she watched Sam cross the grass to her, but everything inside her was dancing with delight. Trepidation. A lot of worry. But still a whole lot of delight.

"Please don't tell me there's a body I haven't yet found." Inwardly she winced at her comment. It had just come out of its own accord, something she was totally unaccustomed to. She *always* considered her words before uttering them. It had often meant the difference between annoyance and anger. Anger and rage. Rage and violence.

But in the past week she had been so sociable that her control had slipped. It was freeing, giving her a sense of normalcy she'd never felt. It also tightened her chest and the nerves in her stomach and sent a vaguely queasy sensation bouncing through her. Her parents were dead. Her secrets weren't.

"No body, please, God. I just wanted to make sure this wasn't any more difficult than it had to be for you."

She blinked, sweat burning her eyes, and automatically swiped her sleeve across her face. "You took time to come here…so I wouldn't have to go into the backyard alone?" The idea puzzled and pleased and touched her, making her next breath hard to come by, making her feel…unworthy. If he only knew…

It was hard to tell whether the flush darkening his cheeks came from the heat or was fueled by self-consciousness. "We aim to protect and serve."

"I—" So much for speaking without thinking. She couldn't find the words to say how much she appreciated this gesture. It was the nicest thing anyone other than Gramma had ever done for her.

She swallowed hard and continued to the gate. The code remained the same, five digits and a pound sign, and when she walked into the yard, it looked the same, too. She followed the path to the back of the house and stopped abruptly, her gaze jerking to the patio and the pool. The water was still, blue and beckoning. Everything glistened with raindrops that hadn't been enough to feed the thirsty soil but had given it a clean shine, and the view was peaceful, beautiful, inviting.

If a person didn't know that one of the lounge chairs

was missing. That a violent act had taken place there exactly one week ago. That the faint stain on the stone was blood. She wondered how porous the stone was, whether that slab would have to be dug up and replaced or if the stain could be sanded out.

Pointless thoughts considering that a man had died.

But sometimes pointless thoughts were the only safe ones to have.

She didn't realize she was holding her breath until Sam touched her shoulder and it whooshed out. Goose bumps rose on her arms as her wide-eyed gaze jerked to him.

"Sorry," she said at the same time he said, "I didn't mean—"

The deep breath that filled her lungs was sweet with flowers and sunshine and rain, and it steadied her almost as much as Sam's presence did. "I'm sorry," she said again. "It's just a little eerie."

"I know. The family went straight to her mother's house in New York. That's where he'll be buried this week. His boss hired a real estate agent, and they'll get everything packed up and shipped east."

"I don't blame her for not wanting to be here again." She didn't believe that souls ripped violently and unexpectedly from their lives haunted places, but she did think they left parts of themselves behind—not good or bad, necessarily, just an essence or imprint of the life they'd lost.

"I know. But someone else will come along and look at it and see a great house, a lot of room, a view, a pool and a garden, and they won't care that a man died here. If they do, it'll just be to negotiate a few thousand off the price for the ick factor."

"That's a good thing, though." Mila set down her trug, pulled on gloves and got the shears. "If nobody was willing to live in a place where someone had been killed, think of all the abandoned houses that would accumulate over time."

When he didn't respond, she looked at him and saw his gaze was on the shears she held. The weapon used on Carlyle, a knife, wasn't part of her tools, but she had multiple pairs of shears. She'd seen the ones sticking in Mr. Greeley's chest, and they were closer to kitchen scissors than garden shears. Still, she held hers out. "Do you want to look at them?"

"No." He shrugged. "We have the weapon."

"Just noticing that I have a similar weapon."

"The witness who actually found the body rules you out as a suspect. She was in the backyard before you. You couldn't have done it."

"Before last week, I'd hoped I would never see another dead body as long as I lived," she muttered. Gripping her loppers, she began checking the flower beds for blooms past their prime yet still taking energy from the plant. Some clients wanted the dead heads collected and thrown away. Mr. Carlyle had wanted them dropped to the mulch, where the seed pods would dry out and raking, wind and rain would scatter the seeds for new plants next year.

"How many bodies have you seen?" There was a touch of disbelief to his voice. Not counting bodies prepared for burial, he would rightly assume people outside law enforcement and the medical profession rarely saw dead people. But she wasn't just a person, and most generalizations didn't apply to her.

There was a lot to be said for never speaking impulsively. She rarely found herself in a situation where she had to come up with a response that seemed reasonable, answered harmless questions and didn't lead to others.

She was moving on to another flower bed when he caught her arm. "Mila?"

She made her expression blank as she looked at him. She ignored the warm, gentle pressure of his hand on her, and the spicy fragrance of his cologne, and the fact that he stood close enough that she could hear his steady breathing. She ignored all that and focused on giving the kind of answer he needed to let the conversation go.

"I told you last night that my parents died when I was eleven." Her voice sounded as flat as a fires-of-hell-temperature beer. "It was a car wreck. Gramma and I were in the car in front of them. We saw what happened and went back, and…" A heaving breath shook her shoulders. The worst/best night of her life stole all her emotions, her breath and sometimes a little bit of her sanity.

Sam's hand gentled even more. "I'm sorry, Mila. I should have let it go. It hurts me that you had to go through that. Thank God you had your gramma."

She let her gaze settle on his hand, right above her elbow, his big fingers holding her so lightly. Monday evening he'd touched her hand. Today it was her arm. If he kept moving in that direction, when would he reach her face? How many first touches could she get from him?

"I don't cry about it," she said, forcing a touch of belligerence into her voice. Gramma had told her that everyone dealt with loss differently. She didn't have to weep or mourn—not because she truly didn't feel that way, but because she was an individual, and if she confirmed that with defensiveness, people always assumed it had been a horribly traumatic experience that she had trouble coping with. That way she and Gramma could keep their secret.

"Nobody gets to tell you how you should feel, Mila. Some things are too big for tears." His thumb moved slowly back and forth with just enough pressure that she could feel her muscles and nerves underneath it relax. Thanks to the shirt, though, she couldn't feel his skin, the texture, the heat.

How bad would she look if she said, "Hold on a moment," then stripped down to her tank top and put his hand right back where it was? Probably like she was a few shades too traumatized for him to pursue any interest in. She knew people thought she was odd. She didn't want them thinking she was freaky, too.

Especially Sam.

Thursday after work found Sam in one of the few family-friendly places to get a drink in Cedar Creek: the Thunder Lanes Bowling Alley. He wasn't the best bowler on the police department's team, but more important, he was better than the Cedar County sheriff and the Cedar Creek fire chief.

The bowling alley was loud and smelled of people, feet and pizza, cheap frozen ones that the owner bought by the dozens and the staff stuck in microwaves. The nachos, also thoroughly processed, were better, the buffalo wings not half-bad, and the popcorn was the best in town, with loads of real butter.

He wondered if Mila liked popcorn. If he showed up one night with a big tub of it and suggested they have a movie night, would she turn him down or invite him in?

Ben sprawled on one side of Sam, Lois on the other, beers in hand. "Is there any reason we have to bowl in order to have an evening out with a drink?" Lois asked, her voice raspy from talking over the noise.

"If we want to keep bragging rights over the sheriff's office and the fire department, we do." Ben was a good bowler, and since he'd broken up with his last girl, most of his nights were free. Lois was a good bowler, too, but her husband wasn't thrilled about her spending her free time with the guys from work.

"You know, Tim could come with you," Sam pointed out.

She made a *pfft* sound. "Yeah, like you ever brought dirty-girl lawyer up here. Like you would bring Mee-*lah*-gro up here."

Sam scowled. "What do you know—"

She waved him into silence. "Oh, please. Gossip is the heartbeat of this city, and I am the cardiologist who monitors it. You know I hear things."

She had a pretty extensive network, too, because Cedar Creek had grown beyond its little-town boundaries a long time ago. "I don't suppose any of your sources can tell you who the new killer in town is."

"That's ugly. We only gossip for good."

"I imagine the victims would have thought it pretty good if you prevented their deaths," Ben remarked.

"People aren't quite sure what to think." Lois tapped her red nails on the base of her beer bottle. "No one knew Evan Carlyle, so they find it hard to get really worked up over that, and just about everyone in town had wished evil on Curt Greeley, so it's hard to get worked up over him, too. It's murder, but it feels like murder with a purpose. Not like someone picking people at random."

She was right. It did feel that way. But Sam didn't have the luxury of caring how it felt. Every death was supposed to be as important to him as the last one.

"Isn't there a rule about not talking business at these things?"

Both Lois and Ben made the *pfft* sound. Cops were biologically incapable of turning off work conversation in gatherings of two or more officers. It didn't matter whether there was anything new to discuss, whether they'd argued the same theories or told the same stories a dozen times. It was their nature.

"Okay," Lois agreed too cheerfully. "Let's go back to talking about Mee—"

"She goes by Mila. Not *MEE-lah*. Just Mila. And let's not talk about her, either."

"Talk about who?" Simpson asked as he joined them on the bench.

"Chief's new…" Ben frowned at Lois. "New what? Friend? Possible girlfriend? Interest? Project?"

Oh, Sam had a project, all right: to get to know Mila better than anyone else in the world. To make her relax. Smile. Laugh. Touch him back. To kiss her, hold her, see her naked, be seen naked by her. To have a—a thing. Not a fling. A relationship, even though he hated the word for its modern-day sensitivity. He wanted to sleep beside her. Wake beside her. To find out if *she and I* could become *us*. To maybe find a future and maybe not, but to have some fun and make some memories along the way.

Lois studied him, her lips pursed, then said, "I think we should call her his new interest. As in love interest."

"As in 'maybe involved with the murders interest,' too." Simpson snickered. "Lock her up downstairs. Sure makes it easy to know where she is any given time."

Someone laughed, but Sam didn't pay attention because his cell was vibrating in his pocket. As he pulled it out, he made his way through various first responders to a relatively quiet place just inside the main entrance. Leaning against the cinder-block wall, he answered.

"Hey, Chief, it's Morwenna. We got a call for you, and she wouldn't leave a message or her name, but you don't normally get those sorts of calls, so I thought maybe you'd want to know about it even if there's nothing to tell. I mean, really, what's the point of calling if you're not going to give your name so you can get called back? But, anyway…"

In addition to answering the nonemergency lines, Morwenna was also a dispatcher, at which times she was perfectly clear and succinct. In casual conversation, though, she couldn't find her way to a conclusion without a road map. "Morwenna," he interrupted. "Just tell me about the call. It was a woman—"

"Yes, how did you— Oh, because I said *she*. Very cop-ly of you, Chief. So she asked if you were in. I said no. She said oh. I asked if she would like to leave her name and number. I told her sometimes you call or stop in in the evenings, and if you did, you might call her tonight, but if not, it would certainly be in the morning. And she said no, thanks, it wasn't that important. Hang on." He heard her on another call, using what he considered her civic-duty-polite voice.

It could have been any of a thousand women calling. A relative. A citizen. An ex-girlfriend. Or maybe Mila.

"Okay," Morwenna said in much too cheerful a voice. "That was Mr. Akins. Said his cat's up the tree again."

Sam grinned. Police work in Cedar Creek had its highs and its lows. "Did you tell him Simpson's brother would come and get it for him?"

"Chief, his cat died three weeks ago. He's having a little trouble dealing with his grief. However, Tank Simpson is going over to talk to the old man. All right, so back to the call for you. I think it was personal, not professional. She didn't sound upset or distraught or anything, and she was very polite, very quiet spoken. However, maybe she speaks softly because she has a big dog."

Hot damn, maybe it *was* Mila. "A dog?"

"With a great big bark. You know, the kind that startles you because you didn't know a dog could sound that big?" Her tone turned teasing. "You know someone with a dog matching that description, Chief?"

"As it happens, I do." He looked back over at the lanes, where his buddies were still hanging around, drinking and waiting for their turns. "Listen, call Ben and tell him just this and nothing else—I got a call I had to take. You don't know from who, you don't know what about, you don't know how long it'll take."

She scoffed. "Jeez, I *don't* know any of that. You want to at least give me a hint in case you need backup?"

"See you tomorrow, Morwenna."

Odds were the call hadn't come from Mila, he told himself as he found his truck in the crowded lot. Plenty of women had dogs. But the call was the excuse he needed to stop by her house. To see her even if for just a few minutes.

When he parked in front of her house, he wondered

idly if she had a car, if there was a garage at the back of the property where she kept it out of sight. It was hard to imagine someone her age not having a vehicle. Cedar Creek was small, but not so small that walking all over town in the weather extremes they were accustomed to was easy. Granted, she lived only a few blocks from a grocery store, a post office, a bank, a pharmacy, a liquor store and Braum's. Most people would say that covered all of life's necessities right there.

Somewhere down the street, kids laughed and called. Playing outside on a summer's evening…that had become rare in his lifetime. If he ever had kids, he wanted to teach them to catch lightning bugs, to lie in the warm, damp grass and watch a caterpillar make its laborious journey, to count the colors in the sunset and listen for cicadas and tree frogs and lonesome train whistles.

If he and their mother weren't too tired at the end of the day to do those things. If they didn't find it easier to park the kids in front of the TV or the computer.

If he ever found a woman he wanted to have kids with who wanted to have them with him. There were so many ifs involved that it really was remarkable how many millions of times it had happened.

His foot was in midair, two inches above the first porch step, when frenzied barking started inside the house. He climbed the steps, grinning, and called, "Hey, Poppy, it's just me. Don't tear the door down." He hoped the words would assure Mila, too.

The porch light clicked on, then the door cracked open. Mila smiled at him shyly, partially, through the space, then stepped back to let him slink inside. One of these days, she was really going to smile at him—one of those giant, spontaneous ear-to-ear smiles when the happiness inside was just too much to contain—and when she did, either his heart was going to break for her or it was going to be put back together.

One of these days.

For this day, he greeted her with a serious smile. "Hi. I'm returning your call."

"I didn't expect her to bother you." Mila leaned against the dining room door frame, arms folded across her chest while Sam gave Poppy a vigorous greeting. She was inexplicably pleased that he'd come by just to see if she might be the one who'd called.

"Morwenna passes on everything. I prefer to know when people call me when I'm out."

"Even when they don't leave their name and number?"

"Aw, everybody leaves their name and number. It made me curious that you didn't."

She shrugged, her hair tickling along her shoulders. "When I dialed, it seemed like a good idea. When she answered, it seemed…not."

"What changed your mind?"

Another shrug. "It suddenly looked silly. Not something to bother the police chief with."

"You can bother the police chief with anything. You can bother *me* with everything." His gaze narrowed, emotion radiating from him with the same intensity of the steam coming off the pavement after the rain. "What happened, Mila?"

Her lips thinned, and her hands tightened where she hugged herself. Without a word, she turned. It took all of eight steps to get from her place in the living room through the dining room, into the hall and into the bedroom. There she backed up close to the open door, leaving plenty of room for Sam to step inside.

When he did, the impact was incredible. The air heated and bristled against her skin. Each breath seared her lungs, and she was pretty sure if her muscles tightened one more degree, at least one of them would break like a giant rubber band and ricochet madly around the room.

He looked around the room clockwise, taking in the side window, the iron bedstead to which a few flakes of pale green paint still stubbornly clung. He glanced at the night table, the wicker chair squeezed into the corner, the old dresser, then at the two rear windows. The blinds were closed on all three windows, but they hung crookedly on the one nearest the kitchen. One slat was kinked, allowing a tiny view outside, and a loop hung awkwardly from the pull cord.

"When I come home from work, I put Poppy out, let her in, shower and change clothes. I keep most of my clothes in the hall closet, so I don't usually come in here until I go to bed." Her voice was steady but had a troubled tone to it that she wished she could scream away.

But because she wasn't a screamer, she calmly went on. "I was cleaning the kitchen after dinner. A breeze came up, and I heard a thumping sound from the bedroom. Poppy came in, whined and went back out, and I came in and found the blinds banging against the window frame in the breeze."

Sam slowly turned to face her, his expression grave. "And you didn't open the window."

She shook her head.

"And even if you had, you wouldn't have messed up the blinds."

She shook her head again. He looked so serious that she felt both validated, for making the call to the police station, and vulnerable, because *he* thought the call valid, as well. He thought someone had been here. Had invaded her sanctuary.

"Is anything missing? Has anything been disturbed?"

She had paced through every room, studied every item, wondering that very question. Last weekend, she had gotten the dead bolt on the front bedroom, its only key with her all day, so that room had definitely been safe, but the rest of the house seemed untouched, too. "No, not unless it was the most meticulous burglar in the world."

"Have you looked outside?"

"No." She should have. She'd thought about it. How many evenings had she let herself into the backyard and just strolled around? She had gotten as far as opening the back door, and she'd stopped, backed up, closed and locked it again.

"You have a flashlight?"

"In the kitchen."

He headed that way, spotting the heavy light on top of the refrigerator before she could point it out. "You wait here, and keep Poppy with you."

She sat in the dining chair he'd occupied a few nights ago and held Poppy between her knees, rubbing her shoulders and wishing Gramma was there to hold her the same way. She'd never cared much about physical contact, probably because with her parents it had always meant pain. But there were times, Lord, when she wanted a warm body next to hers, a hand on her shoulder, an arm around her. Just a little touch that said, *It's all right.*

Bending, she rested her chin on top of Poppy's head. The dog's breathing was shallow; hers was shallow and unsteady. Knowing Sam was only a shout away made her feel safe. Knowing that someone else had been that close troubled her.

She heard his voice before she saw him again. He came in, cell phone to his ear, his expression fierce. "Yeah, I'll be here," he said before disconnecting. "You watered your plants today?"

She nodded. "The system's on a timer. Every other day right now, until we get some decent rain."

"There are footprints in the bed underneath the window, a size or two littler than yours. Maybe a small woman, maybe a kid."

For a moment, her focus went to the fact that he'd noticed the size of her feet. It was silly to even think about. Everyone saw everyone else's feet. But noticing them struck her as…intimate.

"I've got a couple people coming over. While we wait for them, why don't you call Jessica and see if you and Poppy can spend the night there?"

She didn't want to. In her own plain little bedroom, she dreamed in color. In Jessica's guest room, she would dream in vivid, eye-popping Technicolor. Her dreams were scary enough in drab tones.

But she couldn't imagine lying down in her bed tonight, closing her eyes and going to sleep. Every sound would be magnified, terrifying. Tomorrow, after she saw for herself in the light of day that everything was all right—no open windows, no more footprints, no signs of an intruder—and after she wedged dowels into every window to prevent anyone from raising them, she would feel differently.

She stood to retrieve her cell from the living room. At the same time, Sam moved from the kitchen into the dining room, and they both had to stop to avoid a collision. He gazed down at her, and she couldn't look away. That comfort she'd longed for a few moments ago warmed the air around her. Even though his hands were at his sides, even though there were several very proper inches of space between them, she felt safe and protected and reassured just standing in front of him.

It surprised her a look could hold such power, though on reflection it shouldn't have. One look from her father had been powerful, too, and he hadn't needed to come near for her to sense the danger. In fact, the sensations were very similar, except that where one was very good, the other was very bad.

The corner of Sam's mouth turned up in the beginning of a smile, and he lifted one hand, bringing it so near that she thought she felt its heat against her face. But before he actually touched her, Poppy exploded in a blur of furry limbs, barreling between them on her way to the front door. They were lucky she hadn't knocked them into opposite sides of the room.

"I'm guessing that's your guys," she said, managing little more than a whisper. "I'll call Gramma."

Of course, Gramma was upset. Of course, she wanted Mila and Poppy brought over immediately under police escort. She even thought it a good idea that Sam spend the night and shadow Mila everywhere she went for however long it took to feel safe again.

"Yeah, Gramma, I don't think that's going to happen. I'm pretty sure things like real crimes and real victims take precedence over me."

"Not to me, they don't."

"Thank you. I don't know what time it'll be when we get there."

"Doesn't matter. I'll be waiting with cold milk and warm brownies. You stay right by Sam's side. Got it?"

"Got it." After a brief hesitation, she lowered her voice and said the hardest words she'd ever had to learn. "I love you, Gramma. See you soon."

Sam had gone outside with the officers, Detective Little Bear and a woman Mila hadn't met before. Sliding her phone into her pocket, she retrieved a canvas shopping tote from a kitchen drawer and went into the hall to gather pajamas, a change of clothes and toiletries. She packed food and treats for Poppy, shoved her work boots and baseball cap into a plastic grocery bag, then after a moment's thought, added her notebook and ink pen. Times when she couldn't sleep were usually excellent for prying emotions loose from her brain.

Another half hour passed before the officers finished looking around and asking questions about her gate, her fence, her neighbors. The conversation came to a curious stop when the woman—pretty, on the short side, carrying just enough extra pounds to fill out her uniform with luscious curves—asked, "Have you seen anyone or anything unusual lately?"

Mila looked to Sam, whose gaze went to Detective Little Bear, who cleared his throat. "Ms. Ramirez discovered last week's murder victim. She was also present when the second victim was found."

"Oh." The woman flushed, then the enormity of it sank in. "*Oh.* Sorry. I didn't realize."

"It's okay," Mila said. No one besides Gramma could possibly imagine how unusual the past eight days had been. It was safe to say they had changed her. They would mark the time when fear had found her again. When attraction had found her, too. When she'd opened her mind not to the things her parents had taken from her but to the things she could still have. Hope. Laughter. A future. Friends. Maybe even love.

After another moment, the two officers left. Sam hooked Poppy's leash onto her collar while Mila gathered her bags, and they walked out together. He watched as she locked up, and she wondered how effective it really was. A tall fence with locked gates hadn't kept her visitor out. What did it matter if he didn't get in through the door when the window had been so easy for him?

"Do you rent?"

Sam's question caught her off guard, drawing her into a frown as she followed him to the pickup in the street. "Yes. Why?"

"Maybe your landlord will pony up for some better window locks."

"Hmm. I was thinking about picking up some wood dowels at the hardware store."

He laughed, but there was little humor to it. "Wedge them in tight enough, and that should work."

He didn't add the obvious, but Mila heard it just the same: *Until the guy breaks the glass.* She would like to think one of her neighbors would hear the noise and investigate, but no one in her small area was particularly neighborly. She assumed most of them worked during the day, and the heat kept most people who were home inside, with air-conditioning and other distractions.

Sam undid the truck's locks with the key fob, then opened the rear door so Poppy could jump inside. By the time he closed the door, the dog was sitting in the front seat, tongue hanging out.

"She's not as well behaved in a car as she is on a walk," Mila said apologetically.

Sam's disbelieving look was almost enough to make her laugh, though she wasn't feeling much humor, either. At least he didn't point out that *Poppy* and *well behaved* didn't belong in the same sentence.

After a moment spent staring between her and the dog, now grinning and drooling at him from the other side of the window glass, he did laugh. It was weak and born more of stress needing an outlet than anything else, but it sounded good, and it eased the tension in her muscles and made her grateful. Before she tried to sleep tonight, she would make a note of it in her book.

She did have laughter in her life. Not hers, but she would claim it until the time she could find her own.

Sam parked in front of Jessica's building and shut off the engine. He expected Mila to say he didn't need to see them to Gramma's door, but she didn't. He appreciated rationality when it fell in so neatly with his own plans. "Does Poppy need a walk before we go in?"

"Probably." She reached inside one of her bags and pulled out a thin plastic produce bag, stuffing it into her pocket.

"Cedar Creek doesn't have a pooper scoop law."

Her expression was clear revulsion. "You shouldn't need a law. That's just common decency." Sliding to the ground, she gestured to the east. "There's a parking lot on the side street, with a couple of trees that she likes to sniff."

Her demeanor was calm, quiet, controlled. Sam hadn't quite reached that point yet. He hated people who preyed on other people, whether weaker or more vulnerable or simply available. No one should ever have to be a victim of any kind, especially in her own home.

And he hated that the prowler had chosen Mila. Hadn't she been through enough the past week? Did the universe of bad luck have to dump it on her all at once?

It made him feel antsy. Frustrated. He was the chief of police, damn it. If he couldn't even keep the people he cared for safe, what good was he?

The wind began blowing as they walked, shuffling trash along the curbs, picking up fine dust and debris and scattering it midair. There was no cooling in this breeze, though. It stirred the heavy, hot air, then left it hanging where it was, too stubborn to move on.

"It would be nice if that wind was carrying some rain," Mila remarked as Poppy turned automatically at the intersection. Then she made a face. "Such a cliché subject."

"Not for a farmer's son or a woman who makes beautiful gardens for a living." He grinned ruefully. "Oklahoma lives and dies by the weather. And oil prices. And the Sooners."

"Sooners?" She arched one eyebrow as Poppy pulled her toward a small Bartlett pear tree that looked as parched as he felt.

"Not a fan of the University of Oklahoma?"

"Not a fan of sports in general."

"Didn't you play soccer when you were a kid? Toss a baseball around with the other kids in the neighborhood? No, wait, you look more like a dance or gymnastics sort of kid." No matter what she did, she had an air of grace that came from years of body awareness and control.

For a long time she gazed off into the distance, her

features unreadable. Remembering dance recitals with her parents sitting in the front row videoing her? Thinking of all the gymnastics classes they'd taken her to, all the meets, all the encouragement? Or maybe it had been swim classes, her mom sitting patiently through hour after hour of practice and competitions.

Until she turned eleven, when life as she knew it had ended.

He was mentally kicking himself when she gave her head a little shake, coming back from the past. "I was more of an indoor girl. My mother raised a daughter, not a tomboy."

Abruptly she tugged Poppy's leash. "Come on, sweetie, you're just playing. It's bedtime, and you know it."

After a few more sniffs, the dog peed, circled a few times and took care of that, too. Sam took the plastic bag from Mila, scooped it up and tied a knot. He tossed it in a garbage can at the corner disguised as a planter, thick vines of purple sweet potato trailing down to the sidewalk.

Inside Jessica's building, he followed Mila and Poppy up the stairs to the fifth floor, enjoying the view of swaying hips and well-developed glutes for the first two floors, thinking for one floor that she and/or Poppy needed to get over it if they had an aversion to the elevator, then going back to enjoying the view. When they reached the top, Mila pressed Jessica's buzzer, and just seconds later, a harsh voice shouted from behind them.

"Jessica, your granddaughter's being brought home by the police! No surprise there, huh?"

Mila cringed at the shrillness of the voice, and so did Poppy. Sam turned to scowl at the peephole in the doorway. "What have I told you about minding your own business, Miz Wynona?"

"Don't you talk to me like that, Sammy Douglas," she shouted back. "I'll tell your mama at church on Sunday."

He turned back as Jessica opened the door and immediately enveloped Mila in a hug. As he shepherded them inside, he muttered, "Yeah, you don't scare me, you nosy old witch."

Jessica gave him an elbow in the ribs when he drew even with her. "I appreciate the sentiment, but I noticed you said it where she couldn't hear."

He grimaced. "She really will tell Mom, who will ask me why in the world I keep giving Wynona a reason to complain to her."

"Oh, I think that's all Wynona has, is reasons to complain. Welcome to Ramirez Guest Lodge." The apartment was all lit up, not with the soft white bulbs he used in his own house but middle-of-the-blazing-day ten-million-watt-sun bulbs. It made the bright colors—orange sofa, turquoise chair, rug woven of primary colors—even brighter and made him appreciate the quiet calm of Mila's house even more.

"Thank you for bringing my grandbabies safely to me." Jessica hugged him before heading to the kitchen. "I've got milk and brownies. Will you stay and have some with us?"

He wasn't crazy about milk, but he did love a good brownie, enough that he didn't believe there could actually be a bad brownie. But it was late, and he was tired, and Mila looked beyond tired. "Thanks, but five o'clock comes awfully early, and I think your babies can probably use some gramma time."

"Oh, you're so sweet. I bet your mama's proud to burstin' of you, even if you do rile the old hag across the hall. You get an extra one for that." Jessica slid two brownies from the plate on the counter into a plastic bag and zipped it as she crossed to him. "I bake every day of the week that ends in *y*, so if you ever need a sweets fix, drop in here or at the shop anytime."

"Thank you, ma'am." He took the brownies, heavy and gooey, and watched Jessica make a big production of getting Poppy and herself out of the room. Mila slowly approached him, hands loosely clasped in front of him. She glanced up a time or two, catching his gaze, then continued her slow meander around furniture that would be too much for a room twice its size. *Slow* was the only way to get around it.

Finally she stood in front of him, not too close—enough room for an overstuffed armchair between them—and she let her hands drop to her sides before lifting her gaze to his face. "Thank you, Sam." Her voice was barely a whisper. Because she still wasn't recovered from the unwelcome surprise she'd gotten tonight or because she desired privacy within distance of not one but two loud women?

He didn't care. He just matched her whisper. "You're welcome." That jogged a thought in him, and he pulled a handful of business cards from his wallet. Finding an ink pen next to a notepad on a table, he scrawled his cell number on the back of every one. Then, just for an excuse to touch her once more, he put the cards in her hand and folded her fingers over them, just like he'd done with his debit card the other night.

Only this time he didn't let go. "About the only time I'm truly not available is when I'm on the stand in a courtroom testifying. Any other time, if you need something, even if it's just a friendly voice, call me, will you?"

Her gaze locked with his, she nodded. She looked nervous, flushed, awkward, regretful, hopeful… Every emotion he'd seen cross her face was crossing it now, along with some he hadn't seen. Her fingers were motionless within his grip, like she wanted the touch but didn't, couldn't give in to it but couldn't pull away from it, either.

Then her thumb moved. Not a lot. She didn't clench it tighter to her palm. She didn't try to pull it from his hold. She just slid it, bit by bit, until its pad was pressed in that webbed spot between his own thumb and forefinger.

As touches went, it was minor, petty, nothing, but damn, it felt like so much more. So much potential. So much intimacy. So much trust.

So damn much more.

Jessica's crooning to Poppy was getting louder, finally forcing him to speak. "We'll talk tomorrow."

"Okay."

Their gazes held a moment longer before he reluctantly pulled away and turned to the door. "Good night, ladies." He didn't look back over his shoulder as he walked out, or when he said goodbye to Miz Wynona, or when he headed down the stairs.

By the time he reached his truck, his breath was coming in unsteady gulps, not because of exertion. Because he felt…different. There was no other way to say it. The Sam Douglas he was at this very moment wasn't the same one who'd walked into Jessica's apartment tonight. Mila's trust had touched him in a very fundamental way.

Yeah, in the head, he could hear Ben saying.

He wasn't sure exactly what had changed, or if things would return to normal, or if he even wanted them to. Normal was comfortable. It was familiar. It was risk-free. Normal stayed the same, year after year, success after disappointment, heartbreak after relationship.

He'd always been a very normal sort of guy.

He wasn't cut out to be a not-normal guy.

But with Mila in his life, he wasn't sure *normal* was an option anymore.

Chapter 7

The woman's eyes went dark with concern and worry and something else: doubt. She looked around again before refocusing on me. "Honey, are you okay?" she asked cautiously. "Did you have a fight with your dad? Does he know where you are?"

I'm not angry, I'm not trying to get back at him, I'm not lying, I'm trying to save your life! I screamed the words but knew they had voice only in my head. I glanced toward him but didn't see him. That didn't mean he was gone. He always moved someplace where we couldn't see him, not until we walked through whichever door he had chosen and it was too late. This time I could feel him watching me. My skin tingled and burned as if he could use sheer hatred to make me burst into flames. My stomach was so twisted, so filled with helplessness and rage, that I felt as if I was on fire.

"Please," I whispered. "Please believe me. I don't want him to hurt you. I don't want him to kill you. Just run away. Find a security guard or a police officer or someone so you can get out of here. Just go now!"

Slowly she hung the dress back on the rack and turned to face me. I was almost as tall as she was, and I saw the instant it occurred to her that I was big enough to hurt her if I tried. She pretended to be casual about it as she took a step back, but I could see she thought I was crazy, probably dangerous to myself if not to others. Part of her wanted to take my advice and run. Part of her—the part that loved her niece so dearly, the part that made her my father's favorite victim— couldn't just walk away and leave an unstable girl by herself in the middle of the store.

"Come on, honey," she said. She swallowed hard, like she wished she'd never seen me, and took my hand. "Let's go find your father. Whatever's wrong, it'll be all right. I'm sure he's worried sick about you. Come on."

Tears filling my eyes, I wrapped my fingers so tightly around hers, thinking maybe I could stop her, maybe she wasn't up to dragging my seventy-five pounds across the floor. Her hand was so warm and soft. I dreamed of hands like that. Hands that didn't cause pain. That preferred stroking over slapping. That didn't leave marks and nightmares with every touch.

Then I looked up and saw him, and the ice of

his hatred washed over me, numbing me. Defeating me. The little bit of courage I'd found was gone. He'd always said no one would believe me if I told stories about him, and he'd been right. But I'd been stupid enough to try.

And now I was in more trouble than I'd ever imagined.

　　　　　—Excerpt, *The Unlucky Ones* by Jane Gama

Cedar Creek was aptly named, flowing from the woods with cedar trees greedily grabbing every bit of space they could and into Cedar Creek Park, where its banks had been cleared on both sides with a man-made beach on the east.

Mila went there to swim at least twice a week during the summer months, but the past week and a half had thrown her off schedule. This Saturday morning was the first chance she'd had both time and energy.

"You know, we could go the municipal pool," Gramma said as she secured a pair of hot-pink swim goggles over her eyes.

"They don't like swimmers at the city pool."

"If you want to swim, you have to be there when the doors open at six. After seven, the only real exercise anyone can get is kicking at the obnoxious kids when they get too close, and kicking doesn't scare off the kids the way it used to."

"They haven't been raised right." Mila smiled faintly as she dropped her towel on the grass, then stripped off her T-shirt and shorts. Her black swimsuit was one piece—"modest enough for Granny," Gramma had said drily—her water shoes were black, and her hair was pulled back in a tight braid. The only bit of color on her was a thin red stripe on her black goggles.

Gramma, on the hand, was a sight that screamed *Summer!* Her swimsuit, also one piece and Granny modest, was lavender and yellow and lime and electric blue, and her water shoes were pink-and-orange plaid. For a sixty-five-year-old woman, she looked impressively good. She was fit. Despite her penchant for baking and good food, her weight had never varied by more than ten pounds throughout her life, and while she admitted she had some sag, she insisted she'd earned it.

Men in her age range never seemed to mind a little bit of sag. Mila wished that she would start paying back the attention they gave her sometime.

"Did you see Sam yesterday?"

Together they walked into the water, tepid but relatively clear in the shallows, and they both turned to the right. Kids played around the beach, so they always swam upstream, enjoying the quiet.

"No," Mila said, feeling a twinge of disappointment. "He worked late. But Detective Little Bear called and asked me another few dozen questions."

"I like Detective Little Bear. If he was twenty years older…" Gramma grinned lasciviously. "He would still be too young for me, but I wouldn't let that stop me. I wonder if he's got a father or an uncle who's single."

"Have you always stayed single because of me?"

Gramma skirted around a group of preteen girls on floaties. "I had responsibilities—things I needed to do and things I wanted to do. Besides, your grandfather… he was a tough act to follow." She smiled at Mila as they drew near again, the water now up to their waists. "Oh, you would have loved him, Mila, and he would have thought God had blessed him twice. Things would have been different if he'd still been alive, sweet girl. He never would have let Lindy take off with you the way she did. He saw things, your grandfather did, that other people didn't."

They were past the kids now, at a good spot to start their swim along the broad stream, but Mila didn't move. It was so rare they talked about her grandfather. Was it because she didn't ask, or talking about him made Gramma sad, or Gramma thought talking about him made Mila sad?

"What sort of things?"

"Oh, nothing scary or weird. He was the best judge of people I ever knew. He understood that people could be flawed and still do their best. He knew you could love a person who was badly flawed, and that person could deserve it. But he also knew that loving someone didn't mean a damn thing if he or she was bad, and that some people truly were bad." Gramma's gaze settled on the mottled clouds overhead. "He knew Lindy was truly bad. I made excuses for her, so many excuses. She was my little girl! But he always knew. He watched her. He worried over her."

Mila's parents had zoomed past bad straight into evil. For a long time it had scared her that theirs were the genes that created her. They'd given her dark hair, eyes and skin; they'd helped determine her height and weight and, to some extent, her intelligence. Had they also passed on whatever mutant genes they'd possessed? Would she one day lose her sense of right and wrong? Lose her morals and compassion and empathy? Would she become crazy, mean, selfish and cruel?

Her psychologist assured her she wouldn't. He'd been

assuring her of that for fifteen years. Nature versus nurture, he reminded her. Her parents had been horrible people. She'd understood that even when they'd been the only influence in her life. She'd known they were bad and she could be good. If she'd gotten that message while living with them, it had become so much easier to grasp after moving in with Gramma.

"I would have loved Grampa." Mila had seen pictures of the big handsome man whose life had been split so evenly between sheer joy with Gramma and grave sorrow over his daughter. And he would have loved her back.

She still so very much missed every bit of love her parents had kept from her.

They stood in the warm water, sun beating down on their shoulders, the bulk of the people playing in the water behind them. After a moment, Gramma said, "I'll race you to the bend." She pushed forward, gliding smoothly, more graceful in water than on land. Mila watched a moment before shifting to take a long look around. Kids splashing in the creek, parents sitting in lawn chairs or on quilts spread across the grass, other kids running wild around the playground. Smoke from one of the park's grills floated on the air, and from a remote spot of the park, the strains of "Happy Birthday" drifted. It was the quintessential small-town American Saturday morning, and she was part of it, even if in the smallest of ways. All it needed for sheer perfection was Poppy.

And Sam.

"She's leaving you behind," an older gentleman, one of those who'd appreciatively watched Gramma disrobe earlier, called from the west bank, gesturing upstream where Gramma was just bits of colors.

"But she always lets me catch up," Mila replied. With a tentative wave, she slipped lower in the water and started after Gramma.

Swimming equaled peace to Mila. The muted sights and sounds, the water that was refreshing even when it was bathtub warm, the fish that sometimes came right up to her to nibble. She was strong in the water. She could hold her breath forever, and her strokes propelled her forward with amazing ease. She was in her own blissful world, could become a fish that effortlessly swam this way and that, so lost that she was startled when she almost swam into her grandmother.

Abruptly she surfaced. "You beat me again."

"Aw, you didn't even try. You were taking a mental picture of the scene."

No one knew her as well as Gramma did. Physical photos didn't matter much to Mila. Her family pictures started when she was eleven, and there wasn't a lot of happiness in them. Memories were what mattered to her, there in her head where she could call them up whenever she wanted, accompanied by scents and feelings. Where she could treasure them.

"If you beat me back, I'll treat you to hamburgers and fries at Patriot Grill," Gramma offered.

"With onions and jalapeños in the fries?"

"Is there any other way to eat them?" Gramma adjusted her goggles. "On the count of three… Three!"

Mila swam a few yards behind her, then flipped onto her back to gaze up at the sky. She had never been to church in her original life; God didn't escape her parents' anger any more than anything else did. She'd never learned to pray, beyond the lone prayer Gramma had taught her at five.

But she'd developed her own sort of prayer—gazes, gratitude and fears sent skyward. Life was good. It wasn't perfect and never would be, but perfect would get boring in no time. Good, though…good was something to be proud of.

So she'd discovered a dead body. Been present at the discovery of a second one. Had her sanctuary violated. Been driven out of her house Thursday night—though she'd slept there again last night with Poppy's weight comfortably pushing against her.

She was alive. Free. Had her health. Had her gramma. Had met Sam. Had her job and her garden and her whole future ahead of her. Had endless possibilities that intrigued her.

Most of them having to do with Sam.

Life was so very good.

A smile curving her lips, she rolled back to her stomach to finish the swim when something warm and rubbery bumped her arm. A snake was the first thought that came to her mind, and she jerked away, but it wasn't a snake. Fingers enclosed in a glove curled clawlike around her wrist and dragged her beneath the surface of the creek.

Mila's involuntary response was to scream, but she cut it off with the first bit of water that dribbled into her mouth. The attacker's free hand yanked her goggles from her head and let them go. The water stung Mila's eyes, distorting what she saw in the dim, murky depths. There were hollowed-out logs resting on the bottom, tumbled together, with a warning flag attached on their top side so she knew exactly where they were. All she had to do was break away and shoot to the surface, and someone would be close enough to help her, close enough to scare this crazy person away.

Just break away. If only everything was as easy as it sounded. Her assailant was dressed in black, not a wet suit, just snug-fitting black pants, shirt and gloves. His face was obscured by a dive mask with tinted lens. The image of him in Cedar Creek should have been comical, but his grip was so powerful that it felt as if the bones and tendons in her left wrist were being ground to powder, the pain increasing every minute.

Mila's lungs were burning. She'd had no opportunity to take a breath before he'd grabbed her, and she desperately needed one now. She used her free hand to attack his, at the same time kicking her feet, finding a spot on a downed tree to push off. Despite the man's best efforts, her head broke the surface for an instant, long enough to appreciate the sweet fresh air, nowhere near long enough to yell for help. Instead, as he drew her relentlessly back under, she dragged in every particle of air she could.

Kicking and punching underwater was impossible, not with enough force to do any good, so with her stinging eyes barely open, she looked for vulnerabilities. She found a thin gap between one long sleeve and a glove and dug her nails into the skin, scratching, digging, wishing her nails were long enough to do real damage. She twisted in a circle, trying to rotate her wrist away from him, even raised her foot and planted it on his arm to push against the slime-covered surface of the tree. She pulled herself closer and pried her fingers beneath the edge of his mask. He reacted too quickly for her to yank it off, but she had the satisfaction of seeing water bubble where she'd broken its seal.

Her air situation was getting desperate, her breath threatening to explode, her lungs fiercely hungry. She felt blindly, unable to budge the mask a second time so she could gouge at his eyes. Her fingers brushed across his ear, skimmed over a bald head, then went back. Gripping the ear tightly in her fingers, she gave it a vicious twist. His bellow muffled by the mask, the man shoved her away, releasing her hand in the process.

Mila didn't wait to see what he did, where he went. Eyes squeezed tightly to ease the burning, she shot to the surface and emerged, coughing and choking, no more than twenty feet from Gramma. If she could make it to Gramma, she would be all right.

But she didn't make it that far. She heard a man, maybe the one she'd spoken to earlier, exclaim, "What the hell?" followed by an incoherent shout from Gramma. Splashes sounded and arms grabbed her, pulled her to the grassy shore. They dragged her out of the water, then someone pushed her to the ground; someone else wrapped a towel around from her. Gramma crouched in front of her, worry etched deep into her face.

"Baby, what happened? Did you get a cramp? Did you get snagged on something? What happened to you?"

All Mila could do was lift her left arm. Everything fell silent for a moment, then a man, definitely the man she'd talked to about Gramma earlier, spoke in a grim voice.

"I'm calling the police."

"How the hell did this happen with all these people around?" Sam demanded as he stalked across the parking lot and toward the creek bank.

"The guy was underwater. She was swimming. He grabbed her, pulled her under and held her." Daniel Harper matched his stride, not bothering to glance at his notes. "She and her grandmother were the only ones actually swimming. They were racing, but Milagro always let her win because she liked to take her time. When Jessica got down here, she stopped to talk with the geezer brigade, and that's where she was when Milagro suddenly popped up. They said she looked half-drowned, could barely catch a breath. It took three or four of them to get her out. As soon as they saw her arm, they called us."

Sam's heart was pounding as if he were half-drowned, too, like there wasn't enough oxygen in the world to reach the places his nerves and muscles and organs needed it. Who the hell lurked under the water at the local swimming hole surrounded by kids and tried to drown someone in the middle of a busy Saturday? What kind of maniac was after Mila?

He angled off the sidewalk, gave up all pretense of walking and broke into a run across the grass. Six or eight old men were huddled together with two figures in their middle: Mila and Jessica. Both women were pale and shivering, Mila looking unbearably young and forlorn, Jessica's expression torn about equally between grief and rage.

Paramedics were questioning Mila while one gingerly examined her wrist. Sam didn't get in their way, but he stepped up right behind her, laid his hand on her shoulder. It did his heart good when she raised her uninjured hand and rested it over his. "Merry, Kerry, how about some good news?"

The paramedics greeted him with solemn smiles.

"We've narrowed her attacker down to Iron Fist or maybe Bone Crusher. Her wrist is gonna be sore as the devil, and she'll have lovely bruises, but nothing appears broken."

Sam winced when he saw the swelling that doubled the size of Mila's wrist, along with the discoloration that had already occurred. He was so damn angry that it vibrated through him. He felt helpless and impotent and wanted more than anything to pound the man who'd done this into the ground.

No, not true. He wanted more than anything to wrap his arms around Mila and hold her until the shaking stopped, until her breath steadied and her fear faded, until she curled up against him and felt safe enough to fall asleep.

He gazed around the geezers until he found their leader, Charles Brinkley. "Hey, Charles, can you fellows take Jessica here and get her a dry towel and something to drink? Maybe mix a couple of your thermoses together." He knew Charles always carried coffee in his bottle, no matter how hot the weather. He also knew a couple of the others always carried a little mix-in of liquid courage in theirs. Jessica looked like a stiff drink would do her a world of good.

"Be happy to, young Sam." The old gentlemen were pleased to lead her some distance away, though at first she looked like she wanted to resist. It was only after catching Sam's gaze that she went along.

He eased to the ground next to Mila, keeping hold of her right hand, and adjusted the towel around her shoulders. There were a couple of marks across her face that made her look that much more vulnerable.

Merry or Kerry—though not related, they'd been inseparable best friends for so long that he couldn't keep their names straight—followed his gaze. "That's where he yanked her goggles off."

"A kid found them about a hundred feet downstream and brought them over," Daniel said. He sat down, too, choosing a grassy spot in front of them. "Do you feel like answering a few questions?"

Mila nodded.

"You said it was a man. Did you see his face?"

"No. He wore a dive mask that I couldn't see through." Anticipating his next question, she went on, her voice growing a little stronger. "I was looking for a way to hurt him. I thought maybe I could yank his hair, but he was bald, so I tweaked his ear instead. It made him let go."

"Did you see which way he went?"

She apologetically shook her head. "I was out of air. I just surfaced, saw Gramma and tried to get to her."

"Can you make any guess about his size?"

Another rueful shake. "The water was murky, and without the goggles, my eyes were burning. All I can say is he was dressed all in black—shirt, pants, gloves—he was bald, and he had a very strong grip."

Sam looked at the finger marks visible on her arm. As the swelling continued, the marks and colors would run together to make one ugly mass. Damn it, who was this bastard, and why was he terrorizing Mila?

"Could you identify him if you saw him again?"

She was very still for a long time before shaking her head. "No," she whispered. "I wasn't thinking about being a witness. I just wanted to survive."

The statement was so soft, so bald, that everyone around her went still. After a moment, Daniel broke the silence when he closed his notebook and turned his attention to Sam. "You should probably take her to the emergency room. Merry and Kerry offered, but she declined."

"I'm okay." Mila started to move her hand, winced and stopped. "It's not broken."

"You have X-ray vision now?" Sam forced a teasing tone into his voice, though it just about broke his face to smile.

It was worth the look she gave him, though. Relief. Gratitude. Like she would tease, too, if she had it in her.

"It can't hurt to get it X-rayed," one of the paramedics said.

"Of course it can," the other disagreed. "They'll try to put it in all kinds of unnatural positions for the views. But afterward, they'll give you drugs for the pain—and there will be pain."

It was obvious from the paleness of Mila's face that there already was, which made Sam's decision an easy one. "We'll stop by there before we go home." He didn't say it wasn't her home he was taking her to. Her attacker knew where she lived. Might know where Jessica lived.

Merry and Kerry began packing up their equipment. Sam stood and helped Mila to her feet. She nodded to the parking lot across the creek. "Gramma's car is over there. So are our clothes."

His gaze automatically slid down her body. How had it escaped his notice until that very minute that she wasn't wearing anything but water shoes and a black swimsuit that clung lovingly to her body in all the right places? The curve of her breasts, her narrow waist, the flare of her hips and her long, strong, tanned legs…

God, he had it bad.

She was watching him, one brow arched, waiting for…what? Oh, yeah, a response. He tried to remember what she'd said, though the faint snicker from Daniel wasn't helping. Finally, the sound of Jessica's voice as she approached triggered the memory. "We'll drive Jessica over. She can pick up the car and your clothes."

Daniel leaned close. "Or maybe she'll want her clothes before she waits in the ER for the usual couple hours."

This time it was Merry and Kerry who snickered.

Sam's face flushed. "Okay, yeah, we'll figure it out. Daniel, keep me updated."

The detective nodded. He would do his job—interview everyone at the park, walk the creek on both banks looking for tracks, check out all the cars in the lot and so forth. The creek was deep enough in the center that a person could swim all the way past the city limits in both directions, which gave him probably six miles of shore to tramp over, walk into a neighborhood, into the woods, into a house or get into a car and vanish.

Damn it, just thinking about it made Sam less than hopeful.

It was tough for Sam to let Mila walk to the car with her stiff, battered, the-water-monster-almost-killed-me gait. Her wrist was the most obvious injury, but the way she cradled her arm against her suggested she might have strained some muscles or tendons while fighting her way free.

But she didn't ask for help until they reached his truck and she was faced with climbing into the high seat. He gave her a boost and fastened her seat belt, then gave Jessica a hand up into the rear seat.

Gramma looked her age for the first time since Sam

had met her. The idea of someone hurting Mila had shaken her to her core. She was so much the mama bear, and she wanted to put the fear of God into the bastard.

"Are you okay to drive?"

She held out her hand and watched it tremble. "No. Charles is going to meet us over there. I'll get what I need, lock up the Bug and go to the hospital with him. He and his friends will deliver it to me later." She clasped Sam's hand. "What do you know about him, Chief?"

"Charles is a good man. Owned an insurance business just down the block from you. His wife died about ten years ago. They didn't have any children."

Jessica smiled, at least a little intrigued, and patted Sam's hand again.

It was a quiet drive, five blocks to get from the west side lot to the east side. Charles Brinkley was already there, collecting towels, sandals and a string bag with clothing from the grass. After securing the Bug, Jessica and Charles, in his Cadillac, followed Sam and Mila to the hospital.

There in the parking lot, Jessica helped Mila into the shorts she'd worn over her swimsuit. Instead of her shirt, she wrapped their own beach towels, still warm from the sun, around Mila. Satisfied that she'd done all she could, Jessica took a step back. "You walk with her, Sam, in case her knees buckle or something."

"My knees aren't going to buckle," Mila said with an effort at a reassuring smile. Jessica wasn't swayed. Sam wasn't, either. Even Charles didn't fall for it.

Sam took hold of her right arm and started across the street with her. She seemed so fragile. Not because she was skimpily dressed. Not because she'd been attacked.

Because the sad, quiet tones of her voice kept echoing in his head. *I wasn't thinking about being a witness. I just wanted to survive.* The tones of a woman who, at least once, almost hadn't survived.

In less than the two hours Detective Harper had predicted, Mila was snuggled onto the couch in Gramma's living room. She'd wanted to go to her own house, Sam to his, so they'd compromised on Jessica's. Besides the main entrance, there was only one other door into the building, one that led from the tenants' parking out back. Only one person was needed to watch both doors and the stairs and elevator. Unless Mila's would-be killer could scale walls or fly, there was no way he could reach her there.

Gramma pressed a glass of iced coffee into her good hand. "Take a good long drink of that, sweetie, and you'll feel better. Then we'll see about getting you into the shower."

A shower sounded heavenly. She was pretty sure she'd brought home little bits of algae, slime and maybe even some minnows from the creek. Her eyes were still red, her nose smelled of muck and damp, and her mouth—

She gladly took a big drink of coffee and cream to dispel the taste in her mouth and almost spit it right back out. After swallowing, she grimaced and coughed. "What kind of cream is in this?"

"Just the usual," Gramma said innocently.

It amused Mila that Sam already knew better than to trust Gramma's innocent face. He took the glass from her, sniffed it and said, "That's Irish cream. A little heavy on the whiskey, isn't it, Jessica?"

"She's had a tough day."

"Yeah, so let's give her some narcotics, a little whiskey and then put her in the shower. Maybe she'll break something else."

Jessica's face wrinkled. "Well, I was thinking she would have help in the shower, but you're right. We'll save the whiskey for tonight."

She took the glass from Sam and returned it to the kitchen. "I'm going to take a shower, too. I think I'll puke if I smell sunscreen and creek ick one moment longer. I've laid out towels and clean clothes and everything in the guest bathroom, Sam. Mila can help you find anything I've forgotten. I do so appreciate it you doing this, Sam."

Before Mila's mouth finished dropping, Gramma disappeared into her bedroom. Mila stared at the closed door, then whipped around to look at Sam. "I can't believe she just did that."

"You didn't catch it when she said you would have help in the shower? Process of elimination leaves me." He shrugged. "I'm a good choice in terms of not letting you fall. Maybe not so good in terms of modesty and privacy. But we can manage."

She had to admit the idea held enormous appeal under different circumstances. If no injury was involved, if it was totally his idea, if Gramma wasn't down the hall, if they were bathing together…

That last thought was enough to leave her starved for air once again but in a much lovelier way. Being naked, wet, soapy and steamy with Sam, his hands on her, her hands on him, touching and exploring… How many firsts would that mark off her list?

How many other firsts would it lead to?

Her heart was pounding, making her flush with every new influx of hot blood. She wanted a shower, wanted *that* shower, wanted everything with him, but...

He was watching her, his expression level. "We can keep it clean," he said softly. When her face flushed, he chuckled. "I know, *clean* is not my first thought when I think of you naked, but...you're injured. Your grandmother's here. But we're adults, and we can behave appropriately until a better time."

All of that, and she truly heard only one thing: *when I think of you naked*. Before her brain could stop her mouth, she asked, "You think of me naked?"

His only answer was a searing look that warmed her to her toes. He stood and offered his hand. "Come on. Let's test my self-control."

She had no doubt he possessed it in spades. Sadly for her, she had tons of it, too. She could come out of this undressing-showering-dressing again as innocent and untouched as she was right now.

But she took his hand anyway.

She'd left her flip-flops just inside the front door, so her feet padded soundlessly down the hall and to the bathroom the two guest rooms shared. Gramma had left the lights on, the water running to get it nice and warm, and a couple of scented candles burning. For ambience? Seduction?

Then Mila caught a look at herself in the mirror above the vanity, and a look of woe crossed her face. She most definitely needed any help she could get. About 40 percent of her hair was still in a braid, but the rest hung in a tangled mess that looked as if it belonged with the other mucky roots at the bottom of Cedar Creek. The marks on her face from the goggles getting jerked off had turned to purple-hued bruises. Her swimsuit was mostly dry and stiff and smelled rich and ripe, like fertilizer she used in the garden.

Her gaze flickered to Sam, who'd been adjusting the shower spray and temperature. "I guess we start with my hair."

He looked at her head, opened a drawer and pulled out a pair of scissors, his brows arched, his mouth twitching with a grin.

"You don't scare me. The woman who cuts my hair loves me because I let her do whatever she wants." She lifted one shoulder in a shrug. "It always grows back."

"I'd like to see it short someday." He put the scissors back and began searching through the tangle for the rubber band that held her braid together. "Then down to your waist, then really short again, then maybe down past your hips."

A shiver went through her, and not just because he was pulling knots and tangles and the occasional leaf from her hair with such gentle movements. "They say hair grows only about six inches a year." The sort of changes he was talking about would take time. Months. Years.

"I've heard."

"That's quite a commitment."

His gaze met hers in the mirror, his blue eyes serious and intense, his voice gone soft and husky. "I'm very good with commitments, Mila."

Right then, her heart stopped beating. Just for a couple of beats, just enough to make that instant significant. Enough for her to understand Gramma's wistfulness the times she'd asked the boyfriend question.

Gramma had had plenty of boyfriends before she met

Grampa, and he'd won the universe for best boyfriend ever. If he'd made her feel any of the dizzy, breath-stealing, girly things Mila was feeling right now, he'd deserved the title.

Gramma wanted her to feel these dizzy, breath-stealing, girly things, and she'd feared Mila never would. That was the reason for her wistfulness.

"I—I'm…" Heat turned her face crimson. She searched her brain for the right thing to say, but she was too quivery and shivery, the room was too warm, his hands were too deliberate in their touch, and she had no experience with this kind of conversation.

Ruefully, she gave up, almost smiled, almost laughed and said plainly, "Sometimes you take my words away."

"I think that's only fair." He reached the top of her head, combed his fingers through to loosen all the strands, then fixed his gaze on hers in the mirror. "Because sometimes you take my breath away."

Mila wanted that moment to last forever, was preserving it in her brain, every detail of it, when a song from next door filtered into the room. She forced air into her lungs, forced her gaze to move away from his. "Does it surprise you Gramma likes to sing in the shower?"

"It doesn't. Is that… 'How Great Thou Art'?"

"Gospel songs. Loudly. And badly. Wynona Novak calls it caterwauling."

"Wynona would. I hate to say it, but that woman can sing. It probably pains her to hear songs she loves mangled like this." He winced as Jessica blared out a note she couldn't reach with a ladder. "Well. Talk about breaking the mood."

Mila slid her right hand into the waistband of her

shorts and gave them a tug before repeating the process on the left side. Giving her a chiding look, Sam pulled them the rest of the way off.

"How do you want to do this?" he asked, his breath warm on her thighs as he straightened again. "Should I look but not touch? Touch but not look? Put on those vinyl cleaning gloves, drop a towel over my head so I'm blind and play it by ear?" He made a tugging motion on his ear. "Oh, wait, that could be dangerous."

Mila pressed her lips together to keep from grinning and encouraging him. The situation wasn't supposed to be funny. She'd been attacked. And she'd rescued herself, her mind voice pointed out. And she'd wanted more intimacy with Sam. Well, wasn't this scene intimate?

"Just get my splint and the swimsuit off, please. I think I can manage the rest."

"Don't I get to wash your hair?"

She raised one finger threateningly. "Protect your ear."

Removing the plain black splint sobered him. The swelling was worse, and so was the bruising. The pain she couldn't really speak to, since she'd taken a pain pill as soon as they'd picked them up at the pharmacy.

With no more joking, he unfastened the hook at the neck of her swimsuit and peeled it off her. His gaze directed somewhere above her head, he helped her step into the tub, then pulled the curtain between them.

She stood under the warm water, letting it pound her shoulders and spine, eyes closed, feeling better already with the creek water gone.

"Who would want to hurt you, Mila?"

Well, she *was* feeling better. That sounded like Chief Douglas, not Sam. "I don't know."

"A former employer?"

"My previous jobs were online. I work with Gramma in the shop sometimes—doing inventory, unpacking stock, cleaning—but I don't deal with customers."

"A former friend or boyfriend?"

She stuck the shampoo bottle outside the curtain, then flattened her palm so he could squirt some onto it. "They were online, too. The friends. No boyfriends."

There was a moment of silence. Was he wondering the why of that last part? "What about before you lived here?"

She concentrated on lathering her hair one-handed. It couldn't be someone from before Cedar Creek, because so very few people who'd known she existed had lived to tell. If her parents had had friends or fellow freaks, she had never met them. Her father, she supposed, had family somewhere, but she'd never met them, either.

"I was eleven, Sam. Not an age when you usually make many enemies."

"So why the hell is this guy after you?"

Her sigh was almost soft enough to get lost in the rush of the water. "I wish to God I knew."

When the water shut off, Sam's breath caught in his chest. He felt like he was fourteen and about to see his first real live naked girl, his whole body turned to nothing but anxious hormones and lustful thoughts. But he wasn't fourteen, Mila wasn't his first naked girl, and though he was anxious and lustful, he could control it. Hopefully. He handed a thick white towel over the curtain to her, then picked up another one as she swept the curtain back.

Naturally, the bath towel covered more than the

swimsuit, but she was naked under that towel. And beautiful. And wet. Any man alive who didn't appreciate the image of a wet naked woman wasn't really alive.

She held on to his arm as she stepped out of the tub, then he dried her hair with the second towel. It streamed long and shiny down her back and smelled of summer jasmine. "Feel better?" he asked as he blotted thick strands of hair with the towel.

"A shower makes everything better."

Draping the towel over her hair, he rubbed, shaking her head enough to make her giggle. Milagro Ramirez giggled. Another check in the red-letter-day column on his calendar.

She looked so innocent and needy, and so beautiful and sensual, and he was needy, too—so damn needy. His hands stilled, his breath locked in his chest and he lowered his head until his forehead rested against hers. She had stopped breathing, too, and he wondered if she felt the same heat and desire and curiosity and lust that he did. He wondered if she had ever been naked with a man before.

Judging by her edginess and awkwardness when they'd met, he would guess no. He didn't care. He'd never been with a virgin before, but that didn't stop him wanting her, oh, hell, so much.

He wanted to take away the towel that hid her. To look until he'd memorized every part of her. To kiss her. Touch her. Show her. Claim her. He wanted…

In the hallway, Jessica passed, singing a song with the lyrics of "His Eye Is on the Sparrow," but nothing of the melody. Good Lord, if she really wanted to drive Wynona into a psychotic episode, all she had to do was show up at Grace Tabernacle in the morning and sing loud.

He winced, closed his eyes and tried to gather enough oxygen that his voice wouldn't crack like an adolescent boy's. "She puts us in here together, then sings church hymns?"

Mila's breath came out warm against his cheek. "Gramma's…unique."

"That must be where you get it from." Reluctantly, he lifted his head, gave her a regretful smile and laid the damp towel aside. "Are you ready for some clothes?" *Because Gramma or no, either you need to put some on or I've got to take some off.*

"I think I can manage except for the splint." With her good hand, she gestured to the small pile of clothing: black gym shorts, a Cedar Creek Chieftains T-shirt and a pair of plain white but very tiny panties.

"Those obviously didn't come out of Jessica's closet," he remarked as he found a dry bit of towel and patted her left hand and wrist dry. It pained him when she winced, even more that she tried to hide it.

"Why do you say that? Because the colors don't scorch your eyeballs?" she teased. "No, I keep some clothes over here. Gramma's got some at my house, too. Just in case."

He didn't ask what was the just-in-case prior to the last two weeks. He wasn't sure he could handle knowing right now.

With her left arm dry, he slid the splint in place just as the ER nurse had and secured the Velcro fasteners. "Feel okay?"

She nodded.

"While you finish up here, I'm going by your house

to pick up Poppy. I don't imagine she expected you to be gone this long." He might run all the way there, leave the dog's leash behind and do a loop around the city while holding on to her collar, just to burn off some of the excess energy inside him. "Is there anything she needs besides food?"

"No, that's it." She hesitated, biting her lower lip. "I... I would be okay at home, don't you think?" The bravado she was going for lost out to the uncertainty both in her voice and in her eyes with those last words.

"We talked about this, Mila. He tried to drown you. He knows where you live."

"I know, but..." Subconsciously, he thought, she raised her left arm to her chest in a protective manner. "I can't let him scare me out of my house."

"Why not?"

She didn't expect his question. It knitted her brows together, giving her a look of surprise. "It's my home."

"It's a place where you live. You like it, you feel safe and comfortable there, though probably not so much in the last few days as before. But it's just a place, Mila. I know you've lived a number of places, and you might have missed some, and you may have been happy to leave others, but in the end they're all just places. They're not worth putting yourself in danger."

"You're right." She gave up quickly enough that it confirmed what he suspected: her attachment wasn't to the house so much as the independence it represented. Whatever had happened in the past had given her a need to be brave and self-reliant, to stand alone in her world except for Jessica and to keep everyone else at bay. "Can you get me some clothes while you're there? They're mostly—"

"In the hall closet." He grinned. "I listen. Anything else? Books, magazines, crochet, needlepoint, knitting?"

She feigned looking cross, then nodded to the door. "The towel's coming off in five…four…three…"

"Not an incentive to leave," he said with a laugh before ducking into the hall. He imagined he heard the damp cloth hit the floor the instant the door closed, and then he stopped imagining anything, because the last thing he wanted was to face her grandmother with a hard-on.

Jessica was fussing in the kitchen, wearing a pink-and-turquoise plaid outfit that could catch the attention of a blind man. He told her where he was going, and she handed over Mila's keys. When he left the apartment, the door across the hall cracked open an inch before swinging wide.

"What happened to Jessica's granddaughter?" Wynona asked, wearing her customary scowl.

"She was assaulted at Cedar Creek."

"People shouldn't be swimming in the creek. There's a pool over by the high school, for heaven's sake."

"Aw, Miz Wynona, I know you used to swim in the creek. In fact, I heard you used to skinny-dip there and that's how you met your husband."

Her face turned as hot pink as Jessica's outfit, and she sputtered for words before settling on slamming the door instead. Sam's grin carried him down four flights of stairs and to the rear residents' entrance.

"Chief." Liam Bartlett, one of his most reliable officers, had pulled a chair from the building lobby to a point where he could easily see both entrances, the stairs and the elevator. He had a book open in his lap—

The Unlucky Ones—held with his finger marking his place.

"Liam. How's the book?"

"Scary."

"You think it's true?"

"My gut says yes. Scary either way, though, because if she didn't live through it, then she thought of it to write down. You read it?"

"I have a copy. Haven't started it yet. I may wait until things settle down around here," he added drily. "I'll be back soon. Want me to bring you anything?"

"I'm fine, Chief. Mrs. Ramirez brought me some coffee and brownies." He nodded to the wastebasket upended beside him for a makeshift table.

"Enjoy the brownies. They're good." Sam went through the back door and into the parking lot, where his pickup dwarfed Jessica's Bug. The heat was like a slap across the face, leaching the coolness from his skin, hitching his breath. Even with its tinted windows, the interior of the truck was probably near 140 degrees, enough to make sweat pop out on his forehead.

With the windows rolled down and the air conditioner blasting, he drove the short distance to Mila's house, parked out front and heaved a sigh as he crossed the front garden to the porch.

He was digging her keys from his pocket when he was struck by the quiet. No frantic barking came from inside, no scrabbling of claws on wood as Poppy tried to get through the door. Maybe she was asleep, but... No. She was far too excitable to miss the sound of footsteps on the porch. Oh, God, if the bastard had done something to Poppy...

With the hairs on his neck standing on end and a chill

sweeping over him, Sam drew his gun, gingerly touched the knob with two fingers and twisted it.

The door swung open.

The house was eerily still. Remaining in the doorway, he pulled out his cell phone and punched in 911. "Hey, Morwenna, it's Sam. Get hold of Daniel and tell him to meet me at Mila Ramirez's house. Send a couple of uniforms, too."

Without waiting for her response, he put the phone away and took one cautious step inside, his gaze sweeping the room. Nothing was missing, except the eighty pounds of happy dog bouncing off the walls. He listened for a whine, a whimper, a snuffle, anything to indicate Poppy was in one of the rooms, maybe injured, maybe restrained by the man who had tried to kill Mila. He heard nothing beyond the rapid pounding of his own heart.

Small cities were great in one respect: a police officer on an emergency call could get anywhere quickly. He hadn't yet reached the dining room when he heard sirens drawing near, had just checked the kitchen when footsteps thudded on the porch.

"Chief?"

He gestured the officers, both with guns drawn, into the house. "Mila Ramirez lives here. You know someone tried to kill her this morning. They also broke in here. Her dog, Poppy, was home alone, and I haven't found her yet. Brady, check the backyard. Carla, come with me."

He took the lead, moving into the hallway, taking a glance in the bedroom, just enough to see broken glass and no big furry yellow body. While Carla took a closer look, he turned to the left, checked the bathroom, then approached the door to the front bedroom. When he'd been here Thursday night, that door had been closed, and the hall light had glinted off a relatively new-looking dead bolt. Now it stood halfway open.

He eased it open with his foot, but the door stuck partway. A person hiding back there? Poppy, in no condition to greet him?

His stomach roiling, he ducked around the door, leading with his pistol. Relief washed over him. Nothing was blocking the door but the bed. Small as it was, it filled the tiny room.

Thank God Poppy wasn't here dead, but where the hell was she?

The only way Mila's attacker could have struck her in a more vulnerable place was by going after Jessica. That silly, goofy dog meant the world to Mila, and Sam would break in half anyone evil enough to hurt the animal.

"Chief, there's no dog here," Carla said from the hallway, and behind her Brady shook his head. "No blood, no signs of a struggle. Just that broken window."

"Talk to the neighbors, find out if anyone has seen Poppy today, if they saw someone over here, if they heard anything. She's a big yellow Lab mix, about two years old."

As they left, he turned back to the second bedroom. It was as sparsely furnished as the rest of the house. He figured no one but Jessica had ever spent the night there, unless Mila used it for an occasional retreat. The dead bolt indicated a security issue, but there was nothing of obvious value unless...

He opened the closet. She used it for storage: a couple of boxes, some file folders, a pile of loose papers, notebooks, a photo album. The hard-copy stuff that everyone had to deal with in life.

His fingers itched to pick up the photo album. It was old, worn, its pages stuffed so full that they strained at their binding. It leaned against the wall, a depression in the carpet showing it had stood there a long time. Maybe *that* was her treasure, the valuable thing that made her lock an unused room.

But the intruder hadn't cared enough to take it. It didn't look as if it had been touched in ages. Unless Sam had a cop-ly reason for thumbing through it, it would be a violation of her privacy and the trust that she found so hard to give.

"Chief?" The call came from the living room, Daniel's voice. Sam met him in the dining room, where he stood sweaty, dirty, his hair on end, his jeans muddy and ripped.

"You look like you've been traipsing through the woods and fallen a few times."

Daniel's look was flat and unamused. "My dad kept telling me I could make better money in LA, and I wouldn't be combing creek banks. So this son of a bitch tried to kill Mila, then came here and stole her dog."

"Maybe stole. Maybe just turned her loose." God, Sam hoped that was the case. Even though it meant Poppy would be at risk from traffic, getting permanently lost, mean animals and meaner people.

"There's a special place in hell for people who mess with pets," Daniel muttered. "So we need to get the window fixed, secure this place and get some people out looking for the dog. You want me to take over here so you can get back to Mila?"

The thought soured Sam's stomach. How was he

going to tell her Poppy was missing? It would break her heart, and Gramma's, and his own. "Yeah. I, uh… Yeah. Here's her keys."

"I don't envy you." Daniel took the keys on his way to the bedroom.

No, this was going to rank at the top of Sam's worst-moments-on-the-job list.

Chapter 8

My scream—our scream—was still reverberating in the air when a new voice broke into the torment. It came from behind me, from the open barn door, from the center of nature's fury and rage, and it struck a chord hidden deep inside me, buried in years of sorrow and fear. It was my grandmother, red hair and clothes plastered to her skin by the rain. Backlit by car headlights and near-constant flashes of lightning, to me she looked ten feet tall, stronger and braver than any superhero ever imagined. Her name was Anna, and I called her Gramma, and she was an avenging angel come to rescue me.

"Oh, my God. Oh, my dear God in heaven!" She clamped her hands to her mouth as if to keep in her own scream, and for a moment, I thought the horror and shock would drop her to her knees.

Oh, I loved that voice! I hadn't heard it in years, but it was woven into my brain and heart. It was the only voice that had ever sung to me, laughed with me, told me sweet stories about bunnies and puppies and happily-ever-afters. It was the only voice that had ever said, "I love you," and when my parents made it disappear from our lives when I was little, I lost the only light and hope I'd ever known.

My mother whirled to face her, rage making her ugly. "What the hell are you doing here, bitch?" she shrieked. "Get out! Get out! Get out!"

"Dear Lord, Lin." Gramma's voice sounded broken, scraped raw. "What are you—what have you—" Her words trailed off into a wail like a wounded animal.

My mother looked around wildly. I'd seen her do it a hundred times. She was looking for a weapon, something that would cause more pain than her bare hands alone. I wanted to warn Gramma, but my earlier attempt at that had gone so badly. I stood petrified, trying to shrink, to become invisible.

Unable to find anything else, my mother grabbed one of the oil lanterns and flung it at Gramma. It wasn't the first time she'd thrown things at her mother, and Gramma easily sidestepped it, coming a few precious steps closer to me. More than anything I wanted to run to her arms, but I couldn't move.

The lantern shattered, burning oil spreading in a pool that sizzled and sputtered on the wet ground. My mother was looking for something else, my father was just enjoying the show, and his victim hung limply, blood flowing from her wounds.

Gramma didn't take her gaze from my mother. "Sweetie," she said, sending a ripple of hope down my spine. She knew my parents had kept changing our names, though she didn't know why, so that was what she'd mostly called me. "Sweetie, go get in my car."

"No!" With an unholy scream, my mother charged across the barn, the movement so sudden that it seemed blurred.

The shock of it propelled both Gramma and me into motion. "Now!" she screamed, and I lunged to her. We grabbed hands and ran together, out of the barn, into the storm, sliding through the mud and puddles to her car where the engine was still running. She shoved me in the driver's door, and I scrambled across the center to the passenger seat. By the time I sat down, she'd jerked the car into gear, the tires spinning before finding the traction of hard ground, and we were racing down the driveway.

I was saved. Safe. My dearest wish had come true.

And I was so numbed that I couldn't even cry.

—Excerpt, *The Unlucky Ones* by Jane Gama

Mila's pulse jumped when she heard voices in the hallway, but the guests knocked at Wynona's door, then went inside. She stiffened when a car door sounded on the street below and left her chair to look out the window, hoping to see Sam's pickup. It was just a silver car instead.

"You sure you won't eat something?" Gramma asked from the kitchen.

"I had an apple."

"You know apples aren't eaten by themselves in this house. They go in pies or cakes or you dip them in caramel and chocolate and pecans."

That was Jessica's opinion for most fruits. Oranges were for juice, peaches for ice cream, bananas for nut bread, strawberries for angel food cake, cherries for pies. When Mila had first come to live with her grandmother, she had been fascinated by the fresh fruit on the counter. She had seen fruit before—had heard about it, but she'd never had a piece that she could remember, and one night she'd sneaked into the kitchen and eaten until she was sick. Gramma had found her, holding her belly and surrounded by cores, pits and skins, and laughed and then cried, and she'd come home the next day with more fruit than ten kids could eat.

A car passed on the street, and Mila couldn't help turning to look. Sam had been gone an hour, far longer than necessary to pick up Poppy and some clothes. Maybe he'd made a few stops along the way. Maybe he'd needed to check in at the office. Maybe Detective Harper or Detective Little Bear had needed to share something with him. Maybe—

Maybe something had happened.

"Sam is okay."

She didn't realize she'd spoken aloud until Gramma responded. She came across the room and wrapped her arm tightly about Mila's shoulders. "He'll be back soon. He's probably just clearing the decks so he can be your twenty-four-hour bodyguard. He likes you a lot." Her clear gaze studied Mila, and a smile softened her face. "You like him a lot, too."

"I—I do."

Gramma danced her around in a little circle. "Thank you, Jesus. I've been praying for this day."

She was so happy. Would it hurt to let her hold on to it awhile longer? To keep the concerns and worries to herself? The Sam-being-a-cop and Mila-being-a-fraud stuff? The whole ugly story of her past that she hadn't trusted him with? The *This is who I am and what I did and what I bring to the family table*?

Her heart fluttered. Oh. She'd never allowed herself to think seriously about babies, about love, about marriage. Normal life had been such a struggle that she'd thought she would always live on the outskirts of it, almost there but not quite. She'd never imagined a man like Sam taking the time to get to know her. Liking her. Wanting her. Worrying about her. Those things had happened, though. Could he want to stay with her? Have a family with her? Make a life with her?

The very idea made her light-headed. Clinging to Gramma with her good hand, she was returning to her chair when a knock sounded. Gramma went to answer, and Mila knew she should sit down before Poppy barreled in and knocked her down, but her muscles didn't want to work. They'd frozen, leaving her suspended in a moment of breathlessness. Fear.

When Gramma opened the door, her cheerful greeting died unspoken. "Sam, where's Poppy?"

The stone-cold anger on his face would have made Mila's legs give way if they hadn't frozen. He stabbed his fingers through his hair, squeezed his eyes tightly shut for an instant, then spoke in a voice that was as cold and hard as his expression. "She's...missing. He broke into the house and—and let her out or—or took her. We don't know... We're looking... I'm sorry, Mila."

Poppy. Missing. The words sounded so foreign together. Poppy couldn't be missing. She'd been asleep on the sofa when Mila left this morning. She'd opened one eye, given a huge yawn and started snoring loudly before Mila got off the porch. She couldn't be missing. She couldn't be running loose. She was the best dog in the world, but she didn't do well on a leash with Mila hanging on to provide some control. She was too excitable, too silly, too careless...oh, dear God, too important to be missing.

Tears filled her eyes, and her muscles unlocked only to start trembling. "I have to go find her. I have to... she doesn't always come when called, and I've always kept her away from strangers. I don't know if she would trust someone she didn't know. And she doesn't look before she crosses the street. That's my job. It's my..."

A sob choked off the words and propelled her into motion, weaving around the furniture, heading for the door. Gramma tried to stop her, but she pulled free. At the door, Sam caught her around the waist, and she tried to pull away from him, too, but he was too strong. She pushed him; he didn't budge. She kicked him; he lifted her off her feet, spun her around and set her back down inside the apartment, pushing the door shut with his elbow.

"You can't go out there, Mila."

"He hurt me, and now he has Poppy! I have to go!"

"He wants you dead!"

"I don't care! She's just a puppy. She doesn't even

know to be afraid. She's just a baby, Sam, and I need—I need—"

"Is there anything I can do?" Gramma asked, gripping her hands tightly together. "Can I help look for her? She'll come to me. Though, to be fair, sweetie, she'll come to anyone who looks cross-eyed at her."

Sam rubbed the knot between Mila's shoulder blades. She was aware of the action. She just couldn't find the strength to react to it. Everything inside her was numb with fear far greater than she'd felt in the creek that morning. Something happening to her, she could deal with that. Something happening to sweet Poppy…that might be more than she could bear.

"I just need to know you two are safe here," Sam said. "We have a lot of people searching. I'm going out to help. Officer Simpson—" He tilted Mila's face back to meet her gaze. "You remember him?"

She nodded.

"He's coming to stay with you, and Officer Bartlett is still downstairs. Don't leave the apartment, and don't open the door to anyone besides Officer Simpson, understand?"

When she couldn't respond, Gramma did. "We understand." She pulled Mila from Sam and held her tightly as he opened the door. "Call us if you can, Sam. Let us know…"

He gave them a grim nod before leaving.

They stood there in a hug a long time before Mila's back twinged, reminding her she was standing so rigidly. Her eyes were dry, her nose sniffly, her heart breaking. She patted Gramma awkwardly, then pulled away and went to one of the windows.

When Gramma had come to look at this apartment

before renting, both she and Mila had fallen in love with the tall, deep-set windows. Most of the broad sills held collections of colored glass that glimmered in the sun, but the center one was empty because that very first time, Mila had curled up on it to gaze out. She climbed on it now, her right side pressed against the window, her back and feet against the wood jambs, her head tilted against the glass so she could see the intersection of Main and First.

When Officer Simpson arrived, she didn't stir, not even when he assured her that Poppy would be found. Gramma said, "From your mouth to God's ear.

"Your police chief is a good man," Gramma said, "to put this much effort into finding Poppy."

"He is. But man, it makes you wonder what kind of person steals a woman's dog." Simpson shook his head, his dismay tinged with true bewilderment.

Mila knew what kind of person did things like that. She'd lived half her life hoping to survive them and the other half praying to forget them. Evil.

Someone evil had taken the sweetest, most innocent creature in her life. Dear God, how could she stand this?

They were three hours into the search when Sam got a phone call from the mayor. He parked in front of Jessica's building—since he needed to check in and have a face-to-face with his detectives, downtown was a good place—and lifted the phone to his ear. "Mayor."

"Sam. I heard a joke on the ninth tee just now—that you've got the entire police department mobilized to find a missing dog. Please tell me it is a joke. Tell me you're not spending our limited resources looking for somebody's pet."

Closing his eyes, Sam pinched the bridge of his nose. "It's not a joke. The man who attempted to drown the woman at Cedar Creek this morning broke into her house and, we believe, took her dog. I figure two murders so close together have done enough harm to the city's reputation. It would be nice to avoid a third one, and if finding the dog helps us find the killer, that can only be good."

"Or the person who let the dog go is nothing more than a careless burglar who has nothing to do with anything else."

"That's possible, but not likely. I'll make a deal with you, Mayor. You let me and my department do our jobs properly, or we'll make you the official spokesperson for the Cedar Creek Police Department. You announce our successes—" the mayor always wanted in on that "—as well as explain our failures." The mayor tried very hard to distance himself from his own failures, much less anyone else's. "I need a decision now, Mayor, because I've got a meeting to get to."

After a moment of throat clearing, no doubt done to stall while he envisioned himself announcing that they'd found the killer—or that they had another victim—the man heaved a sigh. "I'll defer to your judgment. For the time being, Sam. Don't drag this on too long."

Sam was rarely rude to the mayor, even though His Honor carried no real influence on the job. His was just one vote when it came to the chief's contract, and the other six members of the city council liked Sam just fine. But he hung up the instant the last word cleared the man's mouth.

"Putz," Little Bear said.

Beside him, Daniel nodded. "Major putz."

A moment passed as if to solidify their agreement, then Daniel began talking. "I've seen more of this city today than in the years I've been living here, and I've seen only two yellow dogs. They were both golden retrievers, and their owner offered to keep an eye out for Poppy."

"She also invited him to dinner at that new place on County Line," Ben teased.

Daniel gave him a dry look but didn't deny the date. "None of Mila's neighbors saw anything except the one on the northwest side of the intersection. She was getting her kids ready to go clothes shopping, and she saw Poppy get into a dark car with a man wearing a hat. The only reason she noticed is that the only car ever over there is Jessica's orange Bug, so this midsize dark sedan caught her eye.

"But she didn't see the driver well enough to give any other description or where they went, and she wasn't sure about the time. She was getting her six kids buckled in and settled down. She thought it was between eleven and twelve." He looked as if the thought of having six kids boggled his mind.

"It's fair to assume the guy still has the dog," Ben said. "If he'd just let her go, someone would have seen her. When even the mayor's found out, everyone else in town already knows. So what's his plan? To kill the dog, leave her someplace for Mila to find? To just scare the crap out of her? He's already accomplished that. To send the message that no one's safe from him?"

"And how does it tie in with the other two murders?" Daniel asked.

"I don't know if it does," Sam replied. "In the beginning, you didn't think the second murder had anything to do with the first."

"I know. But Carlyle gets killed, and Mila finds his body. Greeley gets killed, and Mila's there when the housekeeper finds his body. Her house is broken into, someone tries to drown her and someone takes her dog. She's been involved in five crime scenes in less than two weeks. Maybe she saw something at the first scene."

"Like what?" Sam asked.

"I don't know," Daniel answered irritably. "If I'd been there myself, we wouldn't be looking for answers. Maybe a note blowing away in the breeze. Maybe a person in the woods. Maybe something he left on the table, then retrieved when she went to get help. Maybe it was something she really didn't see but he suspected she did."

Sam considered it thoughtfully. When she was working, Mila's focus was pretty tight. It was possible she had arrived in Carlyle's backyard before the killer had time to escape. By her own admission, it had taken her a few moments to notice the dead body. Could she have looked at but not noticed someone going inside the house or making his way to the woods? It was a big backyard with a lot of places to hide behind shrubs and tall, fat flowers.

"We know Greeley was also killed just minutes before he was found," Ben said. "Maybe the killer doesn't know that Mrs. Ajmera found the body. We all heard the call came from the yard service and assumed it was Mila. He may have seen her there and made the same assumption. Depending on whether the guy's crazy or just mean, her showing up at the same place after the second murder could be some kind of omen to him."

Sam lowered the tailgate on his truck, though it would be hot, and braced his butt against it. "Okay, you guys interview Mila again…after we find Poppy. If we find…" He couldn't finish.

His nerves tingled down his spine, and he turned to look up. Mila was sitting on a window ledge in Jessica's apartment, forlorn and sad. She looked so vulnerable. He wondered if that was how Jessica had found her after her daughter's and son-in-law's deaths: a quiet, sad little girl so lost she might never be found again.

He raised one hand, and she did, too, pressing her good hand to the window glass. It hurt his heart.

Behind him a horn blasted once, twice. Irritated, he turned to see a Mustang convertible stopped at the intersection. The two girls inside were standing up, gesturing and shouting at a car across the street.

Sam's gaze never made it to the other car. Its dark color registered, its open passenger door, but the energetic ball of fur making a beeline for the intersection grabbed all of his attention. "Poppy!" He shoved away from the truck, running into the street without even thinking to make sure there was no traffic.

On hearing his voice, Poppy paused for a moment, then spun in his direction, her long legs and big feet eating up the distance. When a car on Main started to drive through the intersection, the driver of the Mustang blasted the horn again, and she and her friend wildly and loudly signaled the driver to stop.

Sam knew Ben and Daniel were behind him, knew they would both have their badges out to deal with the drivers. All he was focused on was the dog, loping along, tongue hanging out, as if she couldn't be happier to see him. He knelt, and she threw herself against him, licking his face and chin all over, then pressing her face to his throat and giving a quiet little whimper. "Oh, puppy, I'm so very glad you're okay," he whispered.

"Poppy?" That shout came from a block back. Sam grabbed Poppy's chain before she could dart off again and trotted to the sidewalk with her, then let her drag him down the street to Mila. She sank to the sidewalk, and the dog climbed into her lap, curling as tightly as she could and still give kisses, too.

Mila was crying, and Poppy was licking up every tear. She vibrated—tired, thirsty, hungry, hot, afraid she would never see Mila or Gramma again? Mila's good arm was wrapped tightly around the dog, and her splinted arm rested gently on Poppy's hip.

Sam slid down beside them, his arms around both of them. Poppy leaned over to lick him once more before sinking with a sigh into their embrace.

Ben came to stand in front of them. "The girls said a car turned west on First from Main, drove a half block, pulled over and the driver opened the passenger door. Poppy jumped out, and the driver took off. They were yelling at the guy that you can't just put a dog out of the car and leave. Now they're elated he did."

So was Sam. Like his heart might finally start beating regularly again. He glanced at the Mustang, parked around the corner now, its occupants still talking to Daniel. "What are they—"

"I think they're asking Daniel out."

Sam shook his head. "Women hit you up like that when you were a young detective?"

"Nope. By the way, I'm your age. When did we become old?"

Sam looked at the females he held. "I think for me it was when I got Daniel's call this morning."

Ben grinned as if the thought was vastly amusing. "We've got a description of the car and direction of travel out for the guy. We'll see if we can pull up video off anyone's surveillance cameras and make sure everything's good at the house."

"Thanks, Ben."

A moment or two passed, his heart rate finally settling, some of the tension that had knotted his muscles easing, before Mila finally raised her face from Poppy's fur. "Thank you." It sounded like the whisper was the very best she could manage after the day she'd had, but the tearful smile that accompanied it made the sweetest thank-you he'd ever had.

"We'd better get you and Poppy both inside," Sam said, but he didn't move right away. The sidewalk was hard and hot, and the stone facade behind them was the same, but with Mila smiling and Poppy sprawled across them, it was the most comfortable he'd been all day.

He forced himself into motion, though. Knowing that her attacker had just been less than a block away made him antsy about staying out here in plain sight. Even though Simpson waited outside the building door—she must have escaped him the minute she saw Poppy out the window—and he was sure Liam was still watching the back exit, Sam wanted her safely behind thick walls. Maybe with bulletproof and shatterproof windows. A tall row of iron bars every foot or so. A place impervious to fire, blast, flood or gas.

He got Mila and himself to their feet, and they both gripped Poppy's collar. A crinkle sounded, and he bent over to find a piece of plain paper tied to the collar with a string. Using the chain to manipulate the paper to the right angle for reading, he scowled at it.

"What does it say?" Simpson had joined them, pulling a latex glove from his back pocket, along with a small multitool.

"I'm glad you're better prepared than I am," Sam complimented him, drawing a grin. Then he added, "Go ahead and pull it off," and Simpson turned serious again.

He crouched, tried to avoid Poppy's spastic *A new person I haven't greeted!* lick, then clipped the string and removed the note, holding both carefully in his gloved hand. "'Next time I won't go so easy on you.'"

Just for this moment, Sam pretended he didn't see the stark change in Mila's eyes. Just for the moment, he wanted everything to be okay, his girls to be safe, the ugliness kept as far from her, from them, as it could be kept. Just for this moment, he wanted to revel in the fact that she had survived the attack at the creek and that Poppy was back home and looked none the worse for wear.

It was so damned unfair that moments passed so quickly.

As soon as they reached the fifth floor, Poppy tore down the hall, skidded sideways into the apartment and brought a delighted cry from Gramma. Mila smiled faintly. She was so sick inside she was surprised she could stand and walk and talk—well, she hadn't said anything since seeing the note. Sam acted as if he hadn't noticed the change, but she knew he had. She felt it in the stiffness radiating from him. Part of it was fatigue, too much worry in too short a time, but part of it was her.

She'd reached the door when Wynona's clicked open. The old lady looked her over thoroughly through the two-inch crack, humphed, then said, "You look all right. And the great-grandbaby looks all right. Good."

Mila was surprised. She hadn't heard Wynona say anything nice in all the time Gramma had been her neighbor. She couldn't even form a thank-you before the door started closing again.

Suddenly it stopped, and Wynona's eyes appeared again. "She might sing because she's happy, but it sure doesn't make the rest of us happy." With a nod, she slammed the door.

Mila looked at Sam, who showed a hint of wry humor. "One of the songs Jessica was singing this afternoon. Apparently, Wynona took particular offense to her rendition."

When they went inside the apartment, Gramma was in the kitchen, hands on her hips, watching Poppy suck in enough water for a camel. "I called Dr. Andrea, and she's coming by to take a look at the baby. We just want to be sure she's okay."

Mila nodded emphatically. While Poppy's behavior was perfectly normal now, what if the man had fed her something that would make her sick later? What if he'd poisoned her? What if he'd brought her back only to taunt them by making her die later?

No. The note said he wouldn't go so easy next time. That implied his intent this time had been to create fear, right? And he'd done that, and he'd let her go, and for the moment they were safe. They had to be safe.

Poppy filled her stomach, made a little room by

burping, took another drink, then climbed onto the sofa and stretched out. Mila bent over the back, rubbing her shoulder, her belly, the soft silky side of her face. "You need a nap, don't you?"

Poppy preened under her attention, offering her belly, her leg, her ear for scratching, the whole time slowly drifting off. Mila straightened when the snores started and found both Gramma and Sam looking at her. Sam had the police-chief look. She was very sure he wanted to ask her questions, lots of them, starting with *What does that note mean to you?*

Gramma had her protective mama face on. "You look like—" The words stopped so fast they caused verbal whiplash.

Mila wore the closest to a smile she could manage. "Gramma's favorite saying when someone looks crappy is, 'You look like death warmed over.' Hits a little too close today, huh?"

Gramma came across the room to hug her tightly once more. "I have a new favorite saying. 'You look like you been rode hard and put away wet.' Don't ask me where it comes from—I just heard it from Charles today—but it means the same thing. Come on, baby girl, let's get you settled in bed. The doctor said rest, and you haven't gotten one bit yet."

"I'd like to—"

They both turned to Sam, and he stumbled with a few uhs and ums. "Can your questions wait until tomorrow?" Gramma asked. "It's been a hard day."

His gaze fixed on Mila, then shifted to Gramma. Mila wasn't sure which one of them garnered the most sympathy. She probably did look the crappiest, but Gramma was looking pretty stressed-out, too.

"Of course they can," he said, everything about him gentling. "I'll be here if you need anything."

Gramma hustled Mila into the first guest room, the one with the queen-size bed. "I usually sleep in the other room," she reminded her, and Gramma grinned.

"Someone might join you tonight. Just to make sure you're okay while you snooze."

"Poppy's used to the twin bed," she said, but her grandmother's look was far too smug to mean the dog. Ah. Sam. That would certainly make her feel better… and maybe she should take the chance before he got to ask his questions. Before she had to tell him *something* about her past.

The prospect wearied her.

She didn't bother undressing; her shorts and T-shirt could double as pajamas. With help, she climbed into the bed, scooted into the middle so Gramma could stack pillows to support her arm, then swallowed a pain pill. She hesitated when Gramma offered a second tablet. "What's that?"

"A muscle relaxant. The doctor said your back, shoulders and midsection will likely be sore from wrestling underwater with that son of a bitch. Next time we swim, we're both taking knives, and don't you argue with me."

Mila swallowed the second pill. "I'm not arguing." She was exhausted, physically and emotionally. Lord, if she could go back to this morning and have this day never happen. She'd known she loved Poppy, of course, but she hadn't realized the depth and the pain of it until this afternoon.

Gramma closed the blinds, turned off the light, then crossed back to the bed to turn on the tiny beaded lamp on the night table. Giving in to fatigue or the medications, Mila smiled, then closed her eyes, shut off her brain and closed off her fears.

She had no idea how much time had passed when she next opened her eyes. The sky outside the window was dark but for streetlights, and her wrist was cold and achy. She tried to draw it under the covers, but something weighted it down. An ice pack, she realized. The splint rested on the night table, and an ice pack had been secured with a rolled towel so she couldn't wiggle it loose.

She made a sound, half frustration, half self-pity, and a shadow moved in the chair in the corner. Sam came into the dim light cast by the lamp, smiling at her. "You've been sleeping like the—"

She brushed her hair back from her face. "Like I've been rode hard and put away wet?"

"Aw, you're prettier than any horse I've ever seen." He checked the ice pack, for iciness, she supposed, then sat on the edge of the bed. "Dr. Andrea brought her mobile clinic over and said Poppy's fine. Did you know that dog's afraid of needles?"

"She needs ice cream to make sure all is right with her world again." Relief sagged through her, making everything from her eyes to her limbs feel heavy. "He didn't poison her?"

"There's no sign he did anything but take her for a ride."

"I hope she threw up in his car."

Sam's laugh was warm and reassuring. "I was hoping for worse myself."

She tried to change positions, but the throbbing starting in her fingertips and working its way to her shoulder made her decide she was okay where she was. After a broad yawn that she didn't even bother to cover, she murmured, "I know you wanted to talk, but I can't remember about what... My mind is kind of..."

He picked up her good hand and squeezed it gently. "Your mind is exactly the way it should be. Sleep is the best thing for you. Take advantage of it."

When he started to stand, she roused enough to hold onto his hand. "Will you stay...?"

"I'm thinking of having my jailer lock us both in a cell so I can always be there."

She wanted to say something nice but couldn't remember for the moment how to put the words together. Before she could tap that part of her brain for a reminder, sleep returned, easy and soothing. For the second time in her life, she had a protector, and she felt safe.

Sunday morning started hotter than hell—Hades, Sam corrected, in deference to the day—but by eight o'clock, the sky had turned dark. Sam stood at one of Jessica's windows, gazing out as the thunderheads started to build. There was a chance they'd break up and move on without delivering even a drop of rain— Mother Nature loved to tease them that way—but it was just as possible they would solidify and try to wash the whole town down the creek in a few minutes flat.

"Glad you're not in the farm business?" Mila came to stand beside him. She'd brought him a cup of coffee before returning for her own, iced in a tall glass, cream added until it was the color of caramel.

"I am. People need cops regardless of drought or flood." He nodded at her glass. "You don't drink hot coffee."

"The only drink that gets served hot in my world is cocoa, and only if there's snow on the ground."

"Coffee's meant to be hot. That's how it gives its kick."

"No, it gives its kick through its strength. Taste."

It was intimate, taking her glass, brushing her fingers, placing his mouth on the rim where she'd drunk. A swallow smashed that intimacy away. "Whoa. That's, what, twice as strong as regular coffee?"

"Three times. Or so. People who consider iced coffee froufrou have never tasted mine."

"No wonder you have the energy to do physical labor eight or ten hours a day outside in this weather." He'd been thinking about her work, and now seemed a good time to ask. "How many days did the doctor tell you to take off work?"

"Until the swelling goes down."

"Three, he said. Or four." Sam had been standing beside her when the doctor made his recommendation. "I'm pretty sure Happy Grass doesn't give paid sick time."

"Or even unpaid sick time."

"A one-handed crew member's not very effective. I don't want you going to work for a few days. Do you think Lawrence will agree to that?"

"I think he'd rather—" she drew a breath, but the next word came out shaky anyway "—fire me."

There were ways to get around someone like Lawrence if buddying up to him didn't work. Sam had seen a number of his business vehicles over the past few weeks, and it would take a blind cop to not find a short list of minor safety violations on every one of them. And there were noise ordinances in town that generally got ignored when it was a yard service company making the noise. But *generally* was no guarantee of *always*.

Then there was Lawrence and the workers themselves. It was common knowledge that at least some of his employees lacked the proper papers to even be in the country, much less hold a job. That detail almost always brought an investigation into how the employees were treated: whether they'd been underpaid, overworked or abused because of their legal status.

A guy as likable as Ed Lawrence, it would be real easy and legal to put him in the crosshairs of a federal investigation.

Sam didn't know what showed on his face—he suspected some pleasure at the thought of a well-delivered smack to a man who'd treated so many so badly—but Mila gave him a chastising look. "I can talk to Mr. Lawrence."

"You willing to let him ogle you and call you that li'l Mexican gal Maria?"

She grimaced. "I'll call him."

"What if he tells you to work or you're fired?"

That word, *fired*, brought a reaction from her again. "I can find another job." She didn't look excited by the possibility, or even convinced of it, but he didn't have any doubts.

"How…" This was one of the hard parts of conversations like this. "What is your financial situation like? Can you afford to miss a few days?"

Her gaze shifted past him to the street, and he became aware of the raindrops hitting the glass. "I've got some money saved."

Define *some*, he wanted to say. Enough to cover her living expenses for a month or a year? Enough to pay for her hospital visit and Poppy's safe-from-the-bad-guy checkup? He had *some* saved, too, quite a bit considering what he was paid, but if he lost his job tomorrow, he would get antsy pretty fast.

She laid her hand against the glass as if she could feel the drop in temperature the rain brought, the rise in humidity, the sticky start of the drops that would turn sweet and fresh soon. "I'll be okay. I have some savings, and Gramma would never let me starve." She said the last with a smile.

"You're lucky to have your gramma."

"More than you know."

Amid the wonderful smells coming from the kitchen, Jessica spoke for the first time. "What time did you tell your boys to be here, Sam? Everything's ready except the eggs, and I only do eggs to order."

He glanced at his watch. "They should be here—" A rap sounded at the door, and he headed that way. "I told you, Jessica, don't go to any trouble."

"I love cooking, so it's no trouble at all."

He opened the door to Ben Little Bear, Daniel Harper and Lois Gideon. The detectives both wore T-shirts and cargo shorts, the baggy pockets providing plenty of carrying space for pepper spray, handcuffs, extra magazines and anything else they didn't carry on their belts. Lois, the only one actually on the schedule for today, was in uniform. She wore her department-issue slicker, while the guys were splattered with rain.

Sam provided introductions, then gathered them around the table. Jessica had already laid out platters of hash browns, pancakes, bacon and sausage patties, biscuits, and toast. On the island were glasses, coffee mugs, creamer, milk and juice. "Jessica, this is too much," he protested.

"There's no such thing as too much. How do you want your eggs?"

"Over easy," Daniel answered, and Ben's "Sunny-side up" was right behind. Daniel caught Sam rolling his eyes and said, "Hey, my many talents do not extend to cooking. I'll take an over easy egg wherever I can get it."

"Yeah, Sam," Lois jumped in. "Your mom still cooks for you whenever you want. Most of us don't have that pleasure. Mine over easy, too, Jessica, please."

Sam wasn't sure he'd done the right thing, inviting the team for a meeting. Maybe it would have been better to talk to Mila alone, to press her about the note left on Poppy's collar and its meaning. But he wasn't the most unbiased soul in the room, and he also wasn't the detective in charge of the investigations. His role was on the periphery, and he liked it that way.

He waited until most of the food had disappeared as if a horde of hungry vultures had fallen on it. Jessica cleared the dishes, and Daniel refilled everyone's coffee, then expectant silence fell over the table. Mila, sitting between him and Jessica, looked acutely uncomfortable. She'd drawn into herself, her head ducked, her shoulders rounded. He was half-surprised she didn't draw her feet onto the chair, hug her knees and try to squeeze into an even smaller space, the very picture of forlorn.

Sam nodded to Ben, who cleared his throat. "We went by the house yesterday, secured the window temporarily, made sure everything was locked up. Daniel stopped by this morning to get some clothes—" Sam had forgotten all about those "—so if nothing matches, it's his fault."

Daniel frowned. "I dress myself every day. I can tell what matches. Besides, I was the only one not afraid of the underwear drawer."

Sam watched Mila's lips press together, as if her mouth wanted to smile even if her head thought it shouldn't.

"Okay," Ben went on. "Let's start with the note on the dog's collar. The paper was standard notepaper, and the ink was common. There were no prints on the paper—no prints anywhere at the house, either—but we know he likes gloves. The paper came from a larger sheet; it had been folded and creased, then torn, and it was tied to the collar with a length of cotton twine you can buy everywhere in town. The message was 'Next time I won't go so easy on you.'"

Beside Sam, Mila tensed, nothing overt, just a quick tightening of her jaw, her shoulders. Daniel, seated across from her, said, "Obviously, that means something to you. Who's told you that before?"

"I—I—" She sounded like she was starved for air but couldn't even make the effort to breathe in. Her gaze, still directed down, darted side to side before she gulped ungracefully. "It just—just scared me. If he'd hurt Poppy, if he came back and took her again, I—I wouldn't… I was…"

Jessica laid her hand on Mila's arm, and Mila's words stopped flowing instantly. After a long, tense moment, Jessica spoke with carefully controlled anger and scorn that sounded like tears were just a heartbeat away. "My son-in-law used to tell her that. He and my—my own daughter abused Mila. By the time I found out…"

Every part of Sam felt raw, like skin scraped roughly away, leaving an open mass of burning nerve endings. He'd suspected it, but suspecting it and hearing it confirmed… If there was any justice, people who hurt kids were punished ten times worse. He hoped to God her parents suffered for all eternity.

Everyone was watching Jessica now, with only brief glances at Mila. Sam could guess by the emptiness sliding across her features how much she hated having her secret known, how exposed she felt, how…please, God, not as if she'd deserved it. He couldn't bear it if she blamed herself for some sick bastard's violence.

His hand shaking, he reached across to take her uninjured hand. Her fingers remained limp for a moment, but then he felt the faintest clench.

"Could…" Daniel cleared his throat. "Could the man who attacked you yesterday—" He didn't seem to know whether to talk to Mila, who looked as if she'd gone away and left nothing but a shell behind, so he turned his attention to Jessica. "Could it have been her father?"

"Oh, dear God, no. My daughter and her husband died fifteen years ago. I'd been searching for them for years, and I finally found them outside Phoenix. I went there. I stole my grandbaby away from them, and they chased us." She abruptly dragged in a deep, unsteady breath. "They died in a horrific crash right before our eyes."

Now the tears came. Sam knew Ben and Daniel were as uncomfortable as he was, but not Lois. She left her chair, moved behind Jessica's seat and wrapped her arms around her, pressing her mouth near Jessica's ear, murmuring softly.

After a couple long minutes, Ben asked, "Were their bodies positively identified?"

Mila raised her head and her gaze, meeting Ben's. Sam wasn't sure he'd ever seen her make eye contact with anyone but Jessica and him. "There was nothing left to identify." Her voice was chilled, flat and emotionless. "They hit a concrete abutment at speeds estimated in excess of a hundred miles per hour. The car exploded. There was barely enough left of *it* to identify. They found parts of bodies. That was all."

Poppy trotted in from the hall, pushed in between her and Sam and laid her head on Mila's thigh. She squeezed his hand a moment longer, then let go and buried her fingers in the dog's fuzzy coat.

Sam had thought it a little sad before that she took such comfort from a dog. Now he was just damn glad she had the dog.

Chapter 9

It was more than twelve hours before we stopped running. Gramma checked in to a shabby motel, parking her car in the farthest corner, holding tightly to me as we sneaked into our room. She'd bought food at a drive-through, and we sat side by side on the bed and ate in silence.

We hadn't talked beyond "Are you hungry?" and "Do you need to go to the bathroom?" I was used to the quiet. It was the way I lived. Gramma was in shock. She had burst into tears at odd moments, given me queasy smiles, squeezed my hand tightly, but words were harder for her to come by.

When the food was gone, I was too tired to hold up my head, but I needed a shower. I needed to scrub the rain and the mud and the ugliness from my skin, and wished I could do the same

to my brain. I'd rather forget everything than remember those minutes in the barn.

When I came out of the bathroom wrapped
in a towel with my hair dripping down my back,
Gramma took hold of my shoulders, stared at
me with grief-stricken eyes and whispered, "Oh,
baby girl. We can't talk about this, okay? It didn't
happen. It's always been just you and me, living
together for as long as you can remember. No
Mama, no Daddy. Just you and me."

Then she wrapped her arms around me and
cried, great heaving sobs of sorrow and guilt and
anger and hate. She cried until only hiccups remained and then they disappeared, too.

Even at eleven, I understood her message. Life
was filled with secrets, and the fewer people who
knew your secrets, the safer you were. Telling secrets could get you in trouble, get you hurt.

Telling secrets could get you dead.

—Excerpt, *The Unlucky Ones* by Jane Gama

For years Mila had imagined what it would be like if
any part of her background came out. She'd thought
people would be horrified, and these four police officers were. She'd thought they would be disgusted by
what an awful child she'd been. They weren't, but the
biggest secrets of all were still secrets.

She was horrified. She'd known the question of the
message would come up this morning, and she'd figured she would explain it away the way she'd tried: that
it scared her. She hadn't discussed it with Gramma. In
her wildest nightmares—or were they dreams?—she

had never thought Gramma would be the one to answer truthfully. *Secrets*, she had so often reminded Mila.

But now, at least some of them were out there, and no one was looking at her with pity or disdain or blame. Sam and the other two men were frustrated and grim, like they wanted to hit something. They were protectors; they looked out for people who couldn't protect themselves. God, she wished she'd had a protector back then.

Her gaze went sideways to Sam. She had one now. Could that have been part of Gramma's reason for telling the truth? She thought Sam needed to know and didn't believe Mila would tell him? The quaver in Gramma's voice when she said *my own daughter...* Gramma had never gotten over the fact that the baby girl she'd birthed, the one she'd raised and loved and taught to be good, had turned out so evil. It had been as hard for her to talk about it as it had been for Mila. She must have thought this was the day for publicly breaking her own heart by telling them.

Fifteen years ago, not Mila's first or even her sixth appointment with Dr. Fleischer, when she'd finally become resigned to the fact that she was going to see him every week whether she said anything or not, she'd thought she would shock him by telling some of the scarier stuff first. He had been shocked, scribbling notes furiously, stopping occasionally to absorb some particularly ugly incident, turning paler and tenser with each moment. She was watching the clock, and when the session ended, she stopped abruptly and just looked at him, and he'd looked back. Stared back.

Finally he put aside the notebook, clasped his trembling hands and leaned toward her. She had shrunk back even though six feet separated their chairs. "My heart breaks for you, Mila. I don't even have the words to say…"

Everyone's heart broke, and no one had the words to say. *She* did. She'd filled a book with nearly a hundred thousand of them. Until recent events, that book had been the story of her life. The beginning, the middle, the end.

But her heart was beating. She had Gramma and Poppy. She was learning people skills. She was learning woman-man skills. She had more living to do before she got to the real end.

It was Detective Little Bear who started the conversation again. "Did your parents have any close friends who knew about or took part in what they did to you?"

She shook her head. "He was all she needed, and she was—" *almost* "—all he needed. We didn't socialize."

"What about parents of the kids at school?" Detective Harper asked.

"I didn't go to school."

"Church folks? Neighbors? Coworkers?"

She breathed slowly through her nose. She needed to be careful. Sam hadn't read *The Unlucky Ones*, and she doubted either detective had had time for it, either, but Officer Gideon—Lois—had read part of it. How much, and how much detail she remembered, Mila had no clue, but she couldn't give them enough information to spark her memory. "No one. They were each other's life. They didn't need anyone else."

Except when it was hunting time. They had tried it with her mother luring the victims, but it hadn't worked very well. She was always excitable, too bright-eyed and a little bit crazy with anticipation. The sort of women who appealed to her father looked at her mother with disdain and distrust. That was why he'd brought Mila into the game. If they had to keep her around, she ought to be good for something.

"She's right." Gramma spoke up, her eyes red but her tears gone. "Lindy and Joshua…they were disturbed. They had their own little world, and there wasn't room in it for anyone else. From the time they began dating, it was just the two of them. She gave up all her friends. I don't know if he ever had any. They fed off each other. It was all they wanted."

As Ben made notes, Mila wondered what, if any, information he would find on her mother and father. Lindy and Joshua weren't the names they had died using, weren't the names they were buried under. If they located a Lindy Ramirez, she wouldn't be related to Mila. And if that led them to search for Milagro Ramirez…

She ground her teeth against the shudders trying to ricochet through her.

Sam settled his gaze on Gramma. "You're convinced that no one who was part of their life could be behind what happened yesterday."

"Absolutely."

"And you, Mila?"

"There was no one. Truly." She decided to risk a play for sympathy. "If there had been, maybe Gramma would have found me a lot quicker. Maybe they would have stopped doing…the things they did."

It didn't feel good, but she did score sympathy in his intense blue gaze, along with regret and sadness and pain. It was in his touch when he patted her arm, and in the air of frustration that simmered the air around him.

"So the wording on the note was coincidence," Daniel said. "It's not like thousands of people haven't said it thousands of times. It wasn't a reminder. Just a warning."

"Which makes the theory that she saw something at the Carlyle house look better," said Ben.

Mila's breath caught in her chest. Was that it? No questions about names or places, no wanting details to confirm their deaths, no digging into her past? She was so relieved that it took her a moment to realize she should be saying something. She shrugged unconvincingly and shook her head. "But I didn't see anything."

"We think the killer believes you did," Sam said.

"Did you hear anything? Footsteps, a door closing, rustling?" That came from Daniel.

She closed her eyes, putting herself back on the scene. "I was thinking how good a quick dip in the pool would feel, and then I stopped to look at the view. I always do. On top of the hill like that, the valley, the town, Tulsa in the distance…"

Now Ben. Tag-team detectives. "Did you look around the yard? Did you notice the fence across the back?"

She opened her eyes again. "Just that it was there."

"The entire back of that house is glass. Did you see anyone inside? Shadows, a hint of movement?"

She shook her head. "The house doesn't interest me."

"Was there any sign that anyone else had been there? A glass on a table? A chair out of place? The smell of aftershave or perfume?"

Just the smells of flowers and blood.

"I don't remember anything. I was there to do the job. I only noticed Mr. Carlyle because he was out of place. But I didn't see anyone or anything else that was worth noticing."

They asked her the same questions about Mr. Greeley's house, and she gave the same answers. Lord, she really had to work on being more aware of her surroundings when working. Like writing, gardening was cathartic for her, but she couldn't relax so much that she could get that close to a murderer twice and be clueless.

"We have to assume the guy saw her," Sam said, his voice quieter, directed to the other officers. "When he saw her again at Greeley's house, he was startled, maybe thought she was there because of him." He rubbed his forehead. "I don't know. There are too many questions and not enough answers."

"It's always like that," Lois said, now perched on the end table nearest Gramma's seat and still holding her hand. "Half the people we deal with are crazy, and the other half are just plain mean. Their actions never make sense to the rest of the world."

Mila's father had been both crazy and mean. She'd spent entire days trying to figure out his games, to see if she did this, would he do that. Sometimes his actions were logical. Usually they came from the brutality that made up his core.

Just as she'd never been able to figure out her father's thought processes, Sam and his people had no clue why the bald man had killed Carlyle and Greeley, no clue why he'd come after her and turned on Poppy. They didn't even know for sure he *was* the killer. He would have to royally screw up for them to catch him. Crazy or mean was scary. Crazy *and* mean was terrifying, and it could also be sneaky and smart as the devil and very, very good at keeping itself hidden.

Until the last couple weeks, she'd believed she was very good at staying hidden, too. Now she knew better.

Emotionally shutting herself off from everyone else, no problem. Being the quiet person on the corner that no one knew, excellent. Slipping in and out of neighborhoods, yards, houses and parks without being seen… not in her skill set.

Luckily for her, surviving was. No matter what.

Liam Bartlett was on duty in the lobby once again when Sam left. Lois had stayed behind to help clean up, or so she said. Sam knew she didn't want Mila and Jessica to be alone just yet. Ben and Daniel would follow their paper-thin leads, while Sam had promised his mother he'd show up for dinner. *You've got to eat. Might as well do it here.*

The Douglases had been meeting at the family farm every Sunday after church for more than a hundred years. The yard looked like a used-car lot, the dining room like a summer camp with its maze of tables and chairs. Maybe not the most comfortable chairs, he admitted, but with his father, his uncles and his cousin Mike at his table, who cared about comfort?

There was relative silence while Aunt Hazel said the blessing, then controlled chaos as serving platters were passed around from diner to diner. "Buffet style," he'd told his grandmother back in the day, and she'd swatted him with a dish towel. "We're a family, Sammy. We eat family style."

"So tell us what's happening," Uncle Vance said.

"You know I can't. I came here to listen." The men in his family usually had a lot to say.

"Ol' Curt Greeley," Samuel, Sam's father, remarked. "He was a piece of work. His own mama used to say she should have sold him to the circus at birth."

Sam looked around the room for his cousin Zee, the only person in Cedar Creek who might mourn Greeley's passing, but there was no sign of him. Samuel caught his eye and shook his head faintly. So Zee was either drunk somewhere or high, and his parents didn't want to discuss it. Sam had to give Zee credit; at least he hadn't done anything arrestable in Cedar Creek since Sam got the chief's job.

"Any of you ever do business with Greeley?" his father asked around the table.

"I repaired some holes in the Sheetrock in his bedroom," Uncle Stan volunteered. "He watched over my shoulder and complained every step of the way. I put on too much mud, I sanded off too much mud, the paint looked funny if he stood in the corner on one leg and leaned over backward to see it with one eye closed." He paused for the chuckles he knew he would get. They'd all had too much experience with difficult people. "I told SuSu don't accept any more jobs from him. If I'd had to go through that again, I would've killed him."

One of Sam's aunts passing by stopped. "Y'all are terrible. Are you talking about that man who was murdered?"

"Yeah, the second one."

"Oh, Curt Greeley. Everyone would have killed him given the chance. It's really sad about that other guy, though."

And his aunt thought *they* needed chiding.

There were more stories about Greeley showing his greed, his need for control, his disdain for everyone. Firing people, stiffing them on money owed, acting out of spite. The gossip was right. Everybody hated Greeley.

As the conversation moved on, Sam leaned closer to his father. "You have anything to add?"

"I quit selling to him at the nursery. He'd order truckloads of plants, leave 'em sitting in the sun without water for a week before getting around to planting them, then want his money back, claiming I sold him weak stock. He was an idiot and a jerk."

"What do you know about Ed Lawrence?"

"The man gives fertilizer a bad name."

"You ever do business with him?"

"Nah. He's too cheap to pay my prices." His dad took his time chewing a piece of roasted chicken, his head tilted to one side to indicate he was thinking. "He underpays his employees and overcharges his clients. He cheats on his wife. That's why she started working in his office last year. He pretends to be a smarter, better, richer man than he is, and he doesn't know squat about growing anything, but he's good with showing a profit. I wouldn't believe him if he said it was raining until I felt the drops on my face and made sure it wasn't the Jolly Green Giant taking a pis—"

"Samuel." That came from Mom, coming to rest her hand on Sam's shoulder. "Not at the dinner table."

"Aw, Mom, how do we ever manage to carry on a conversation without you?" Sam asked, earning a light smack on the back of his head for the question. His grandmother had done that to her sons so many times that, as kids, Sam and his cousins thought she was the cause of the bald spots most of them sported by the time they were forty.

"You've been busy, I hear," she said. "Two murders, one attempted murder…but you found the dog. Yay."

"Sarcasm doesn't suit you."

"Maybe not. But setting the mayor straight suited me very well after Sunday school this morning. I guarantee you, he'll look twice to make sure no Douglases are around next time he opens his mouth."

Sam stood and kissed her forehead. "Thanks, Mom." He picked up his empty dishes, plus his father's and Mike's. "How's business?"

"Busier than usual for July," Samuel answered. "Kat's baby is due in a couple weeks, and she won't be coming back, and Trista is heading back to college the middle of August, and we're starting to get our fall products in."

"So you'll be hiring someone soon."

"We-ell," his father began, and LeeAnn scowled and spoke over his drawl.

"Yes, he's hiring someone. His part-time help is *not* going full-time. Why? Do you know anyone looking for a job?"

Sam thought of Mila, of how quickly his father would take to her, how intensely his mother would be interested in her. Was it fair to subject her to more than one intensely interested Douglas? "I don't know. I'll ask around." It was always good to have an option.

Holding the dishes in one hand, he hugged his mother, then his father and said his goodbyes. No one was surprised that he was leaving so soon. Of course, they'd all heard about the two murders, one attempted murder and the found dog. Some of them thought he'd already handled the important part: finding the dog. Fellow dog lovers would make fitting in easier for Mila, wouldn't it?

Whoa, Sam. You haven't even kissed her yet.

The reminder surprised him. The list of things they

hadn't done was long, but it *felt* like they'd done so much more than they had. It felt like he *knew* her. Not all the details, not the facts and statistics, but the person she was inside. It felt...

He couldn't even describe it. Like this was something he'd wanted without knowing he wanted it. Like there was some bond there before they'd even met, just biding its time until God or fate or whatever brought them together.

Damn, when had he damaged such a huge part of his brain? He liked her. He liked her a lot. He wanted to get closer to her. He thought they could have a future together. He wanted to protect her and keep her safe and make her smile and laugh and forget all the bad in her past.

But...

But they'd known each other such a short time. But she had trust issues. But she was damaged by her past. But he hadn't even kissed her.

But he still felt he knew her in all the ways that counted, and he still liked her a lot, and he still thought they could have a future, and he still wanted her, damn it. Everything about her, easy and tough, good and bad, the pretty beyond description and the ugly beyond pain.

It still felt *right*.

Mila was sitting on the windowsill in Gramma's living room when Sam came back. He let himself in—she hadn't realized Gramma had given him a key—and hung up his damp hat on the coatrack near the door. She tried to tamp down the warmth and comfort just the sight of him created. She'd spent so much of her life alone. She could handle a few more hours of solitude. "Still raining, huh?"

He grinned. "You have a talent for stating the obvious." He started toward her, stopping to give Poppy a rubdown where she half slept on the couch. "Where's your gramma?"

"She's visiting Mrs. Bushyhead on the third floor. Officer Gideon escorted her down there, and she'll call Officer Bartlett when she's ready to come back."

"Mrs. Bushyhead…why don't I know her?"

"Well, she's probably about 107, and she doesn't get out very often, but she has every sports channel known to man, so she's good with that."

"Oh, yeah, I remember. You have a gift for exaggeration, too. I have it on good authority she's not one day over 104." He smelled sweet as he came nearer, of rain and fresh air and home-cooked something or other. She imagined him at his family's weekly dinner, in a crowd so big he hardly stood out, loved by all, liked and respected by most. She didn't envy him. She was just glad he had it.

And she wondered if she could ever have it. She could envision a lot of things she'd never experienced before, but being a welcome member of a big family just wouldn't form. Not enough experience, not enough knowledge how those things worked.

Small steps, she reminded herself. She'd sat at a table just this morning with five other adults, eaten and talked. That had been a huge deal for her. There were a lot more firsts between that and meeting his family.

Assuming that he would stick around long enough to want them to meet her, and that she could overcome enough fear to want to meet them.

Little tiny baby steps.

He nudged her, and she dropped her feet from the sill, straightening to make room for him to sit beside her. "I love these old buildings—the tall ceilings, the deep windows, the woodwork, the floors. The mayor wanted all of them torn down and rebuilt so we could have more consistency in styles, methods and materials in our downtown area."

"He's a putz." Mila smiled when he narrowed his gaze at her. "He may have come up in conversation with Officer Gideon, and someone may have called him that, though it could have just as easily been Gramma. He tried to stop her from having her garden, and I believe she compared him to a cow—full of crap and shouldn't be holding office."

Sam's responding smile was tinged with smugness. It was always nice when someone you liked disliked the same people you did. "I thought she gave me the complete tour last night. I didn't see a garden."

"Would you like to?" Mila slid to the floor before he could say no. She'd been inside more than twenty-four hours, and it felt like an eternity. She hadn't even been allowed to take Poppy on her bathroom runs. She needed to breathe fresh air soon, or her skin might start mummifying.

He stood, too, and she headed for the door. Poppy raised her head and looked, then laid it down again. Maybe it was because of her own traumatic experience at Cedar Creek the day Gramma found her, but wet wasn't something she particularly enjoyed.

Mila took an umbrella from the coat stand, then had to stand back while Sam checked the hallway first. He locked up, and she directed him to the door at the south end of the floor, accessible with the house key. There a flight of stairs led upward, opening onto the roof, where he stopped suddenly, eyes wide.

"Mine is for show," she said, opening the umbrella and stepping out into the steady rain. "Gramma's is a cooking garden. She has about thirty varieties of herbs, a bunch of heirloom tomatoes and carrots, some garlic, cucumbers, bell peppers, lots of lettuce, and this year she's even growing corn."

There was also a small seating area, four chairs around a fire pit that doubled as a table. The chairs and cushions were drenched now, and there would be no way to keep a fire going in the pit even if they needed the heat, but on a cold winter night, it was a wonderful place to sit and be still.

"I had no idea this was up here." Sam took a few steps, then sniffed. "I smell lemon."

"That's lemon basil. Gramma planted it around the path so it releases its flavor when you step on it." She walked at his side, holding the umbrella high enough for him, too. "Quite a few of the buildings down here have rooftop gardens. You just have to be high enough to see them."

They took the short tour—the only kind possible with a garden of that size—and wound up by the fire pit. He gave her a sly, good-natured grin. "This being the tallest building besides the courthouse and having the camouflage of the plants, you could do all kinds of things up here and no one would ever know."

They were already standing close to stay dry, but when he said the words, he caught a handful of her T-shirt and snugged her even closer. Goose bumps raised all over her body, and her heart began pounding the way it had in the creek yesterday, though with a so very much more pleasant effect. She was torn between looking at him hungrily and suggesting he show her some of those things, and letting the familiar awkwardness take over and finding an excuse to go back inside. Instead, feeling a little shy, a little embarrassed and a whole lot unsure, she managed a smile and an uncomfortable admission. "I haven't done all kinds of things anywhere. By the time I had the chance to meet other kids, I...didn't know how."

Meeting his gaze was one of the hardest things she'd done, but she forced herself. The look he gave her was tender, affectionate, sad, lustful, promising. A lot of things she'd never seen directed to her. Never imagined directed to her.

"It's never too late to learn," he murmured, sliding his arms around her, pulling her so close their bodies touched, his transferring heat to hers, and tingles, and butterflies, and fear of the good *I don't know what's going on, but I like it* kind.

Though mere inches separated their mouths, a lifetime passed, maybe two or three, before he kissed her, and all of them were good and happy and sweet. His lips were soft and warm, his body muscular and heated, his arms wrapping her in privacy and safety. Then he slid his tongue inside her mouth, and she was pretty sure her brain imploded. So much sensation, surprise, need, desire, weakness, curiosity, elation, shock, anticipation, greed. Oh, yes, greed. She'd never felt this way before, and she wanted more. She wanted it to never stop, wanted it to consume her, to make her a part of him. She wanted...oh, God, she didn't know how to put it into words. She'd read about sex, of course. She'd read about incredible sex. But for a woman who had equated a man's touch with pain her entire life, she thought maybe she hadn't believed in it, or maybe it had been just one of those many things she wasn't entitled to in her life.

Her lungs grew tight, her body started to tremble and tears burned her eyes. It was humbling, such need, such want. Was she worthy of it? After all she'd done, all the heartache she'd helped create, did she deserve this?

Sam stroked his tongue over hers, slid his hands beneath her T-shirt in back, caressed her skin. Lifting his head slightly, he nipped her lip, pressed his forehead to hers and laughed, but there was a strained quality to it. "We're getting rained on."

She looked blankly at him, aware of the damp on her cheeks, of the tears, then felt the heavy drops plopping on her head. The umbrella dangled upside down in her right hand, totally useless in the moment, but she didn't care. "I—I—"

With the pad of his thumb, he dried a large drop from her cheek. "How long will Jessica stay at Mrs. Bushyhead's?"

He touched her, held her, kissed her and then expected a coherent answer? She stuttered the same sounds—"I—I…"—while trying to force her brain into some sort of recovery mode. "She—she said—"

His beautiful blue eyes opened wider, encouraging her, and she almost forgot again, but the words slipped out on a last breath. "Call her."

"She said to call her when you're ready for her to come home?"

Mila nodded. At the time, she'd thought maybe Gramma was suffering from enforced captivity, too, and not thinking clearly. Now she knew Gramma had been thinking perfectly clearly, thank you, and doing a whole lot of hoping. Which was probably the reason, she realized now, that she'd left for her visit downstairs right after Sam called to say he was on his way back.

"Then let's go back to the apartment." He grinned again. "You can do all kinds of things in the privacy of a bedroom and not have to worry about getting rained on. Okay?"

Not trusting herself to speak, she nodded, but her brain didn't give her body the command to start moving. Sam took the umbrella from her, shook out the water collected inside and snapped it shut, then laid his hand on her hip and nudged her toward the door. Faint scents of lemon wafted around them, pale and insubstantial compared to all the wonderful smells that were him, her, them. Heat spread from where his fingers touched her, and with it came something else, something more. Certainty. She wanted to do all kinds of things with him, no matter how it scared her, because he would be careful and tender and would never, ever hurt her. No matter that she had no experience to offer him, he would be satisfied with what she could give, and he would teach her the rest, and she would be a better person for it.

Oh, hell, yeah, this was definitely okay.

Poppy was still stretched out on the sofa, paying them no mind as they came in and hung up the umbrella. The air-conditioning raised gooseflesh on Sam's skin and changed his shirt from coolly damp to uncomfortably cold in seconds. He closed and locked the door and thought about scooping Mila into his arms and carrying her straight to the bedroom with no chance to change her mind. Too overeager?

Of course, he couldn't do that. Even if she had changed her mind, the wanting might kill him, but he would accept it. He knew what he wanted. This had to be her choice.

She stepped out of her sandals, glanced at him with that young, shy, innocent look and smiled a shy, innocent smile before she turned and walked away, across the room and into the hall. The sway of her hips mesmerized him, and her long, lean, muscular legs made the muscles in his own legs go unsteady.

He followed her, skirting around furniture, passing the dining table and walking into the hallway just in time to see her disappear into the first guest room. He paused in the doorway to watch her watch the rain out the window. One-handed, she released the clip that held her hair in a loose braid, combed her fingers through it, then gave her head a shake to send her hair tumbling free, and his breath hitched in his chest. She was so damn beautiful. So...

Words failed him. Instead, he moved into the room, closed the door behind him and threw the room into dim shadow. "Poppy—" His voice was rough and husky. He cleared his throat. "Poppy won't mind?"

She gave an expressive shrug that included a who-knows twist of her face. Right. She'd never been alone in her bedroom with a man for any period of time. How could she know how her dog would behave?

She'd never been with a man. Any man. And he was the one she'd chosen. Wow. Just...wow.

He walked slowly to her, circling the bed, stopping in front of her, reaching past to close the blinds for privacy. "You don't, um, carry condoms?" He meant it as a statement—why would she?—but his voice went up at the end anyway.

Lips pursed, she shook her head. "You don't, either." The idea pleased her. "Gramma said I'd find anything I need while I'm staying here in the nightstand drawer."

The night table was pine, old and battered from years of living, and the drawer stuck when he pulled the handle. It slid out crookedly, revealing a package of tissues, her pain pills, a bottle of ibuprofen and a box of prophylactics. "You need to blow your nose?"

"No."

"Got any pain?"

"No."

"Then I guess the only thing we can use here is…" He lifted out the box. "Which bothers you more—the fact that your grandmother might have an active sex life or that she might have bought these specifically for you?"

Mila pulled the box from his hand and slid the top open with one slender finger. "I hope she has an active sex life. She's given up so many other things for me." She tilted her head to one side. "Don't you hope your parents still have sex?"

He made a *ew* face. "I've tried very hard not to ever think about it. I mean, they're my *mom* and *dad*. I can't let those images in my brain, or I'll be forever scarred."

He was going for a light tone—though totally serious—but she answered quietly. "There are far worse things parents can do to their kids than have private sex together. Scars scab over, and some of them go away. Eventually."

He slid his arms around her, holding her as close as he could in a nonthreatening way, and gently rocked her side to side. "I'm sorry, Mila," he said, his voice muffled by her hair. "I don't know the right words to say, but I'm sorry for what they did, and I'm sorry for what you had to endure, and I wish I could just magically turn it into less than the faintest of memories. It hurts me that I can't, but I can promise you this—I'll do my damnedest to protect you from now on. To make sure no one hurts you. To put the past in the past and make the present and the future happy and safe and loved."

She returned his tight embrace for a moment, then eased back a bit as she looked up. "Happy and safe and wise to the ways of sex," she suggested. The trust in her face, softening her eyes, could have been his undoing, but no, that came an instant later when she cupped her hand to his face, touched her mouth to his and the tip of her tongue delicately sought his lip. He'd just been officially broken by this woman, heart and all.

Now all she had to do was put him back together.

Sex was good. A little painful. Far more personal than Mila had expected. Of course, intellectually she had known how it worked, but in reality, having Sam deep inside her was…breath stealing. Mind-blowing. Incredibly intimate and sweet and impossible.

He was bracing himself over her, most of his weight on his arms, but their bodies were still in contact everywhere. And she'd thought holding hands with him was such a big deal. This…this was incredible. Just to prove it, she tightened the muscles deep in her belly and watched the color drain from his face. His expression was stark and pleasured and complicated, and she felt all that times ten.

"Don't tease me," he ground out, and for good measure, he thrust his hips a few times against hers, touching her in ways that drained the color from her own face. She was pretty sure there was no blood flow above her neck at the moment. She had become a mass of aching, throbbing, needing. No thought required when he kissed her nipple and made her groan. No message from her brain when he withdrew, leaving her bereft, then filled her again, the sensation of all that was good cradling her, cradling them both.

Sweat beaded on his forehead, and the muscles in his arms quivered as he stared down at her. Staring back, she raised her hand to his cheek, and he turned his head to press a kiss into her palm. There was a feel to the moment, a sense of awe, a sense that after years of wondering, she was becoming a real person. Right here, right this moment, she wasn't her parents' daughter. Wasn't their victim. Their unwitting accomplice. The stupid girl who made them hit her. The odd girl people stared at, who lived with her grandmother but rarely came outside, who pretended to be invisible.

She was the lucky one. The normal one. The one Sam wanted. The one he'd chosen to make love to on a dreary Sunday afternoon, the one whose life he had irrevocably changed, the one he was overwhelming now with his touches, his kisses, his thrusts, his labored breathing, his muttered words. Every move he made, every place he touched, she ached, throbbed, her muscles so taut they hummed, until it became too much, or maybe just exactly enough, and pure pleasure burst through her.

Pure, incredible, twitchy pleasure.

It was a long time before she found her voice. Her body still trembled, her left wrist hurting with the shudders, and her lungs were grabbing whatever molecules they could, giving up on the futility of a full, deep breath. "I didn't know," she whispered.

Sam sank onto the bed, shifting so he didn't smother her with his weight. "Didn't know what?"

She pushed her fingers through his hair. "You can read everything you can find on a subject, use your imagination and think you know…but you can't really, truly know until you've experienced it, with all the little feelings, for yourself."

He gave her a smile in equal measures sweet and satisfied. He thought she was talking about sex, and she was, but other things, too. For a long time, she'd made no effort to follow Gramma's and Dr. Fleischer's advice and open herself to new experiences because she'd read about life. She'd thought she knew what it was, and she hadn't thought it worth taking the chances necessary to have it for herself.

Having someone other than Gramma in her life mattered. Having Sam in her life and her bed and her heart mattered. Even if this thing between them didn't last— she still had secrets, the worst ones of all—even if he broke her heart, she would be better for having taken this chance with him.

Oh, God, that sounded sappy and sentimental and just plain goofy, but it felt awesome. After all, she'd never been allowed to be sappy or sentimental or just plain goofy.

He mattered. And she mattered, too.

Chapter 10

Gramma knew better than to think that because we made it to the road, we were safe. My mother would fling herself to the ground in an all-out fit of temper, screaming out her frustration and breaking anything within reach. That was her way.

My father would take action—violent action. That was his way.

The storm was the worst I'd ever seen. Rain blew sideways, and tree branches flailed in the wind like feathers. Pops sounded on the flat surfaces of the car as hail pounded, and the lightning came so bright and so often that the image of one strike still burned on my eyes even after the next flashed. I didn't know how Gramma managed to see the road, fight the wind and watch the rear-view mirror.

I was huddled in my seat, hot and cold and wet, starting to shake inside, not daring to think or speak or even look around, when Gramma caught her breath. "Dear God, no."

I twisted around, my stomach cramping when I saw the headlights veering wildly behind us. It was my father. Ours was the last house on the road, the biggest reason he'd chosen it. I had never seen another car on the road in the months we lived there, and it was too much to believe it was someone else now. He was coming after us, and if he caught us...

Faster. I wasn't sure I'd said the word aloud, and I tried again. "Faster, Gramma. Please... faster..."

The car skidded, the tires fishtailing, but she didn't slow down. No, she drove as if Satan himself chased us. But he drove even faster, coming closer. I felt the danger, the threat. *If you try to run away, I'll kill you.* He always kept his promises. This time would be no different.

Ahead I caught a glimpse of a stop sign, but Gramma didn't slow. Swinging the steering wheel tight, she turned onto the highway, the rear tires fishtailing again. She narrowly missed a car going the other way. Its horn blared, but she just stomped harder on the gas pedal.

I wanted to believe that we were safe now we were on the highway, but the feeling wouldn't come. Didn't he call himself the luckiest man in the world? Hadn't he committed crime after crime, murdered woman after woman and never gotten caught? He was more motivated than

Gramma. He was crazier than her. He would catch us. If he couldn't stop us, he would force us off the road. He couldn't let her escape, and he wouldn't let me go.

We skidded, crossed the center line again, ran another stop sign. Gramma looked like a wild woman, still an avenging angel but a frightened one now. The only thing she knew to do was drive faster, no matter how dangerous it was, and she knew, just as I did, that probably wouldn't be enough.

It's all right, I wanted to say. *You came for me. You didn't forget me. You tried to save me.* That was enough for me. It was more than anyone else had ever done.

But I couldn't find my voice as we sped past a yellow sign signifying curves ahead.

"Seat belt, sweetie," she said, her voice frayed, and I grabbed the strap and buckled it over me.

The right tires went off the road on the first curve, and she overcorrected, sending us onto the opposite shoulder. She was saying something under her breath, not meant for me, a prayer. "I begged you to help me find her, Lord. Now that I have, dear God, don't take her away from me."

Tears burned my eyes. My parents had lied to me. Someone did love me. Someone did want me. It was the best gift I'd ever been given.

She did better on the next curve, but I saw his headlights behind us, closer than before. *Please, God.*

The road straightened, lightning showing a long stretch ahead. The wind was letting up, the rain now falling down instead of blowing to the side. Easier for her to drive. Easier for him to catch us.

We flew like a desperate bird with a predator on its trail, the road sounds changing as we sped through an underpass. A hundred feet ahead, there was a second tunnel that we whipped through so fast I didn't notice the momentary blocking of the rain. A blink, we were protected. Another blink, and we were back in the weakening storm.

I twisted again in my seat to watch as he entered the first underpass. He was driving so fast that I fancied I heard the engine over all the other sounds, revving, straining. He sped back into the open, and that was when it happened.

His car slid, the right tires leaving the road like ours had done, but he didn't seem to notice. The vehicle continued racing forward but at an angle now, in a line that would take it straight into the bridge abutment.

"Please, God," I whispered over the pounding of my heart. "Please."

Maybe he tried to steer away. Maybe he didn't care. Maybe God had hold of the wheel. I didn't know.

But one thing I did know as his car crashed into tons of concrete, as it exploded into a brilliant, breathtaking ball of flame, was that my terror had ended, and my life—my real life, the one I was meant to live—had just begun.

My father was dead.

Tears of joy ran down my face.

—Excerpt, *The Unlucky Ones* by Jane Gama

Sunday evening, Mila got a call from Ed Lawrence. As she wandered down the hall to talk, Sam watched her until he felt Jessica watching him. Their dinner plates were stacked in front of her, and she was pushing a few leftover peas around the top one with a fork. "He'll probably fire her. He's kind of heartless that way."

Sam figured she was right but didn't want to jinx anything by agreeing out loud. One of the good things about Jessica, though, was she didn't need a response to continue the conversation.

"Though, I have to admit, when you have a small business and an employee takes off unexpectedly, it's not always heartlessness. I can manage the store alone if I have to. It just means I'll be busier and customers may have to wait a little longer. But when you need a working body riding that mower or using that trimmer, it's harder to make do. Which doesn't make Lawrence any less a jerk if he fires her. Where's the loyalty? The appreciation? It's sure not in her paycheck or the benefits she doesn't get."

Sam shifted his attention fully to Jessica. "You always argue both sides of the story, or only when you're upset about something?"

Putting the fork down, she sighed wearily. "I'm not upset. Just…worried."

He had to admit, he was still flustered by the fact that she'd so obviously pushed him and Mila together. Giving them privacy, providing condoms… He was thirty-five years old, and his mother didn't want to hear that he had a sex life, much less do anything to facilitate it.

But since coming back from visiting her neighbor, Jessica had seemed as satisfied with how things had gone as he and Mila. *Almost*. No one who hadn't been in bed with them could possibly feel as satisfied as they did. But maybe reality was settling in with Jessica. Maybe she'd gone from oh-great-day-Mila's-not-a-virgin-anymore to oh-dear-Lord-Mila-might-get-her-heart-broken.

He reached across the table to hold her hand. "I would never hurt her, Jessica," he said, putting all his sincerity and trustworthiness into the promise.

For a moment, she stared at him, then jerked her hand away and swatted him. "I know that! Do you think I don't know that? Just how flawed do you think my judgment is? Just because I didn't know what was happening to her back then… It was a long time ago, and I've learned buckets about people since then. I know who to trust and who not to. I just never dreamed I couldn't trust my own—"

Pressing her fist to her mouth, she shoved her chair back, stood and escaped to the kitchen with the dishes.

Sam stared after her. Talking about what Mila's parents had done to her had been even harder for Jessica than he'd realized. Like Mila had said, he could read, talk and learn. He could imagine himself in a situation and think he knew what it was really like, but truth was, all he could do was imagine. Empathize. But he couldn't *know*.

Jessica *knew*. She'd been struggling deep inside all day with knowing and doing and escaping.

Listening to the pad of Poppy's feet as she wandered to the kitchen looking for a treat, Sam headed that way, too.

Jessica was slicing something in a square pan. She shoveled a huge piece of it onto a plate and pushed it into his hands. "Fruit cocktail cake," she said, her voice thick with unshed tears. "It's the reason God invented fruit cocktail. Whipped cream's in the refrigerator, vanilla ice cream in the freezer. You'll have to share with the baby if you have ice cream."

Ignoring Poppy's thumping tail at the mention of ice cream, he set the saucer aside, leaned against the counter and studied her. "You never talk about it, do you?"

She scooped out two smaller pieces, then covered the rest with foil. "I prefer to pretend it never happened."

"Does Mila talk about it?"

"Not with me. We should. And she's willing. It's me who's failed. But she's seen…talked to… There's someone…"

Mila came into the room, her bare feet making no sound. "She's trying to say I've seen a psychologist ever since I came to live with her without giving away too much of my right to patient privacy." She set her cell on the counter, then slid her arm around Jessica's waist and smiled at her, a sweet and amazingly serene smile given what she'd been through the past few weeks.

The past weeks? Hell, the first eleven years of her life. Sam didn't think he would ever forget the emptiness in her voice that morning when she'd said, "They found parts of bodies. That was all."

Her mother and father had died right in front of her, and she'd talked about body parts without a shred of sadness. Dear God, what had they done to make her care so little about their deaths? Did he want to know? Could he handle knowing?

If she needed to tell him, damn right he could handle it. If his knowing made it easier for her to bear, he would listen to every tiny detail. If he could take her burden and she could be free… His heart was strong. He was strong.

But maybe not as strong as she was. She'd been through hell, and she was gentle, kind, loving and compassionate. Awkward with people? Preferred solitude over a social life? When the people who were supposed to love you the most hurt you the worst, who wouldn't find peace with a garden and a dog and four walls?

Mila hugged Jessica before her small hand pushed Sam out of the way to open the freezer and get the ice cream. He was so lost, because even that brief touch made him want to pull her close and never let go.

"You didn't fail, Gramma. You saved my life. You gave me a home. You loved me. You found Dr. Fleischer for me. You gave me Poppy. *And* you make the best fruit cocktail cake in the world. You're my superhero."

"Wow." Sam joined her in trying to lighten the moment. "She sets high standards. If I want to be your hero, too, I'm gonna have to work hard, aren't I?" He hadn't saved her life or given her a home, though he had one he could offer. He hadn't found a psychologist for her or a puppy who needed her exactly as much as she'd needed to be needed, and he couldn't bake any kind of cake that didn't come out of a box.

But he loved her. That counted for something, didn't it?

Mila pried the lid off the carton, then paused, wielding a big scoop. "I do have standards. And you've exceeded all of them. Your tights, bodysuit and cape will be arriving in the near future."

He grinned. "Just no pink. I don't look good in pink."

"I've made a note of it."

He traded spots with her and dished ice cream onto

each of the three plates, then a final scoop in Poppy's dish. They moved into the living room, where Mila alternated taking a bite of her own dessert with spooning up ice cream for the dog. Poppy was surprisingly well behaved as long the scents of sugar and cream remained in the air. When Mila showed her that both dishes were empty, she immediately turned to Sam with an eager smile.

"What did the ogre say?" Jessica asked, reminding them of Ed Lawrence's call.

Mila pulled her feet onto the sofa, patting the cushions, and Poppy, who wasn't having much luck getting Sam's ice cream, jumped up and flopped out beside her. "He said I could have Monday and Tuesday off, that he would just make the guys in our crew work a couple extra hours both days. If I'm not back by Wednesday, I'm fired." She buried her hand in the dog's fuzzy fur. "I told him I quit."

Sam's eyes widened as something sweet and fragrant bloomed in his chest. "Really?"

Jessica's reaction was less subdued. After putting her dessert on the end table, she jumped up and danced circles around the chair. "Oh, I've been wanting you to look elsewhere for so long, but you're twenty-six. I can't make you do what I want. This is a wonderful day!"

Mila's gaze shifted to Sam, her expression a mix of relief, uncertainty and possibility. She raised her brows, as if asking if she'd made a mistake, and he gave her a thumbs-up. The uncertainty eased but didn't go away completely.

"You'll be able to take off long enough to let your wrist heal fully," Jessica said, "and then you'll find someone better to work for." She grinned broadly before grousing, "It would be hard to find someone worse."

Jessica danced her way into the kitchen to get drinks for them. While she was gone, Sam reached toward Mila, resting his hand lightly on her fingertips. "Just today my mother asked me if I knew anyone interested in a job at the nursery."

Her brows narrowed. "She just asked? You didn't suggest anything?"

"Nope. Two of their employees are leaving soon. One's having a baby, and one's going back to college. Apparently, Dad thought maybe Mom would step in and work full-time, but she made him understand that's not going to happen. So, if you're interested…"

She chewed on her lower lip. "You wouldn't say anything to them? You wouldn't say, 'I like her and she needs a job so please hire her'?"

"Not if you don't want me to. But they'll figure it out soon enough when I bring you to work every morning and pick you up every night."

"Why would you do that?"

"Because I'm not gonna be comfortable with you out of my sight as long as the killer is free. Even after we catch him, I'll still be so traumatized by what happened yesterday that I'll probably need to see you a dozen times a day to make sure you're safe."

The words brought her a small smile of nothing but pleasure. "And you think your parents would put up with that better than someone like Mr. Lawrence."

"Oh, hell, yeah. They love me. They'll love who I love."

The last three words hung in the air between them, making her eyes softer, the smile smaller and more intimate. She opened her mouth to say something, but Jessica's return with three glasses and a bottle of wine deterred her. Jessica poured and passed the glasses around, then lifted hers in salute.

"To life. Ain't it grand?"

When Sam got to the station Monday morning, Ben was waiting, a sheaf of papers clutched in his hand and a grim look on his face. He followed Sam into his office and sat down while Sam set his hat aside and quickly scanned the messages he'd picked up on his way in: the usual minor complaints, scheduling and other petty stuff. So much of his life was spent dealing with the petty.

Or the life-and-death important.

He'd been feeling pretty damn good before he got here, considering the circumstances—funny how waking up next to a beautiful woman could brighten a man's outlook before he even got out of bed—but disquiet simmered around his detective. Knowing how unflappable Ben was, Sam's own good mood dissipated like water down a drain.

"Is this something Daniel needs to hear?"

Ben nodded. "He'll be here in a minute."

It probably *was* only sixty seconds before Daniel came through the door, but it seemed an eternity. Before he got settled in the only other chair, Ben started.

"I called the Phoenix Police Department to ask about the car wreck that killed Mila's parents. There was a bad wreck near there fifteen years ago. Car hit a bridge at a high speed, exploded, huge fireball, killed two people. They sent me the report."

That was on top of his stack of papers. Sam knew

they were organized, from the first one he needed to the last, because that was the way Ben did things.

"The victims were identified as David Brumley and Teresa Mackay. Brumley by logic, mostly—the car was registered to him, and he had a driver's license in that name. With Mackay, they used dental records. A third person was thrown from the car, a woman who called herself Mary Jackson. She was badly injured—almost didn't make it. It was two months before she could talk with the police. She said she didn't know Brumley and Mackay, that she was hitchhiking and they gave her a ride."

Ben laid a printout of Brumley's driver's license on the desk between them. He was an average-looking guy: slight, five nine, 150 pounds. Brown hair, blue eyes, big smile, but there was something off about him. Even without the information Sam had, something about Brumley—aka Joshua—would have roused his suspicions.

"Okay, so David Brumley didn't exist before he came to Arizona to live. His driver's license was a good-quality fake. Social Security number was, too. He rented a house out in the country, him and his wife, and had been there about three months. Landlord ID'd him from the driver's license but had only ever seen him the time he showed them the house. They paid the rent on time in cash, never asked for anything."

Ben handed over another driver's license photo, a pretty blonde. Just on sight, Sam would plug her as married, kids, soccer mom, cheer mom, as busy in the kids' activities as her own.

"Teresa Mackay was a dental hygienist in Phoenix. She went shopping for her niece's birthday present the day before the crash and never came home. Surveillance footage from the mall showed her leaving with David Brumley."

A series of grainy photos showed the two coming out of a service entrance at the mall and getting into a white midsize sedan. David pushed Teresa into the back seat, then slid in beside her, and the driver, unseen on the footage, drove away. One thing Sam did see in the final picture: a small, slim figure in the front passenger seat. She huddled against the door, head bent so her black hair covered her face, and her shoulders were rounded as if she didn't have far to go to disappear into a ball of arms and legs.

Nausea rose in his gut as he raised his gaze from the photos to the detectives. "Mila's father and mother went to the mall to kidnap this woman, and they took her with them?"

Ben's nod was sour. "Makes sense that they were just body parts to her, doesn't it?"

More than he wanted. "So Teresa Mackay was real. David Brumley was a phony. I'm guessing Mary Jackson is also a phony."

Another nod from Ben. "She claimed when she realized they were going to crash, she jumped out of the car and lost everything she owned, including her ID. Hitting the ground at that speed, she broke half the bones in her body. The doctors were amazed she survived."

Sam tilted his head back to study the ceiling. He was ignoring the single most important part of what Ben had discovered. He needed a moment to make sense of the lesser stuff first.

Like the fact that Mila's father had kidnapped a woman, and his wife had helped him, and they'd taken their eleven-year-old daughter along for the ride. What had been the point of that? Had he planned to rape Teresa Mackay? Had he intended to kill her? Was his mistreatment of Mila just a warm-up for his real pleasure in life—kidnapping, abusing and killing a strange woman for the fun of it?

A strange woman? Or women?

For an instant, Sam thought he might lean over and puke into the trash can. Whatever Joshua/David's intentions had been toward Teresa Mackay, he'd caused her death, and he'd done at least part of it in front of his little girl.

Jessica's words whispered menacingly in his head: *They were disturbed...their own little world...fed off each other.*

"So the person who tried to kill Mila Saturday is most likely her mother," he said, unable to leave it unsaid any longer.

Ben nodded, but Daniel frowned. "Mila said it was a man. And don't you think she would have recognized her own mother?"

Ben pulled out two more photos, a copy of a driver's license identified as Traci Brumley and a photo of a woman in a hospital bed. The one was a bright-eyed, attractive black-haired woman, easy to believe as anyone's mother. The other...

She hadn't just jumped out of a speeding car. She'd landed close enough to the vehicle to suffer the agony of the flames, her body too broken to scoot, crawl or claw away from them. The doctors were amazed she'd survived. In this photo, she looked as if she hadn't.

God help her. Even knowing what he did, Sam

couldn't squelch his sympathetic wince as he passed it on to Daniel.

"Damn." After studying it a moment, Daniel thumbed through his own file folder for a picture. "This was taken off a surveillance camera at the feed store two blocks down from where the driver put Poppy out of the car. Seems the owner's got a problem with kids tipping over that giant cow out front, so he put in a camera. The license tag was stolen in Arizona, the car in Texas, and the driver…"

Very easily could be Mary Jackson, aka Traci Brumley, aka Lindy whatever the hell her name was. Sam was pretty sure right now neither Jessica nor Mila had come by their names by marriage or birth. Upon escaping her parents, they'd probably thought changing their own names was necessary for their survival.

"So Mila's mother survived this horrific crash. After a long recuperation, she tracked down her mother and her daughter. She killed Mila's two clients to send her a message, then went after her personally. Does that sound reasonable to you guys?"

"The day murder starts to sound reasonable to me is the day I change jobs," Daniel said, leaning to the side to remove his buzzing cell from his pocket. He stared at the screen, alarm darkening his face. "Damn, Chief, make it three clients. Ruben Carrasco just called in. He found another dead customer, this time out in the county. The sheriff wanted you to know."

Well, hell. Sam had joked about putting Mila in jail to keep her safe, but it was looking more appealing by the moment. "Go. Tell Jan I appreciate her letting you look over their shoulders." Jan Latimer was a good sheriff, and part of that was her willingness to accept help. She would be open to input from Daniel.

Daniel had barely made it out the door before Lois came in. Her graying hair wasn't yet smashed under her ball cap, but it was standing on end as if she'd been pulling at it, a dead giveaway that she was upset. She neither knocked nor waited for an invitation, circling to Sam's side of the desk and dropping an open book in front of him.

"I knew that note bothered me, but I couldn't figure out why until this morning. This is the book I was telling you about, the one that creeped me out so much I had to quit reading. Listen to this." She cleared her throat, but it was still shaky, still heavy with emotion. After a few words, she pushed the book to Sam and stabbed at the place where she wanted him to start.

He read aloud, haltingly, sickened, the muscles in his body winding tighter with fury. "'I knew the result would be the same… The next thing I knew, I was on the floor, certain that this time he'd broken my jaw, my cheekbone, a tooth or two. "It's always your damned fault. But you'd better learn good because…"'"

He stopped for a long, heavy moment before finishing. "'Next time I won't go so easy on you.'"

Lois's gaze locked with his. "The girl in that book, Sam, that's Mila." She flipped the book shut and read from the cover, "The girl who survived the 'harrowing ordeal of being raised by serial killers' is Mila."

Ben made the protest Sam wanted to but couldn't. "It's slim evidence."

"That girl is twenty-six now. So is Mila. Her parents were killed in a fiery crash in Arizona fifteen years ago. So were Mila's. That girl's gramma—*gramma*, Sam—

searched for her for years, just like Mila's gramma. Gramma in the book had red hair—so did Jessica. The girl calls her her superhero. Mila says the same about Jessica. Gramma in the book calls her daughter Lin. Jessica's daughter's name was Lindy."

"Maybe Mila knew…" Ben broke off halfway through. Ben and Sam—hell, everyone in the department—had trusted Lois's instincts way too many times to count. And this time it felt…

God help him, it broke his heart to even think it, but it *felt* right.

Mila was sitting on Gramma's couch, an old quilt spread over her, an ice pack on her wrist as she breathed deeply the savory aroma of chicken broth simmering in the kitchen. Jessica was a big believer in the caring and healing properties of food, and homemade chicken and noodles was at the top of her list. A hen filled the big pot, carrots and onions and celery bubbling along with it. Later she would pull out her rolling pin and the flour and make her own noodles. If they didn't feel better after the meal, it wouldn't be for lack of trying.

When the knock sounded at the door, Jessica waved her aside and went to check the peephole. Wearing a smile as bright as her orange capri set, she opened the door to welcome Sam, Ben and Lois inside. Mila's smile that came automatically at the sight of Sam faded when she saw the rigid set of his face. It curled and dissolved into ash when she recognized the book he carried. *The Unlucky Ones.*

Oh, God, they knew. She wanted to throw back the quilt, rush into the bedroom and hide in the darkest corner of the closet, or maybe she could make it past them out the door and up to the rooftop garden. There was a rickety old fire escape still clinging to the back side of the building. It would surely hold her weight long enough to reach the ground, and she could run like hell.

But there was nowhere to run. Her whole life was right here in this apartment: Gramma, Sam and Poppy. She couldn't leave them no matter how desperately the need clawed at her.

Jessica had seen the book, too, and her face went blank. She stood awkwardly, as if everything in her world had suddenly tilted askew and she didn't know how to right it. She gestured toward the sofa and chairs but couldn't come up with the words to invite their guests to sit.

Ben and Lois sat down, and Gramma joined Mila on the couch, but Sam remained standing. Though he didn't move a muscle from his spot between his two officers' chairs, there was an air of tension about him, as if he were moving so hard and so fast that not even a blur betrayed him.

He looked as if he might break if he eased his control one whit. She knew the feeling, and she was so very sorry for bringing it into his life.

After a moment, he stepped forward and set the book on the coffee table. She imagined, if she lifted the dust jacket, she would find the impressions of his fingertips on the cover from being squeezed so tightly. "Is that—" His voice was hard, as tightly controlled as his emotions. She almost didn't recognize it.

Gramma scooted closer to Mila, grasping her right hand tightly. With a whine, Poppy got up from her spot across the room and came to sit in front of them.

"Yes." The air rushed out of her lungs on a sigh.

She'd never thought she would admit that, not ever, and it felt…freeing. As if muscles she hadn't been aware of had released their tension, as if worry centers in her brain had taken a great sigh of relief. Her biggest, ugliest secret was out, and she hadn't dropped dead. She hadn't freaked out, she wasn't trying to escape, her heart wasn't exploding.

It might break later, but right now it was beating steady and strong.

"Jane Gama? Is that—"

"*Gama* is Spanish for a type of deer. A doe. Jane Doe."

He nodded once. She was surprised he could do that much without shattering. His emotion was that intense. She couldn't tell if it was good or bad or a combination of both. If he pitied her, was repulsed by her, feared she might be as crazy and evil as her parents, if he was horrified he'd kissed her, made love to her and even wanted to introduce her to his family.

She couldn't tell if he blamed her. Surely his police training would temper that, but in a case like hers, didn't it always creep into the shadowy edges of people's thoughts: *What was so horribly wrong with her that* made *her parents do what they did?*

He opened his mouth, couldn't find words and closed it again. Pivoting on his heel, he went to stand in front of her favorite window, staring out, his hands clenched tightly. And then he said the last words she'd ever expected to hear. "Your mother's not dead."

Lois gasped. So did Gramma, but hers turned into a sorrowful prayer. "Oh, dear God, no."

Mila stared at Sam's back, willing him to look at her. "That can't be," she whispered. "We saw them recover two bodies. The newspaper the next day said they both died on impact."

After a long moment, Ben looked Sam's way, then took over. "Your… Joshua did die. But the dead woman was the one he'd kidnapped. Lindy jumped out of the car at the last instant and was very badly injured. It was years before she could leave the hospital."

Tears slid from Gramma's face as she keened, low and mournful. Mila tugged her hand free and wrapped her arm around her. They had thanked God for fifteen years that Lindy was dead, and all that time she'd been out there, recovering, regaining her strength so she could punish them.

"She's the one who tried to kill me," Mila said flatly. It was a shock that her mother was alive, but not this part of it. Lindy had always hated her, always wanted her destroyed. She must blame Mila for Joshua's death, for her own injuries. Blaming others was what Lindy did.

Lois came to sit on the other side of Jessica, hugging her, too. Did any of the officers understand that it wasn't just the shock of finding out that Lindy had survived, but also of learning after years of freedom that she and Gramma had failed in their grand escape? They'd just had a fifteen-year-break from the terror that was her mother.

As if reading her mind, Sam finally turned, finally locked gazes with her. She couldn't read anything in his but that taut control. His words, though the tone was harsh and stiff, were encouraging. "You're not a child anymore, Mila, and you're not alone."

She would have felt less alone if he'd embraced her

or touched her shoulder or held her hand. But first he'd have to unknot those fists that whitened his fingers.

Papers rustled as Ben opened a folder. He leaned forward to show her a photograph. "Is that your father?"

It was hard to look at the demon from her past, but she forced herself, a little voice in her head chanting, *He's dead dead dead.* And *you're not alone.* "Yes."

Another photo. "Is that your mother?"

This time it was hard not to look. The woman who had brought her into the world. The woman who had fully intended to take her out of it. The woman who wasn't *dead dead dead.* Pressing her hand to her mouth, she nodded.

One more picture. "This is what she looked like three months after the accident."

Scars, lone wisps of hair, a face that didn't fit together right, bandages, raw places that hadn't yet healed... In an impersonal only-human way, it saddened Mila that the woman in the photo, who'd once been pretty, friendly, high energy—manic, Dr. Fleischer said—now elicited only shock, fear, pity or morbid curiosity.

One last picture. "That's just before she let Poppy out of the car Saturday."

"Oh." Mila's gasp was more vehement than she'd intended, and it made both Sam and Ben look at her expectantly. "I—I, uh, saw this woman. Just down the street. A week ago. The night we—" Sam hadn't tried to hide anything from his officers, but she wasn't sure if he wanted that to change. "The night Poppy and I ran into you and we went to Braum's."

She recounted the meeting for them, shuddering to remember how empty the street had been. The

woman—her mother—had even commented on it. She
also recalled how unnatural her hair had looked. A wig
to hide the fact that much of it had never grown back?
Even then, Mila had been torn whether the stranger
was a man or a woman. Fast-forward to Saturday at the
creek, no wig, convincing her the attacker was a man.

Her mother. She had been that close to her mother.
How could she not have sensed something?

Because Lindy had always hated her, and she had
always feared Lindy. And because last week she'd still
believed Lindy was dead.

Sam dragged his hand through his hair, then pinched
the bridge of his nose. "You two don't leave this apartment for any reason. Lois, you're staying here. If Poppy
needs to go out, you have the officer downstairs take
her. Okay?" He took a few steps, then turned back, his
gaze connecting with Mila's again. "You should know…
Ruben and the crew discovered another body this morning. Mrs. Baker, out off Pickett Prairie Road. Lindy's
going to be angry that you weren't there to see it."

Sadness welled inside Mila for Mrs. Baker, who baby-
sat her great-grandkids every weekend and relied on
Mila every Monday to undo the damage they'd done
to her garden. And emotion welled for herself, too, and
Gramma, Sam, Lois and everyone else.

Mila had survived this awful nightmare once, but
her relationship with Sam might not. Lindy was out for
vengeance, and if Sam was right, Mila's absence this
morning would have infuriated her. Normal Lindy was
a formidable force. Furious Lindy was a tragedy waiting to happen.

Mila prayed that this time she was her own victim.

* * *

Monday was officially a horrible day that should never be remembered again. Jessica had tried to make things as normal as possible, but tears kept coming, and Lois kept wiping them away. They were close in age and seemed as if they'd known each other forever instead of a few days. Watching them made Mila, for quite possibly the first time ever, fully yearn for a best girlfriend, not an idealized, read-about-it version, but the sort of deep connection she watched with Gramma and Lois.

Mila was missing a lot of things this evening. Sam was chief among them, but there was more. Her fledgling sense of normalcy had flown right out the window and wasn't coming back. The guilt she'd largely managed to avoid for the Carlyle, Greeley and Baker families' losses. The pride that she and Gramma had salvaged wonderful lives out of the destruction of their own.

The confidence that her mother could never hurt her again. Just the fact that Lindy had survived took some of the shine and accomplishment out of their lives. The idea that she would kill people she'd never even met just to get at Mila…

What *was* so horribly wrong with her that her parents had become monsters? They'd been okay before her birth, and killers after. Was she somehow responsible for that?

It was nearly nine o'clock when Ben Little Bear arrived, a duffel slung over his shoulder. Lois had left when her shift ended, replaced by another officer. Mila had hoped Sam would at least come for dinner. She'd hoped he would call and say, "It's okay," even if it might not be true. Even if he'd just come by, squeezed her fingers and given her the sorriest excuse for a smile he could summon, she would have felt stronger.

But he hadn't.

Jessica reheated the chicken and noodles for Ben, served him a huge slice of fruit cocktail cake, and offered him the third bedroom. He opted for pillows and blankets on the sofa instead.

Mila dithered for a moment, knowing the polite thing to do was go to her room and leave him to rest in peace. She just needed to know…

Finally, standing on one foot in the hallway, her other foot poised to head to her room, she glanced back. "Is… is Sam…"

Something crossed Ben's face. She didn't know him well enough, didn't know people well enough, to make a guess at it, but it made her want to run to the guest room and hide in the shadows.

"It's been a long day," Ben said cautiously, but then he seemed to be a man who always spoke cautiously. "He's known the Baker family a long time, and he's still got all the chief things to do, and now we're coordinating with the sheriff's department, too, and… He was still at his desk when I left."

She swallowed hard. "Is he…reading that book?" She couldn't say *my book*, not yet. It was odd, how writing it could have lifted such a burden from her, but having someone she loved read it created an unbearable burden of its own.

Ben's nod was quick, making her heart sink.

"Well…good night."

She was six feet down the hall when he spoke. "It'll be all right."

She smiled tightly but didn't speak until she was

inside her room, the door closed at her back. "I wish I could believe you," she whispered.

Sam closed the book and set it on his desk, but he was half-afraid to shut his eyes, even though exhaustion dragged at him. He would have found the story unsettling under the best of circumstances, but this...

How did someone do those things to another human being? To a *child*? How did they lose the capacity to recognize right from wrong? Mila's parents had had so many chances along the way, but at every turn they chose the bad thing, the mean thing, the unforgivable thing. Even now, after the miracle recovery she'd been through, Lindy's only apparent goal was to punish her daughter for Joshua's death. She was a sick individual who shouldn't be walking around free.

But they had to find her before they could lock her up.

The numbers on the wall clock showed it was only midnight, but his body felt as if he'd been battered in combat for thirty hours straight. He needed to go home. To get some sleep. Or run ten or twenty miles to exhaust his anger. He needed to scrub away every image conjured by the book—every insult, every hurt, every slap, every moment of terror those monsters had put Mila through.

He needed to see her, touch her, tell her how incredibly proud he was of her, of her strength and resilience and courage. To apologize for the shock and impotence that had kept him at a distance today, until his brain had processed some of the outrage, heartache, the helplessness.

He left his office, calling goodbye, and walked out

into the hot, still night. His truck sat under a streetlamp in its usual spot, but he walked past it. He continued west until he came to the intersection where a right turn would take him to Mila, a left would take him home. He could see her bedroom from there, looking mostly dark until his eyes adjusted and caught the faint glow of the night-light. It was a wonder she could bear the dark at all.

His heart hurting, he turned left. If she'd managed to find sleep tonight, he wouldn't disturb it. He would send her a text to await her in the morning.

It was funny that he was only a block off Main Street but his neighborhood was as quiet as if it sat on the fringes of town. Lights burned at every house—porch lamps mostly, or a living room light softened by blinds. His house was dark inside, but a single green light shone next to the door. Green-light a vet. While he was out of the army, he still offered support where he could.

He pulled the keys from his pocket as he climbed the steps and was half an inch from inserting the house key in the lock when the glider at the far end of the porch creaked and a figure stood. For half an instant, he hoped it was Mila, needing to see him as much as he needed her, but the feel of his muscles going rigid, his hand automatically going to his gun, told him it wasn't.

"Hello, Chief."

Sam had never heard the harsh, raspy voice before, but his gut identified it. His first thought was *Thank God she's here and not after Mila*. Then he turned to face the stout figure. In the glow of the light, it was hard to determine gender. So much damage to the body, the voice, the mind…though the mind had been damaged beyond repair long before the rest of her.

What wasn't hard to determine was the nature of her weapon tonight. The nine-millimeter Ruger looked small and her grip was awkward, but the red dot of the Crimson Trace laser sight sat true right above his heart.

He lifted his hand away from his pistol. There was no way she would miss with the laser at this distance, no way he could draw and get off his own shot before she killed him. "Your mother, your daughter and I were all very sorry to find out you were still alive. We liked the world much better without you in it."

She barked a laugh. "You're one twitch away from certain death, and yet you still make insults. I'd want to kill you even if you weren't her boyfriend."

The odds of an officer passing on routine patrol, or a neighbor going out or coming home, were slim. Sam would give a lot for any kind of distraction that would give him a chance with her. He would settle for keeping her talking. "We know your real name, and Joshua's. What was her real name? She doesn't remember."

Lindy made a gesture that might have been a shrug, or the closest she could get to it now. "Who the hell cares? She's had a hundred names. My mother can tell you. She always did love the stupid brat more than me." The next gesture was a farce of a smile. "But not Joshua. He loved *me*, and I loved him. We were one."

"Yeah. You were so devoted to him that when you knew he was going to die, you jumped out of the car and saved your own life."

"That's not true! It wasn't like that at all!" Tremors rocketed through her, making the red dot on his chest dance.

If he made her angry enough, maybe he would get the opportunity to charge her and get the gun from her.

Or maybe she would shoot him at point-blank range. The Ruger might be small, but it was powerful. Who knew he should have worn a bulletproof vest to walk home from work?

"Then what was it like?"

"She killed him, as surely as if she'd shot him with this gun. He was the only reason she was alive—he wasn't done with her yet—and she killed him. Ungrateful little brat. I was damned if I would let her kill me, too. She had to be punished, once and for all."

Though he'd skipped lunch and barely touched his dinner, nausea rose in Sam's gut. Had he said he was proud of Mila before? *Proud* didn't even begin to cover it. It was nothing less than a miracle that she wasn't locked in a psych hospital somewhere, totally incapable of dealing with life.

Milagro, Jessica had told him the first time they met, was Spanish for miracle. They'd chosen the perfect name for her.

Sweat trickled down his back. Fifteen minutes ago, he'd thought he would come home, shower and hopefully sleep a few hours in a cold room, then get up too soon to restart the hunt for this woman. She'd moved his schedule ahead a few hours.

"How many people have you and Joshua killed?"

"Killed? We didn't kill anyone. We freed them."

Great. Not just evil but crazy, too. "From what?"

"Existence in our world." She made that odd attempt at a smile again. "We didn't want them here."

Not just evil and crazy but mean. God help them.

She shifted toward the porch railing, keeping the laser sighted on his chest. "We didn't count. It was enough to keep us happy. When we got unhappy, we killed someone else." Abruptly, she jerked her left hand, enclosed in a dark glove, toward the door. "I know you're trying to distract me, Chief, but it won't work. The brat's inside. You need to go join her so I can finish this."

Sam's heart stuttered to a stop before bursting into a full gallop. "Mila—" He twisted the knob. It turned easily, the door swinging in without a sound, releasing the powerful stench of gasoline. Green light fell in a narrow wedge through the opening and showed his living room, everything in its place except the wooden dining chair that stood where the coffee table should be. Mila was sitting on the chair, wide strips of duct tape over her mouth, her wrists, her ankles. And five one-gallon gas cans were strewn on their sides around the room.

Of all the ways Lindy could kill them, she'd picked the absolute worst Sam could imagine. How the hell were they going to get out of this?

Mila should be frantic, in a panic, desperately trying to find a way to get out of this nightmare that she'd found herself back in. She should be trying to work her hands free, tearing through the tape, praying to God, but her brain had shut down the instant she'd awakened to find the one person she feared most leaning over her bed. Where was Gramma? Poppy? What had Lindy done to Ben? What about the officer keeping watch in the lobby? Were they hurt? Dying? Dear God, please not dead.

In that rusty voice, Lindy had whispered, "The cops might survive. Your stupid dog…she remembered me from before and let me walk right past. Your precious gramma…she'll definitely survive. That'll be her punishment. Living without you. Knowing that in the end, when it mattered most, she didn't help you. She'll hear your screams for the rest of her life, just like I hear Joshua's."

Her choice of weapon had surprised Mila. Her father had always used knives. He'd liked the feel of the warm, rich blood as it ran over his hands. In the latest killings, her mother had used blades, too, but tonight she held a gun. Of course, she'd had to face police officers and her own mother, who would claw her eyes out to keep Mila safe.

She'd let Mila put on flip-flops, then taken her from the apartment with the gun barrel nestled in her rib cage. Muffled sobs had come from Gramma's room; Ben had lain motionless and bleeding on the couch. The officer in the lobby was toppled onto the floor, his chair upturned beside him. Mila couldn't see what Lindy had done to him.

She would have known this house they'd come to was Sam's even without being told. It felt like him. Smelled like him. A cowboy hat rested on the fireplace mantel. A pair of familiar running shoes had been kicked off between living and dining rooms. Pictures—him with family, with cop friends, with army friends—hung on the walls.

How wrong it was, seeing it for the first time tainted by *her*.

Lindy remained in the doorway, the gun now pointed at Mila. She couldn't see the red dot on her forehead but guessed it was there from the way Sam's eyes widened with fear. Producing a flashlight, Lindy grappled with it in her gloved hand and shone it on a knife on a sofa cushion. "Cut her loose, then move over by the fireplace."

Sam hesitated before approaching Mila. His brain must be running a thousand miles a minute trying to find a plan to somehow free them both. She was no expert, but she knew a knife from a distance of twelve feet was no match for a gun her mother didn't even have to aim. He took extra care loosening her left wrist—the splint was back at Gramma's—then crouched to get her ankles. "I'm so sorry." His mouth barely moved. His words barely reached her ears. The next words were even softer. "I love you, Mila."

Such sweet words that she wanted to hear them again, but he was standing, walking toward the fireplace. Lindy made a sound and pointed with the flashlight again, and he stopped, tossing the knife onto the sofa as she indicated. "Your gun, too."

He obeyed.

Mila stood, pulled the tape from her mouth with a wince and eyed the two weapons. She had no clue how to use a gun, and she couldn't imagine herself plunging a knife into a living being's body. But she could do it to save Sam. To save herself. Even if it did prove that she was her father's daughter.

"Now you go over there." Lindy pointed to the opposite side of the room as she stepped all the way inside and closed the door. The odd green tint vanished, along with virtually all the light, but she flipped a switch and a low-watt bulb, not much brighter than Mila's night-light, came on overhead.

Gasoline squished in the carpet as Mila crossed the room. She scanned for some kind of weapon and found nothing. Of course. Lindy had probably started planning this from her hospital bed. She would have accounted for every possibility.

"Have a seat, Chief. We're gonna let you wear the tape for a while."

It made sense in a Lindy sort of way. She didn't trust Sam to meekly let her restrain him, knowing it would mean his and Mila's deaths. This way she could keep the gun on both of them while Mila did the restraining. After all, Mila with hands free was far less dangerous than Sam was.

The smell of the gasoline was turning Mila's stomach in sour flips, threatening to bring up her dinner any minute now. Her head pounded with an ache, her eyes burned, but she picked up the duct tape her mother had left on the coffee table, along with the knife.

"You look pukey, brat. Bad smells don't bother me anymore. Thanks to you, my nose was scraped right off my face. I don't have eyelashes, either. Eyebrows. Hair. I have to wear a damn wig everywhere I go, and people still stare me like I'm a freak. Hell, *they're* the freaks. They have no idea who they're dealing with."

How much damage had she suffered? They'd thought she wouldn't survive, Ben said. The question in Mila's mind was why had she wanted to. She'd known her precious Joshua was dead and Mila was gone and her mother had helped make both happen. Why hadn't she just given up? Why had she fought so hard to live in such a damaged shell?

To kill me.

"Come on. I don't have all freaking night."

Mila walked behind the chair, sat on the edge of the couch and pulled Sam's hands to the back center of the wooden seat. He squeezed her fingers tightly and, she wanted to think, hopefully. She used the knife to cut a strip of tape and used Sam's broad chest to hide her actions as she wound the tape through the vertical slats of the chair back. She secured just the ends around his wrists, making sure they didn't overlap.

Cutting the next piece, she grunted in pain from using her left hand. It made her mother laugh. "A sprained wrist, for God's sake. That's all you have. You want to hear the injuries you gave me?"

Yes. The longer Lindy fixated on the wrongs done her, the more upset she would get and the less attention she would pay to anything else.

"I left half my skin on the roadway when I jumped from the car. My entire body was a mass of torn, oozing, bleeding scrapes with bones poking out. I broke my collarbone, my upper arm, my elbow, my lower arm, my wrist, my hand and every bone in my fingers."

Mila wrapped a second piece of tape, again securing most of it to the chair. Sam could easily break free of what touched him.

"Every one of my ribs," Lindy went on. "My hip, my pelvis, my femur, my lower leg, my ankle and my foot. I didn't crack open my head, though. Can you believe that? That means I lay there in the weeds, in more red-hot agony than you could ever imagine in your stupid little brain. I lay there, and I listened to his screams, and I watched the flames coming closer, and I couldn't do a damn thing to save myself while I burned alive."

Mila continued cutting and wrapping pieces of tape, praying it looked like his hands bore the brunt of it. Done, she moved to the front of chair, tape and knife in her good hand, and spoke for the first time since Sam had arrived. "My wrist hurts too bad. If you want me to tie his ankles, you're going to have to cut the tape for me."

Lindy swept a pile of books from the table nearest the door. "It's a damned *sprained* wrist!"

"If you wanted me to have two good wrists for tonight, you shouldn't have tried to kill me Saturday." Mila knew the mere fact that she'd spoken angered Lindy. She saw it in her eyes, heard it in her gasp, recognized it in the sudden clenching of her fist. Family rules: Mila never spoke to Lindy unless it was necessary, never criticized her, frowned or scowled or rolled her eyes at her and never asked for or expected anything of her.

Lindy stalked across the room, and it took all of Mila's strength not to cringe or shrink away. It was a small source of wonder that she didn't want to as badly as she always had before.

"I should have drowned you at birth." Lindy's breath was fetid and hot on Mila's face.

A smile slowly curved her mouth. "Look at the fun we'd be missing if you had."

She'd never seen Lindy so enraged. Spittle flew from the corners of her mouth, and she gulped shallow breaths through her rebuilt nose, tremors rocketing through her from head to toe. The shaking of her hand was enough to make Mila dizzy from the up-and-down swirls of the pistol's red dot.

"You're a coward," Mila said, her voice drawing strength from someplace else. Behind her, Sam murmured her name, a faint warning. She glanced at him and recognized worry and concern and love and faith. He trusted that she knew how to handle her mother better than he did.

"Bitch!" Lindy staggered forward, switching the gun to her other hand, slapping her open palm against Mila's face. She had always been so fast before, spinning, circling, landing a second punch before Mila could refocus her eyes after the first. But broken bones and skin contractures from scarring made for slower movement.

Mila's cheek stung, but she didn't touch it. "My father knew how to kill. He took his time with it. It was art to him. He made tender slices, delicate cuts and savored the lifeblood he released. You…you sneak up behind people. You stab, butcher, and then you run away like the coward you are."

"You think this isn't art?" Lindy spread both arms to indicate the room. "I've lain on the grass and smelled my own flesh roasting off my bones. Now I'm going to sit outside and smell your flesh roasting. I'm going to listen to your screams, like the most beautiful music ever played. And I'll know no one will save you, because your boyfriend will be dying right beside you. It'll be beautiful."

Mila scoffed. "That's not saying much, given how amateurish the rest of them were. My father would be embarrassed."

Lindy lunged again, her fingers curved into claws, her rage too great to control. Mila stepped back too late. Her mother slammed into her, and they fell to the floor. Vaguely Mila heard scuffling—Sam freeing himself, please, God—but it was lost in the furious wounded-animal screams coming from Lindy's mouth.

When Lindy charged, she'd dropped the pistol, but Mila still held the knife. Lindy grabbed it with her fingers, the blade slipping and slicing, cutting deep into her skin. Blood flowed down the hilt and onto Mila's

hand, drained farther onto her arm. The smell, so ter-
rifyingly familiar, made her want to join Lindy in her
mindless screaming rage, to drop the knife, but her fingers were locked around the handle. If she let go, she
would die, so no matter the revulsion gathering inside
her, she held tight, but she was losing her grip one slick,
wet blood drop at a time.

Lindy jerked the knife from her hand, flipped it
around and pressed the blade to Mila's throat before,
suddenly, thankfully, she was gone, lifted into the air
by the strongest, angriest man Mila had ever seen: her
protector. The man she loved. Sam.

He hefted Lindy three feet off the floor, one hand
gripping her waistband, the other her neck, then threw
her aside. Mila didn't care where she landed or how
hard or whether she was hurt. She didn't care about a
thing except they were alive.

As easily as he'd picked up Lindy, he lifted Mila, too,
cradling her in his arms, staring intently at her face.
"Oh, my God, Mila." That was all he could say. That
was all right. It was enough for her.

Her clothes and hair were soaked with gasoline, and
giving in to the fumes, she rolled away and vomited.
As she straightened, Lindy stirred near the fireplace,
rolling to one side, digging her ungloved hand into her
pocket. Light glinted dully off the item she pulled out,
then a tall slender flame flared.

Mila stared in horror, unable to form even the slight-
est of sounds, but Sam turned, following her gaze.
Tightening his grip on her, he lunged toward the door
as Lindy dropped her hand and the cigarette lighter to
the carpet and flames whooshed to life. Heat scorched

their backs as he leaped down the steps and hit the sidewalk, then the street, at a hard run.

The last thing Mila saw before the world exploded was a figure standing in the doorway of Sam's house, arms raised to the sky, as flames consumed it.

Epilogue

Dawn that morning was all delicate pinks and lavenders, breathtaking in their beauty, such a contrast to the ugliness where Sam's house had stood. The blaze had been out for an hour or more, but firefighters still lingered, spraying the ashes, watching for hot spots.

I sat in a yard across the street, Sam at my side. Within minutes of escaping the house, we'd been hustled back to Gramma's to shower off the gasoline and change into clean clothes. I scrubbed and scrubbed but was pretty sure the smell would linger in my imagination for a long time.

Ben Little Bear and the officer on duty in the lobby were both taken to the hospital, both in good condition. Gramma was taken, too, hysterical from her run-in with Lindy, from banging on her bedroom door screaming for help while she thought Sam and I were dying. Despite the hour, Lois Gideon went to the hospital to sit with her after they sedated her.

Without discussion, Sam and I went from the hospital back to his block. We watched the last of the flames, the curious people gathered around, the eerie flashes of red-and-blue lights. We didn't talk. Sam held my hand, and I clung tightly to his. We just…were. Together. The way we were meant to be.

As the sky lightened, I gave the burned-out remains of his house one last look, then leaned my head against his shoulder. I'd always believed it would come to this: my life or my mother's. Except for those lovely fifteen years when I'd believed her dead, I'd always thought she would kill me. I'd sometimes dreamed I would kill her instead.

There was no doubt of her death this time. We had watched her as she burned, doing a macabre little dance—Sam and I, the arriving firefighters, a neighbor who'd been roused from his bed.

And she had laughed. At least, I thought it was a laugh. With her damaged throat, it was hard to be sure, but it seemed she would find her kind of sick, twisted humor in the situation.

Daniel Harper approached us, using his shirtsleeve to scrub the sweat from his face. "It's gonna be a while before we can recover…" Glancing at me, he shrugged.

Her body. What was left of it.

"Why don't you go home? Get some rest. We've got everything here."

Sam's fingers clenched a little tighter around mine, a question. Should we go? Could I?

I squeezed back and moved to stand up. Sam and Daniel were quick to help me. "Rest sounds good."

"Home sounds better." Sam gave the ruins a wry look. "Though I don't seem to have one of those anymore."

Daniel offered us a ride, but I shook my head. I wanted to walk. To let the dawn peace seep into our souls. It was a new day for us, in more ways than one.

Hand in hand, Sam and I started toward Gramma's. I could go home again. I could pick up Poppy, and we could return to our little house. Sam would go with us. We would be his home now.

A block passed in silence. I felt…content. "Is it wrong that I don't feel sad or guilty?"

He gazed down at me, his blue gaze moving over my face tenderly. "Nothing you feel could be wrong, Mila. She was an evil, damaged person, but at the end of the day, she was still your mother. She gave you life, and she tried to take it away. But you're a survivor, Mila. You're the strongest person I've ever known."

I'd never considered myself particularly strong. Warped. Broken almost beyond repair. Almost. But Gramma hadn't believed that. Sam hadn't believed it.

"You know I love you." I said the words simply, with certainty, words I'd never imagined myself saying to anyone besides my grandmother. They were sweet and lovely and felt so especially right.

He smiled, and that rightness filled me to overflowing. "I love you."

We were less than a block from Gramma's now, and I could imagine Poppy jumping at the bedroom window, delighted to see us, unbearably hurt that we'd gone outside with her. "I heard you ask about my real name. Does it matter?"

"Not in the least. Whatever name you use, you'll always be my miracle." He grimaced, then grinned. "That was incredibly sappy, wasn't it?"

I bumped shoulders and hips with him. "It's the sweetest thing anyone ever said to me."

Now I didn't have to imagine Poppy barking. I could hear her as the blinds in my window jiggled. As long as someone was that happy to see me, my life mattered. Sam would be that happy for me, and I would be that happy to see him, for the rest of our lives.

A new day, but not a new life. My old life made me the person I am today, and I wouldn't give that up for anything.

—Excerpt, journal of Mila Ramirez Douglas

* * * * *

Don't miss out on any other suspenseful stories from Marilyn Pappano:

DETECTIVE DEFENDER
NIGHTS WITH A THIEF
BAYOU HERO
UNDERCOVER IN COPPER LAKE

Available now from Harlequin Romantic Suspense!

ROMANTIC suspense

Available April 3, 2018

#1987 COLTON AND THE SINGLE MOM
The Coltons of Red Ridge • by Jane Godman
Brayden Colton refuses to participate in Esmée da Costa's true-crime documentary, but then the K-9 cop rescues her child and she begins to see him in a new light. Now a killer thought long gone is back, and Brayden must save Esmée and her son for them to become the family they long for.

#1988 CAVANAUGH VANGUARD
Cavanaugh Justice • by Marie Ferrarella
Bodies start appearing when the historic Aurora Hotel is demolished, and it soon becomes evident the killer is still active. Brianna Cavanaugh and Jackson Muldare are on the case—but will they be able to build the trust they need to catch a killer?

#1989 NAVY SEAL RESCUE
Team Twelve • by Susan Cliff
Dr. Layah Anwar and her nephew need to get across the Zagros Mountains, and mountaineering expert navy SEAL William Hudson is the only man who can help. Neither of them ever expected to fall in love, but Layah is keeping a secret that could have devastating consequences for them both.

#1990 HER ROCKY MOUNTAIN DEFENDER
Rocky Mountain Justice • by Jennifer D. Bokal
A chance encounter—and a search for a missing person—pits med student Madelyn Thompkins and undercover agent Roman DeMarco against a murderous gangster. Will they learn to rely on each other in time to save themselves?

Get 2 Free Books,
Plus 2 Free Gifts—
just for trying the Reader Service!

HARLEQUIN
ROMANTIC suspense

YES! Please send me 2 FREE Harlequin® Romantic Suspense novels and my 2 FREE gifts (gifts are worth about $10 retail). After receiving them, if I don't wish to receive any more books, I can return the shipping statement marked "cancel." If I don't cancel, I will receive 4 brand-new novels every month and be billed just $4.99 per book in the U.S. or $5.74 per book in Canada. That's a savings of at least 12% off the cover price! It's quite a bargain! Shipping and handling is just 50¢ per book in the U.S. and 75¢ per book in Canada*. I understand that accepting the 2 free books and gifts places me under no obligation to buy anything. I can always return a shipment and cancel at any time. The free books and gifts are mine to keep no matter what I decide.

240/340 HDN GMWV

Name _____ (PLEASE PRINT)

Address _____ Apt. #

City _____ State/Prov. _____ Zip/Postal Code

Signature (if under 18, a parent or guardian must sign)

Mail to the **Reader Service:**
IN U.S.A.: P.O. Box 1341, Buffalo, NY 14240-8531
IN CANADA: P.O. Box 603, Fort Erie, Ontario L2A 5X3

Want to try two free books from another line?
Call 1-800-873-8635 or visit www.ReaderService.com.

*Terms and prices subject to change without notice. Prices do not include applicable taxes. Sales tax applicable in N.Y. Canadian residents will be charged applicable taxes. Offer not valid in Quebec. This offer is limited to one order per household. Books received may not be as shown. Not valid for current subscribers to Harlequin® Romantic Suspense books. All orders subject to approval. Credit or debit balances in a customer's account(s) may be offset by any other outstanding balance owed by or to the customer. Please allow 4 to 6 weeks for delivery. Offer available while quantities last.

Your Privacy—The Reader Service is committed to protecting your privacy. Our Privacy Policy is available online at www.ReaderService.com or upon request from the Reader Service.

We make a portion of our mailing list available to reputable third parties that offer products we believe may interest you. If you prefer that we not exchange your name with third parties, or if you wish to clarify or modify your communication preferences, please visit us at www.ReaderService.com/consumerschoice or write to us at Reader Service Preference Service, P.O. Box 9062, Buffalo, NY 14240-9062. Include your complete name and address.

HRS17R3

"I fled to Syria to escape war," she continued. "I returned
to Iraq for the same reason. I do not wish to settle in
another unstable place. Armenia has known many years
of peace, and our people are welcome there."

"Do you speak Armenian?"

"A little."

"How many other languages?"

"Four or five."

"Which is it? Four or five?"

"I am fluent in English, Arabic, Assyrian and Kurdish.
I also know a bit of Farsi and Armenian."

He counted on his fingers. "That's six."

"But I only speak four well."

"I only speak one well. If that."

"You can learn another."

He turned toward her and studied her face. A week ago, he'd had no interest in learning Arabic. Now he wanted to learn her ways. He wanted to know every inch of her. When he cupped her chin with one hand, she didn't pull away. He rubbed his thumb over her parted lips. "What is the word for this?"

"Mouth or kiss?"

"Both."

"*Bosa* is kiss."

"*Bosa,*" he said, then touched his lips to hers.

"Mouth is *fum.*"

"Fum." He kissed her again.

"*Tongue* is *lisan.*"

"*Lisan,*" he said, and gave it to her, plundering the depths of her mouth. She returned his kiss with a low moan. Her tongue touched his shyly and her fingers laced through his hair. She tasted like Yazidi liquor and female spice, a delicious combination. He settled against her, learning all her sensitive places. His lips traced the silky column of her throat while his hands roamed. Her hijab fell away, and he pulled his shirt over his head. Her fingertips danced across the surface of his chest.

Don't miss
NAVY SEAL RESCUE by Susan Cliff,
available April 2018 wherever
Harlequin® Romantic Suspense books and ebooks are sold.

www.Harlequin.com

SPECIAL EXCERPT FROM

A serial killer is on the loose on a military base—
can the Military K-9 Unit track him down?

Read on for a sneak preview of
MISSION TO PROTECT by *Terri Reed*,
the first book in the brand-new
MILITARY K-9 UNIT miniseries,
available April 2018 from Love Inspired Suspense!

Staff Sergeant Felicity Monroe jerked awake to the fading sound of her own scream echoing through her head. Sweat drenched her nightshirt. The pounding of her heart hurt in her chest, making bile rise to burn her throat. Darkness surrounded her.

Where was she? Fear locked on and wouldn't let go. Panic fluttered at the edge of her mind.

Her breathing slowed. She wiped at the wet tears on her cheeks and shook away the fear and panic.

She filled her lungs with several deep breaths and sought the clock across the room on the dresser.

The clock's red glow was blocked by the silhouette of a person looming at the end of her bed.

Someone was in her room!

Full-fledged panic jackknifed through her, jolting her system into action. She rolled to the side of the bed and landed soundlessly on the floor. With one hand, she reached for the switch on the bedside table lamp while her other hand reached for the baseball bat she kept under the bed.

Holding the bat up with her right hand, she flicked on the light. A warm glow dispelled the shadows and revealed she was alone. Or was she?

She searched the house, turning on every light. No one was there.

She frowned and worked to calm her racing pulse.

Back in her bedroom, her gaze landed on the clock. Wait a minute. It was turned to face the wall. A shiver of unease racked her body. The red numbers had been facing the bed when she'd retired last night. She was convinced of it.

And her dresser drawers were slightly open. She peeked inside. Her clothes were mussed as if someone had rummaged through them.

What was going on?

Noises outside the bedroom window startled her. It was too early for most people to be up on a Sunday morning. She pushed aside the room-darkening curtain. The first faint rays of sunlight marched over the Texas horizon with hues of gold, orange and pink.

And provided enough light for Felicity to see a parade of dogs running loose along Base Boulevard. It could only be the dogs from the K-9 training center.

Stunned, her stomach clenched. Someone had literally let the dogs out. All of them, by the looks of it.

Don't miss
MISSION TO PROTECT by Terri Reed,
available April 2018 wherever
Love Inspired® Suspense books and ebooks are sold.

www.LoveInspired.com

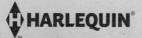

LOVE
Harlequin
romance?

Join our Harlequin community to share your thoughts and connect with other romance readers!

Be the first to find out about promotions, news, and exclusive content!

Sign up for the Harlequin e-newsletter and download a free book from any series at **www.TryHarlequin.com**

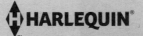